Blackbird Rising

A Novel of the American Spirit

Gary Earl Ross

FULL COURT PRESS
BUFFALO, NEW YORK

Imprint: Full Court Press
A division of FCPress
PO Box 342
Buffalo, NY 14223
Web site: fcpress.us
E-mail: info@fcpress.us

ISBN-10: 0-9817070-4-1
ISBN-13:978-0-9817070-4-4

Library of Congress Control Number: 2009922252

Printed in the United States of America
ALL RIGHTS RESERVED

Book design by Linda Lavid
Front cover male face courtesy of the Library of Congress

In memory of my first reading teacher, my mother, Marlene:

I am grateful you lived to read the first draft of this novel. ·

In the kindest universe, you read the final draft over my shoulder.

And in memory of my father, Earl:

When I was ten and said I wanted to be a writer, you gave me your

old typewriter. That day you made this book possible. Thank you.

Illustrations:

Acknowledgments:

This novel would not have been possible without the efforts of the many persons to whom I am indebted for access to old newspapers, artifacts, source material, and the like. I thank them for all that they did to lessen my mistakes:

Bill Loos, Elaine Barone, Patricia Blackett, Bob Gurn, and Barbara Soper (retired) of the Buffalo and Erie County Public Library; Doris Ursiti, Ann Marie Brogan, Mark Comito, Suzanne Pilon, and Joseph Rennie of the Theodore Roosevelt Inaugural Site; Mary Bell, Virginia Bartos, Yvonne Foote, Cathy Mason, and Pat Virgil of the Buffalo and Erie County Historical Society, and special thanks to the late Mabel E. Barnes, for bequeathing to the Society her unpublished notebooks detailing her many visits to the Exposition; Gary Shorter and Madeline Metz of the Library of Congress; Jim Sucy of the George Eastman House Museum of Photography and Film; the staff of the Smithsonian Air and Space Museum; Susan J. Eck's web site *Doing the Pan* and Peggy Brooks-Bertram and Barbara Nevergold's web site *Uncrowned Queens*.

Also, I extend thanks to the family, friends, and colleagues who made suggestions (taken or not), offered assistance or research material, commented upon parts of the manuscript, allowed me to examine old photographs and antiques, and listened to me in the endorphic sleepwalk of the fiction writer: Patrice Ross; Steven Ross; Robert and Wendy Edwards; Gertrude Ross; Joanne Fenton; Heidi Kueber Wilson; Trudy Munford; Mary Robinson; Steve Bennett; Scott and Glo Williams; Sherryl Weems and Shaf Rahman; Sherry Byrnes; Jim Peck; Amrom Chodos; and Dr. and Mrs. Jesse Nash, Jr.; and a special thanks to Linda Chodos and Mysha Webber-Eakin, for help with the title.

Finally, I'd like to thank my agent, Ellen Levine, for her faith, guidance, and persistence, and Linda Lavid of Full Court Press for her generosity, insight, and support.

1901 Street Map Courtesy of the Buffalo and Erie County Public
Library, Buffalo, NY

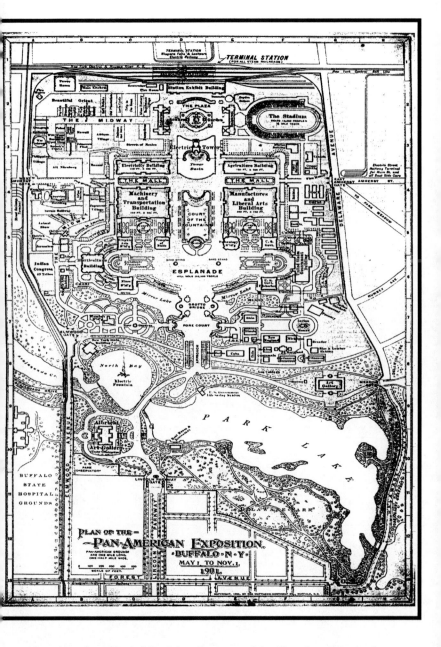

Pan-American Exposition Map Courtesy of the Theodore Roosevelt
Inaugural Site, Buffalo, NY

Flight—A Prologue

I had reasoned this out in my mind, there was one of two things I had a right to, liberty or death; if I could not have one, I would have the other.

—*Harriet Tubman*

May 1851

Across the water, amid the flickering lights of the Canadian village, lay freedom.

Thirty yards above the river bank, William MacAtley waited for the moon to hide. If it did, he would escape having to return to the narrow secret room in the Quaker family's damp cellar, in the wood-frame house against which he now pressed himself. The wooden pallet there had been his third and most hospitable bed in two weeks but he was ready to leave it. If the moon slipped behind clouds, his sponsors—with an urgency born of a possible thousand-dollar fine and six months in prison for harboring a runaway slave—would hurry him down the hill to the river. The abolitionists were supposed to have a boat down there, hidden amid overhanging trees and carefully arranged branches. If the moon withdrew and three signal lanterns flared on the Canadian side to guide the oarsman, William would lie in the bottom of the boat and weep as he was carried to his new life.

If . . .

A twig snapped, and the slap of wet grass broke the whisper of the water. Footsteps. Dressed in black, William crouched and worked his large body into the space between the house and the woodpile. His hands sifted through the pile in search of a weapon and finally closed around a sturdy stick, perhaps a foot long, with a ragged point at one end. His arms and his back were strong from his years in the Carolina cotton fields. He knew that even if he missed an eye, he could still bury the sharp end of the stick deep inside the skull of the first slave catcher to lay hands on him. If there were more than one, they would have to kill him. They would have to shoot him dead and lose the ten dollars his return would bring. He would kill or die before anyone took him back.

Uncertain footsteps drew closer, just around the corner from the woodpile at the rear of the house. Whoever had come near stopped, and there was a slight rustle of clothing, as if he was turning to look in one direction and then the other. Then his movements stopped too. William pushed his broad-brimmed hat back with one hand and held the weapon against his thigh with the other. Balancing on the balls of his feet, he swallowed and waited. For a long time the only sound he could hear was the other man breathing.

"William?" The voice was deep but hesitant and belonged to the last man William had expected to lead him to the river tonight. "You s'pose to be here somewheres, but I can't see you nowhere." Joseph Lockhart, the blacksmith's apprentice, was himself a negro—a quiet but not especially friendly man— and like William in his early twenties. "I don't know where you be but I hope you can hear me. The other folks can't come. They sent me to take you 'cross."

"Here," William said quietly. He climbed to his full height. His shoulders too broad and torso too long for regular suspenders, he had knotted a rope around the waist of the trousers the abolitionists had given him upon his arrival five days earlier. Now he slid the stick between the rope and the fabric. Then he stepped into view and offered his hand to the dark-clad man who would row him to freedom. Though half a head shorter, Joseph was as powerfully built from blacksmithing as William was from plantation work. But his sinewy fingers gave a handshake less steady than William had expected.

Releasing William's hand, Joseph said, "You got to go tonight." Then he tugged his hat down tighter, as if for emphasis.

William narrowed his eyes at him. "What about the moon?" It was bright enough that he could see the lines in Joseph's face.

Joseph shook his head. "That stranger paid 'nother visit to Hosea at the blacksmith shop. A federal man name o' Sparks, an' he got a warrant for you. Don't matter how bright the moon be, you got to go tonight."

William moved away from the house and gazed toward the village on the other side of the river. "No signal lanterns yet."

"Don't matter," Joseph said, his voice rising with impatience and maybe fear. "Sparks been all over the riverfront axin' 'bout you. He talk to the hostler an' the barge men an' the tavernkeep. He talk a long time with Hosea—an' his daughter."

William turned back to him. "Augusta?"

Joseph nodded. "He say he gon' take a negro back to North Carolina—if not you, then somebody else. Hosea too old. He look at me for a long time, but I always got my papers say I was born here, free. Then he say some judge really want you and I don't know nothin' 'bout cotton no ways so he won't get no money from takin' me."

If the slave catcher had questioned Augusta, William had

reason to be afraid—not because she would have betrayed her father's secret work but because of the looks they had exchanged during his time at the blacksmith shop. This morning he had taken a long last look at her smooth brown face and the smile of her lowered eyes. At that moment he might have risked capture just to touch her hand. But Hosea, insisting that he get to the safety of the abolitionist's cellar, had urged him toward the door. Leaving, William had seen the ghost of himself staring back from Augusta's face. Hosea had seen it too. Surely, Sparks had seen it when he questioned her.

"We got to hurry," Joseph said. He started down the path to the river, coattails flapping about the backs of his thighs.

William fell into step behind him, the whisper of the river growing to a murmur as he drew near. Halfway down the path, he glanced left, then right, eyes taking in the lamplight and firelight that stretched unevenly in either direction. Were he anything but a runaway subject to the provisions of the Fugitive Slave Act of 1850, he might remain in this small lakeside city. He liked its feel, liked Hosea and the abolitionists who had risked their own freedom to help him—and he especially liked Augusta. Buffalo was his last station on the way to Canada, which prohibited not only slavery but also slave catchers. Once there and working in the job that had been set aside for him, he could begin to build a life free of fear. When he was able, perhaps when he had land of his own, he would write to Augusta, maybe even send her money and an invitation to join him.

At the river's edge the apprentice hesitated before going to where the boat was hidden and looked about so often he made William uneasy. Was this his first time taking a runaway across to Canada? Was this the first time that he, freeborn, had ever faced the possibility of prison? But then Joseph waded into a pile of limbs and began to drag the larger cuttings aside. William followed suit, and Joseph said, "Move just enough to pull the boat out. Got to hide it quick when I get back." William took hold of the bow with both hands and began to pull the boat from beneath its dark oilcloth covering. Joseph squeezed behind it and pushed. Presently, the boat slid free, its underside scraping limbs and muddy leaves. The work of an abolitionist who was a cooper, the boat was crude, scarcely large enough to hold two average men, much less a pair *their* size. Two narrow boards served as seats, oars wrapped in oilcloth stretched across them. William realized he would have to sit up, in full view of anyone—if his and Joseph's combined weight didn't push the boat beneath the surface. But if he wanted to get to Canada . . . Teeth clenched, he stepped backward, into the cold water, pulling the bow in after him. As water filled his boots, he ran his fingers along the seams of the boat, as if searching for softening oakum or gaps in the planking.

"Don't look like much but it's a fine boat," Joseph said. "Cooper say his barrels never leak and neither do his boat."

The distinct click of a gun being cocked pierced the soft rush of the river. Silence fell over both men.

"Bet it'll leak when I put a hole in it."

The figure that separated itself from the shadows of a knot of maples five or six yards away was lanky and clad in a long dark coat and floppy-brimmed hat. It approached them unhurriedly, almost soundlessly, a casually held long-barreled pistol glinting in the moonlight. "You there in the water," the man said, his Southern drawl slow and gritty. "Stay right where y'are and don't so much as bat an eye or this here Colt Walker will blow your head clean off." He paused and rotated his neck, which produced a faint crack. "William MacAtley, I 'spect. I'm Deputy U.S. Marshal Cobb Sparks. You're under arrest."

William felt a burning bile crawl into his throat and pressed his lips together to keep from screaming. He was too close give up now and mentally measured the distance between himself and the slave catcher. He would take a lead ball, happily, to keep from going back to the South, but he wanted to be close enough to get a hand on the slave catcher's throat as he pulled the trigger. If William was meant to die tonight, the slave catcher would die with him. That William promised himself, but at the moment they were too far away from each other and he resolved to wait for the chance he knew must come. As the blood in his legs began to thicken in the cold, he raised his hands slowly.

"Been after you for weeks," Sparks said. "Trackin' you through the wet and the cold in one Godforsaken place after another." He hawked and spat. "I don't know what you did to Judge MacAtley but he wants you back so bad he's payin' me fifty dollars extra." He studied William for a moment. "What'd you do to him?"

William said nothing.

Sparks raised his gun and extended his arm so that the barrel was pointed right at William's head. "I'll let the money go 'fore I take disrespect from a nigger. I asked what you done, boy?"

"Learned to read," William said.

"That a fact?" He snorted, then chuckled and lowered his gun a few inches. "Lot of good white men can't read. What good's readin' to a slave?"

William knew better than to answer, that the proper thing to do here was cower, then lower his eyes. But he refused to give the slave catcher that much ground, to look frightened or downward. Whether or not he could reach Sparks, he would die a man. Presently, he noticed that Joseph's hands hung loosely at his sides, that his face showed no traces of his earlier fear. In fact, the slave catcher paid no attention at all to Joseph, which could mean only one thing: the blacksmith's apprentice had betrayed him. William unsealed his lips to take in and let out a deep breath. Then he looked from Joseph to the slave catcher to the river. Perhaps he could move in the other direction, throw himself under the water and begin to swim. He had learned to swim when he was a child, on Sundays in a small lake on the MacAtley property. He was confident of his strength but was unable in the moonlight to estimate either the distance to the Canadian bank or how much his clothing and the temperature of the water would slow him.

"You try to swim and I'll kill you." Sparks sucked his teeth. "Make me get in that water to drag your carcass out, I'll kill your friends too."

Confused, William turned back to Sparks and saw Joseph looking at him too.

"Most of your abolitionist friends are under lock and key. And if the sheriff knows what's good for him, he'll keep 'em there till I get back."

Joseph murmured, "Y-you said—"

"Don't worry, boy. I didn't let him lock up your belly-warmer." Sparks nodded to William. "Federal law says your friends got to be punished. Up to you whether they live to go to prison. What's it gonna be?"

Shivering, William said, "I'll do whatever you say."

"Good." Sparks pointed his Colt at the bottom of the boat and fired, then cocked and fired again, each burst of flame illuminating his gun hand, each explosion making Joseph flinch. Before the sound could fade, the gun was trained once more on William, whose shoulders were shaking. "Cold, are you?" Sparks grinned. "Serves you right. Now why don't you sit down and stay sittin' till I tell you to get up. When your ballocks are numb enough you'll beg me to take you back where it's warm."

William glanced across the river and saw a signal lantern ignite on the opposite bank. Then he sat, the water soaking through his coat and shirt, stinging his ribs.

Sparks seemed not to have noticed the lantern. "You," he said to Joseph. "Push that boat out in the water."

Joseph shoved the boat into the river, guiding it past William. The holes in the bottom spouted, then bubbled as water covered them. When he was just past knee deep, Joseph let the current take the boat and stood back, trembling from the cold himself, to watch it drift away and sink. Then he moved back toward the bank, careful to stay away from William.

The previously gentle evening breeze felt sharper against William's face and chest, and his shivering intensified. He dug his fingers into the mud to brace himself. Then he shifted his weight to his left arm and pulled his right hand free. His fingers fluttered the mud away and crawled inside his coat to close around the sharp stick still held by the rope around his waist. He heard his own teeth chattering. "I'm p-powerful cold," he said.

"Just stay put, boy, till I say you can come out."

William worked the stick free and with his fingertips began to ease it, blunt end first, into the right sleeve of his coat, pushing it as far inside as his middle finger could stretch. The point pressed into the palm of his hand. He moved his hand against the point until it bit into the skin—until, finally, he felt pain pushing the numbness out of his hand, out of his arm. He pushed the point in deeper, twisted his hand to enlarge the hole he was making. He closed his eyes and willed the pain to spread, to warm his belly and his other arm and his legs.

"Wonderin' how I knew you'd be here?" Sparks said.

"N-no," William said, eyes still closed.

"Look at me when I speak to you, boy."

William blinked, saw that Sparks had moved closer to him, leaving Joseph several paces behind him.

"If you wasn't such a dumb nigger, you'da seen it already," Sparks said, taking another step. "Though I'll never understand white men who do so much for worthless niggers, I do expect you people to help each other. But another nigger turned you in." He glanced over his shoulder at Joseph, who said nothing. "Imagine that! Seems the blacksmith's daughter got a mite too friendly with you for *his* liking." Now Sparks stood so far down the bank that water ran over the toes of his boots. For an endless moment William and he held each other's gaze, slave and slave catcher, neither man willing to avert his eyes first. Only Sparks smiled. "And with the blacksmith locked up, Joseph here'll get his gal and his shop."

William moved his hand to disengage the point of the stick from his flesh. He thought of Joseph Lockhart and needed only his anger to warm him now.

"I'm s-s-so c-cold," he said.

"All right." Sparks backed up a few paces. "Come on out."

William rolled to one side and climbed to his feet, dripping and unsteady. He paused to gain his balance, then trudged out of the water, stooped by the weight of his wet clothing. He took an unsteady step toward Sparks and shuddered, hands and arms and shoulders shaking almost uncontrollably. His lower lip quivered and he could barely feel the spit running down his chin. The whole time his eyes never left Joseph, but the useless dog would not look at him directly.

Sparks produced a pair of heavy-looking manacles from a deep coat pocket and dangled them in his free hand. "Put out your paws, William, and keep 'em still."

As Sparks drew near, William lifted his arms and extended his hands away from his chest. But he continued to stare at his betrayer, then cried, "Hit him, Joseph! Now!"

As Sparks spun on a surprised Joseph, William splashed forward, stretching to cover the distance that separated them, and brought up his right fist as if he were swinging a bale of cotton into a wagon. The fist caught Sparks under the chin as he turned back to William and would have sent him reeling backward if William had not shaken the sharp stick down into his hand. Blunt end braced against his bleeding palm and shaft steadied between his second and third fingers, William drove the point of the stick into the soft flesh between the chin and Adam's apple. He felt the tip rip through the thickest region of the tongue, then break off somewhere inside the roof of the mouth. The force of the blow sent Sparks's hat flying and briefly lifted him off the ground. Twitching and gurgling, he tried to raise his gun. But his eyes rolled back, his head lolled to one side, and his finger tightened on the trigger. The gun went off close to William's left ear, the explosion sending pain through his head. Stunned, he let go of the stick. The body, gun still clutched in one hand and stick lodged in the throat, toppled backward—into the arms of Joseph Lockhart.

William pressed the heel of his hand to his ear to subdue the murderous throbbing. He saw Joseph ease Sparks to the ground. Joseph's eyes rose to meet his and shifted to the gun. Both men went for the Colt at the same time. Joseph reached it first, but before he could uncurl the fingers from the grip, William was on him, hurling him backward. Clawing for possession, they heaved themselves off the body, together tearing the gun out of the dead man's grasp. Hand slick with blood, his own and the slave catcher's, William clutched the barrel. Beneath him, Joseph held the cylinder, but neither man could work a finger inside the trigger guard. Twisting his body into him and pushing his right elbow into his adversary's mouth, William managed to get a second hand on the barrel. Joseph pounded his free fist into William's back, then swung it up and down into the side of William's head, into his draining ear. The pain that blossomed along William's jaw made his hands go slack for just a moment.

He felt the gun wrenched away from him but he was still

on top and twisted so that again they were face to face. His right hand closed around Joseph's throat. His other hand trying to pin Joseph's flailing right arm, William squeezed, his thumb digging into the softest pocket of flesh beside the Adam's apple. The apprentice gagged, his eyes bulging as if trying to gulp air themselves, the fingernails of his free hand clawing skin off the back of the hand choking him. But William continued to tighten his fingers, even as his clenched teeth began to ache and he heard the sound of the hammer being cocked and sensed Joseph's gun hand angling toward him, even after the barrel cracked thunder and his left shoulder caught fire. Only when Joseph slackened beneath him and the fingers clutching the hot pistol unfolded did he relinquish his grip and, gasping, roll onto his back.

No longer able to hear the rush of the river, William lay unmoving as new pain spread through his arm and chest with every shallow inhalation, as the stink of blood mixed with mud and river water reached his nostrils. Unblinking, he noticed for the first time that evening how beautiful the stars were. He had spent so much of his fugitive journey with his eye on the North Star, following its light to a new life, that he had never stopped to consider the splendor of the heavens themselves, the endless miracle of everything. Now he remembered what his granny, long dead, had told him one hot summer night when he was a child seated on her lap. Stars were God's diamonds flung across a great expanse of black velvet heaven, reminders of the earthly treasures slaves could never have. The moon was His silver, the sun His gold, and only through death could a slave inherit the riches of the sky.

William smiled at the memory and knew at last the true value of the sky's treasure. Above him, amid the flickering diamonds of the Kingdom of God, lay freedom.

Part One

A Dream of Wings

My grandfather was a big man.

Papa Joe stood more than six and a half feet tall, his shoulders so broad from fifty years of blacksmithing that any coat he wore seemed an uncomfortable fit. Even when he was in his seventies and beginning to complain of arthritis, his arms were hard and corded, his skillet-sized hands still remarkably strong. Beneath a sprinkling of white hair, his face was weathered and dark, with a wide nose and lips so full they looked as if they had been carved from volcanic rock. But it is his eyes I remember most. They were the deepest, wisest eyes I have ever seen, and they glittered like diamonds in the night sky. My grandfather was a dreamer, you see, a man who gazed into the future as easily as most men look back at the past. And he was in the perfect place to dream—America, where some dream of riches, others dream of freedom, and a select few dream of doing wondrous things.

In another time and another skin, he might have been a teacher or a college professor. He read more books than anyone I have ever known. And he remembered what he read, quoting not just long passages of Scripture with the skill of a practiced preacher but also Shakespeare and Douglass, Dunbar and Dickens, Don Quixote, *Williams'* History of the Negro Race in America, *dime novels about the Wild West, Jules Verne, astronomy books, even pieces he had read twenty or thirty years past. He would have been wonderful in a classroom, a great bear of a man holding students enthralled with his deep voice and tireless stories. Instead, he was a blacksmith successful enough to own his own carriage, an ex-slave who somehow had acquired the documents of free birth—which I still keep in the family Bible. To the world that never saw him gazing at the stars or reading in his favorite chair or urging his son and grandsons to stand tall, my grandfather was a simple man. To my brother*

Will and me he was an inspiration. He made dreamers of us both.

  —*From the unpublished manuscript* Flight of the Blackbird *by Augustus Lockhart*

One

On the second day of April, 1901, early in the afternoon, Captain Hayward Driscoll settled himself behind the tiller of his new horseless carriage and waited. The station master had promised him that railyard hands would be quick about securing a gangway so he could drive the gleaming Packard off the flatbed rail car that had carried it to Buffalo from the factory in Warren, Ohio. But the yardmen were taking much too long. Away from home since the previous October, he was eager to see how his son Daniel had kept up the estate in his absence. And he could hardly wait to show off his remarkable acquisition, not only to his son but also to all those he motored past on his way home.

Pulling up the collar of his black coat, the station master, a pale, broad-shouldered man with huge brown mustaches, emerged from the railway office. "Captain Driscoll," he called. "Just a few minutes more, sir."

"Very well," Driscoll said, resigned. "And you'll arrange to have the rest of my things carted to my home."

"Yes, sir. And if I may say so, sir, that's a fine-looking machine you have there."

The Packard was certainly eye-catching. The polished black body with red trim sat on a black spring chassis with red wheels and white tires. A wide fender curved above each tire, and a brass lantern was on either side of the front. Driscoll most appreciated the carriage-style top that would permit him to drive in the rain and the cushioned leather seat that would ease the pressure on his piles. But he knew it was the white tires that would draw attention on the street. When the business side of his travels had taken him to Warren, he had seen a Packard on display. Before then he had never given much consideration to owning an automobile. But struck by the absolute beauty of it, he ordered one identical to it, impractical tires and all.

The virgin look of the tires would be short-lived on the streets of Buffalo. He decided, then, that his first drive would be beneath the oak and maple canopy of Delaware Avenue, past the ivy-cloaked mansions of the lawyers and businessmen and political bosses who had deprived him of two opportunities to increase his wealth. First, they had shut him out of the 1899 lakeshore land purchases south of the city. What a sweet deal *that* had been! If those owners had known their property was being snatched up for a long-term investment like a steel mill instead of a six-month fair, they would have sold at much higher prices. Second, Driscoll's estate, north of the Rumsey spread, had been under consideration as a site for the Pan-American Exposition. But Rumsey had held more sway with the planners and got his own property chosen. Driscoll had resented standing on his own land and watching the construction of an enterprise that would put the city on the map and should have put money into his pockets. Added to the death of his wife a year earlier, the loss of the Exposition had been too much to endure. So he'd traveled, following his varied business interests all the way to California and back. Time had made his losses more bearable, but a slow drive up the Avenue, where all could see his prosperity and nonchalance, would do wonders for his sense of well-being.

*   *   *

The ride was bumpier than he expected, and the April air

bit into his topcoat with winter-sharpened teeth. Moreover, Delaware was quieter this Tuesday afternoon than he had hoped. He feared his proud motoring had gone largely unseen, except by carriage drivers and the occasional servant. Even if his automobile had been noticed, he himself had been obscured by the framework that supported the bonnet. And after several miles of dirt, mud, and manure, his tires were no longer pristine. Worse, his piles were inflamed and in need of the medicated ointment he'd got from a hotel doctor in Chicago. Disappointed and uncomfortable, he was in a surly mood when he tillered onto the carriage path that ran through his property.

I see Daniel has not yet hired the landscapers, Driscoll thought, shaking his head. His son was a romantic, narrow-chested and dreamy-eyed. He had no sense of the practical; in his thirty years he'd made no mark upon the world, despite the advantages of money and education. Driscoll shifted uncomfortably in his seat as his motor car bounced over carriage ruts.

The path wound through ice-laden underbrush, past elm and maple trees, and ended at a rambling clapboard farmhouse with a gabled roof and a long L-shaped porch. Beyond the house, across a rising expanse of muddy grass, stood the oversized barn. The hundred plus acres had been a farm once but had been abandoned as such by the time he purchased it, with the idea of surrounding himself with land to safeguard his privacy. Anna had wanted to tear down the house, to replace it with a modern home befitting their wealth. But he had talked her out of it. However much they prospered, he had said, they were simple folk who enjoyed a simple life and were not the sort to throw their money around. Such behavior demeaned a man.

The rise of monied classes over the past several decades had pushed the city northward, to swallow the undeveloped land that stood in its path. Driscoll had been a part of that expansion. Even so, he had found himself unwelcome in the burgeoning upper class. Like Driscoll, the wealthiest men in town had made their fortunes in commerce, in the manufacture, transportation, or sale of goods. Like him, many had started elsewhere and in the course of business had settled in Buffalo because of the railroads or Great Lakes shipping. Unlike him, too many had come to view their newfound wealth as providential privilege, an entitled detachment from the lower classes. Driscoll was proud to have risen through the ranks, both in the army and the business world, and was grateful for the labors of those who had helped his climb. Now he was an irascible ex-soldier with a calm contempt for opulence and an indifference to the functions of obscure pieces of tableware. Perhaps he was too much a reminder of the past they wished to escape to find a place among the newly rich. If not for his business shrewdness in general and railroad prosperity in particular, his insistence that opportunity for success was the birthright of even the lowliest American might have led some of his peers to call him an anarchist.

But today anyone who saw him stop his automobile in front of his house and climb down as sore in spirit as he was in posterior would simply have called him an old man, home at last and tired after his long journey. He mounted the steps and stood in the doorway a moment, hesitant to set foot in the front hall with even slightly muddy boots. In all their years together, he had tracked enough dirt and mud onto Anna's carpets and floors to fill a dozen graves. It struck him as strange that it should take her death to make him learn to wipe his feet. The absence of her fussing was even louder than the frustrated oaths she had hurled at him when she was alive and bitter about the absence of a proper mud room. He dragged his soles across the rough mat just outside the door and took a step inside. Then he pulled off his gloves and woolen cap and dropped them on the window seat.

"Daniel!" he called. "Come see what I have brought home."

There was no answer.

"Jonas!" Jonas Newcomb, the live-in hired man who looked after the needs of the house, had served under him at Gettysburg. "Sergeant, where are you?" But Jonas made no reply either.

Unbuttoning his coat, Driscoll strode down the hall toward the kitchen. His heels echoed on the wide floor planks. "Mrs. Ridgewater," he called to the colored cook and housekeeper who had been with his family for years. "It's Captain Driscoll. I'm home."

Still there was no answer.

He found the iron cookstove still warm, as was a covered black pot on the sideboard. Mrs. Ridgewater must have stepped outside, though for what he could not imagine. April was too early to pluck herbs from the garden or to plant new vegetables. Everything she needed to enhance those wonderful meals she made was inside, dried and hanging on twine stretched above the stove or in cans and jars or the ice box in the pantry. Long ago, he had run a line from the well into a deep tub in the pantry so she could pump water without leaving the house. Where, he wondered, could she have gone?

For that matter, where was Jonas? And Daniel?

Driscoll looked out the rear window and saw the side of the barn facing the house. He opened the backdoor and descended the porch steps. To his left, lashed to the rear post reserved for the nags of deliverymen, stood a massive brown horse hitched to an old stanhope four-wheeler that seemed too small for such an animal. At least seventeen hands high, it was an old but powerful-looking horse with a jagged white diamond beneath its forelock. He wondered who the owner was.

Trudging through wet grass, past the carriage shed that sat between the barn and the house, he rebuttoned his coat and jammed his hands inside his deep pockets. Following the footpath which rounded the barn to the front, he noticed for the first time additional windows had been installed high in the walls. *What the hell?* He stepped back to get a better look and saw a rail, thinner than train rails but a rail nevertheless, running down from the peak of the roof to his right. And over the doors of the barn hung a large pulley device that had not been there before. He continued around the barn and saw that there were in fact two rails which began at the peak. They formed a narrow track that extended down the north side of the barn, which faced away from the house, and followed the slope of the ground into the hollow for perhaps two hundred feet, where they ended abruptly in a ramp that looked like an unfinished trestle.

What in God's name is going on here?

Confused and angry, he marched to the doors and threw them open.

The tableau that greeted him left him speechless. Eight pairs of eyes swung up or around to meet his. Silence settled over the assembly. Daniel was there. So were Jonas Newcomb, narrow-shouldered and slightly bent, and heavy-bosomed Mrs. Ridgewater—and five negro men of various sizes and complexions. Yet it was neither Daniel nor the negroes that fully captured his attention. It was the enterprise in which they were engaged.

The interior of the barn was unrecognizable. The planks that comprised the loft floor were gone. The packed earth floor of the barn itself had been cleared of hay, except along the walls, where blankets suggested it was being used as bedding. The dividers between stalls had been removed. Wooden racks that held tools and what appeared to be machine parts stretched across the far wall. Near the racks, a boxlike wooden contrivance the length of two coffins lay atop another trestle-style structure. Elsewhere were sawhorses, boxes, spools of rope and wire, workbenches, and a drafting table. One corner held a firepit, a bellows suspended above it and an anvil and cooling tub positioned beside it. But all the barn modifications imprinted themselves only peripherally on his mind. What transfixed Driscoll was the object that lay in pieces in the center of the floor, caught in the light from windows that once had lit the loft.

Driscoll swallowed, clearing the tension in his throat but failing to find his voice.

The larger wings were in four sections, each a ribbed wooden framework about twenty feet long and covered in dark gray material that appeared to be sateen. They were laid out in pairs, the outer end of each section curved to a point. Spread open between them was something that resembled a seaman's hammock cut in half. Around it lay a confusing configuration of cables, handles, and stirrups. Off to the side were three more wings, each half the width and length of the others and curved to points on both ends. Scattered around the wings were struts and slats, wheels and sled runners, gears and chains. On the nearest workbench were lengths of polished dark wood that resembled oars fastened together at the handles. But these curved blades were single pieces of lumber which had been fashioned by a hand with a grand purpose.

My God, Driscoll thought. *Daniel has made a flying machine!*

Abrupt comprehension left Driscoll dizzy. For a heartbeat or two he felt the muscles slacken in his legs. But he still held the iron ring fixed to the door and was able to remain on his feet. Eyes moving from one face to another, he took stock of Daniel's silent colored helpers. Three of the men were young, like his son, one about six feet tall, the other barely five, and the third in between. His lips parted as he realized he knew the middle-sized man after all. A slim coffee-skinned fellow in a heavy gray coat and faded trousers, he was standing near Jonas—Mrs. Ridgewater's son, Andrew. Driscoll had not seen him in a good many years, not since he had accompanied his mother to work when he was a boy and sometimes played with Daniel. The middle-aged man in preacher's garb was also familiar, as was the broad-shouldered old man well over six feet tall. But before Driscoll could tie either face to a memory, Daniel, in short coat and work-worn trousers, came toward him and spoke.

"Good to see you, Father." He held out his hand. Driscoll released the iron ring to take it. "You're home earlier than I expected. You must be wondering about the horses. I've stabled them nearby." His Adam's apple bounced on the top button of his shirt. "We needed to have the barn completely empty."

Driscoll grinned wildly at the son who had failed to find a niche in his business or any other endeavor. "I've ruined your surprise?" He pulled Daniel to him and embraced him. "That's only fair since you ruined mine too." He chuckled. "But yours is bigger and much better than mine."

Daniel stepped back. "Father, this is not as it appears."

Driscoll shook his head. "I've read enough about Lilienthal and Langley and that von Zeppelin character to know that this is exactly what it appears to be, a flying machine—an aeroplane."

"Yes, but—"

Driscoll moved past him to study the contraption. He walked around it, back and forth in front of it, paying little attention to Daniel's colored work team—who, as if one, had stepped back to give him room to conduct his inspection. Brow furrowed and lips pursed beneath his shaggy mustache, he knelt beside a wing, put a fingertip to it as gently as he would have to the wing of a fallen bird. The sateen skin was tight but resilient, the wooden skeleton beneath it firm but lightweight. He was impressed by the craftsmanship and wondered whether the wings would work, if they could flap with enough force to carry a man aloft. Then he smiled. Even if the wings were too weak, Daniel would be joining a select group. Driscoll had read about aeronauts in a couple of the illustrated weeklies. Like Daniel they were men wholly unsuited to the rigors of business or the waging of war. Yet however daft they appeared to the rest of the world, they earned respect with their hot-air balloons and winged suits and unwieldy machines. Their dreams enabled them to attempt what other men dared not. Driscoll felt pride swell in his gut at the notion that Daniel might make a mark on the world after all.

Finally, he stood and looked at his son. "Daniel," he said, suppressing his excitement, "tell me how it works."

Daniel flushed and ran a hand through his strawberry-colored hair. "It is . . . difficult to explain." He looked toward one of his negro assistants, then back at his father.

"How does it take flight?" Driscoll pressed. "What is the principle upon which it is based? Is the framework hollow, like the bones of a bird? Do the wings move on hinges to lift it from the ground? What powers your aeroplane? A steam device? Human exertion?" His eyes suddenly widened. "I'll wager it's powered by an engine such as the one that might be found in a horseless carriage." He shrugged. "That was my surprise. I've brought home an automobile." Then he smiled broadly. "But what *you're* doing could make you one of the greatest men in history."

Daniel opened his mouth as if to speak but no words emerged. He sighed and shoved his hands into his coat pockets and lowered his eyes, which had begun to glisten.

Driscoll did not understand why his son should seem ashamed or embarrassed. He took a single step toward Daniel, hoping that his proximity would lend a measure of comfort. "Son, this is a wondrous undertaking—no doubt a secret endeavor, lest someone else learn your principles and take to the air first. I will safeguard your secrets with my life. Now, how does it work?"

Daniel raised his wet eyes to meet his father's and said, "I don't know how it works."

Driscoll winced, clenching against renewed pain in his piles. "I don't understand."

"Perhaps I can explain."

Driscoll was surprised to see one of the younger colored men he did not recognize step forward and pull off his cap. Tall with chestnut brown skin, he had widely spaced shoulders and short hair that arced over a large forehead. The forearms visible beneath the rolled coat sleeves were thick and corded. His dark eyes were penetrating, and for an instant he seemed amused.

Driscoll frowned at—but quickly dismissed—the possibility that this negro might be laughing at him. "Who are you?"

The negro smiled, the corners of his eyes crinkling. "Will Lockhart, sir," he said. "That aeroplane is my creation."

Two

Though he had heard the explanation at least a dozen times, Papa Joe Lockhart still had difficulty comprehending exactly how his grandson's flying machine was supposed to work. Whenever Will spoke of generating beneath the wings a concentration of air strong enough to lift the aeroplane off the ground, Papa Joe did not understand how such a thing was possible. But his faith in Will was deeper than his grasp of mathematics or aeronautics. A designer at heart, Will could see clearly what others would not imagine. At ten he had built a roller-mounted floor sweeper to help him finish his chores faster, at twelve a five-eyed camera that took photographs in rapid succession. When he was in his early teens he designed a track-and-pulley system, which he anchored to the crossbeams of the blacksmith shop, to permit his aging grandfather to move loads that might otherwise have required three men. Papa Joe knew that the aeroplane, when finished, would fly.

Today Papa Joe studied his grandson's newest listener more than he watched Will himself. Captain Driscoll was known as a shrewd but fair man. Papa Joe knew too well that fairness did not necessarily extend to negroes and looked for indications that Captain Driscoll would respond to the dream by ordering everyone off his property. His astonishment that Will had stepped forward with an explanation was evident to everyone in the barn. Will answered the open-mouthed silence with his drawings, his calculations, the sequenced photographs of birds in flight. He described his bird dissections; clarified his idea about curving the upper surface of an artificial wing; explained the wind shaft along the back wall; detailed how the ramp would help increase the aeroplane's speed. Driscoll listened intently, the skin above the bridge of his nose knotted in contemplation. He seemed to be giving Will's ideas the full measure of his consideration. Why shouldn't he? He had been willing to believe that his son had forged a path to the sky. Why not Will?

His explanation finished, Will withdrew to permit Daniel to introduce his father to the others. Papa Joe studied Driscoll as he moved down the line to shake hands. He already knew Andrew Ridgewater, an apprentice mason whose mother, Sister Sophie, had introduced Will to Daniel. Next came Papa Joe's other grandson, Gus, and Portius Banks.

"And this is Mr. Lockhart, Will's grandfather."

Driscoll gazed up at him as if trying to place his face, then held out his hand. Papa Joe smiled and decided the man's handshake was firm enough to earn anybody's respect.

The introductions complete, Driscoll turned to Sister Sophie. "I noticed a pot on the sideboard, Mrs. Ridgewater. I could do with a hot meal." She nodded and disappeared from the barn. Next Driscoll motioned to Jonas Newcomb to follow him. Outside, he paused and lifted his face to the sky, perhaps imagining the aeroplane in flight. Then he started down the soggy stretch toward the back porch, grizzled, bowlegged Jonas two steps behind him.

Papa Joe caught up with them halfway to the house, just as—ahead—the back door closed behind Sister Sophie's long black coat. Jonas was explaining in apologetic tones how Daniel had resisted his advice against changing the barn and getting himself mixed up with the colored men. "But then when I talked to this Lockhart boy, I got to thinkin' maybe he had somethin'.

Maybe he could make this thing fly. Anyway, I figgered these folks didn't know nothin' about business, but I was sure you'd want to be part of somethin' like a flyin' machine."

"Captain Driscoll." Papa Joe passed Jonas and shortened his stride to match Driscoll's. "I must apologize for my grandson."

Driscoll shrugged. "Why? He's a remarkable boy."

"That is exactly his failing," Papa Joe said. "Sometimes he is so lost in his own dreams that he forgets his upbringing."

"I don't understand."

"He never expressed his gratitude for the use of your barn. On his behalf, I thank you."

Driscoll stopped and turned to Papa Joe, who stopped also. "I *have* seen you before," he said. "You're a blacksmith, aren't you? I believe you put a shoe to one of my carriage horses some years ago." He glanced over his shoulder at the horse hitched at the rear of the house, then turned back to Papa Joe.

"That old cart-hauler's mine," Papa Joe said. "Name's Mac."

Driscoll nodded. "And your shop is located . . ."

"On Broadway, near Michigan."

"Yes, that's right." Driscoll scrutinized Papa Joe for two or three seconds. "But I know you from somewhere else." Then he snapped his fingers. "It was one of those Pan-American Exposition meetings in the Ellicott Square Building. In the Vitascope Hall in the basement. Last autumn, before I began my . . . extended travels." He wagged a finger to underscore his certainty. "You were there. You didn't say anything but a man tall as you kind of stands out in a crowd."

Papa Joe smiled. "So I've been told."

Driscoll looked back toward the barn. "And your minister friend Banks was there too."

"Portius and my son were close friends. He invites me to

accompany him on many occasions."

"You were both there with some other negro leaders, another minister and a Mason. Reverend Banks, I think, did a lot of the talking, something about trying to get support for a negro exhibit for the Exposition and negro church groups to march in the 20th Century parade on New Year's Eve. I seem to recall there was considerable resistance to both ideas." Driscoll narrowed his eyes. "Then some fool pulled out a newspaper article that said negroes were a menace. Something about under-living a sewer rat." He frowned. "When your people protested you were asked to leave."

"You have an exemplary memory, sir."

Now Captain Driscoll smiled. "It wasn't long afterward that John Milburn and the rest of the Exposition committee asked *me* to leave that same meeting." After a pause, he said, "Did you perchance go to the parade?"

Papa Joe shook his head. "We were in church for our watch night service. Afterward we stood outside and watched the fireworks light up the sky." In fact, he now remembered, the combination of fireworks and countless electrical lights powered by nearby Niagara Falls had seemed to erase the midnight stars. When the celebration was finished and most of the congregants had walked to their nearby homes, Papa Joe and Portius had stood in the lightly falling snow, watching overcrowded streetcars clack past and horse-drawn cutters and the occasional motor car skitter over slick cobblestones. Papa Joe did not share with Driscoll the question the minister had asked that evening— *What do you think this new century holds for the negro people?*—and the answer he had used to draw Portius into the secret circle building the aeroplane: *This century will be ours, son. Will is going to give us the wings to claim it.* Instead, he said, "We didn't go to the parade on principle. 'Never stand begging for that which you have the power to earn.'"

Driscoll furrowed his brow in confusion and looked at Jonas, who shrugged.

"Cervantes," Papa Joe said, looking from one to the other as Driscoll nodded and Jonas continued to look perplexed.

Driscoll was silent a moment, then said, "You seem well educated—for a blacksmith."

"Not formally, sir, just well-read—for a blacksmith."

"Well, Mr. Lockhart, what does your reading tell you of drinking whiskey with a man?"

"My experience tells me I can withstand modest quantities—when I am in the company of a friend."

Driscoll laughed. "Then for a glass or two, I shall be your friend." Turning to Jonas, he said, "You were right, sergeant. I am interested in this aeroplane. Go back to the barn, then. Help young Lockhart however you can and keep me informed of any progress. This could be the start of a new industry and we must move carefully but I suspect these men are not as unschooled in business as you believe."

Jonas loped back toward the barn.

"Mr. Lockhart," Driscoll said. "Come with me."

Papa Joe followed Driscoll up the back porch steps, wiped his feet on the mat outside the door, and stepped into the warm kitchen. Removing his cap, he inhaled the smell of smoldering wood and simmering food. Sister Sophie stood at the cookstove, swirling a long-handled wooden spoon through a huge black pot. For an instant, surprise crossed her face when she saw Papa Joe in the doorway. Then, as Captain Driscoll moved past her, she lowered her eyes, never breaking the rhythm of her stirring. She raised them enough to catch Papa Joe's eyes as he walked through the kitchen in the Captain's wake. Feeling devilish, he winked at her.

Driscoll led him to a book-lined room off the parlor and extracted a bottle and two glasses from a shelf. He set them on a small circular table and uncapped the whiskey, pouring two fingers into each glass. Then he handed one glass to Papa Joe and gestured him into one of two chairs beside the table. Driscoll took the other chair.

For a time they sipped in silence. Cap perched on one knee, Papa Joe let the whiskey ignite the tip of his tongue and slip down his throat in a fiery thread. He had never been much of a drinker but was willing to share liquor with any man whose help would carry Will's dream an inch closer to reality.

Involving the Driscolls had been a risk from the beginning. In October, Gus had argued against permitting any whites into their undertaking. "Anything you do they'll steal and claim as their own," he said. But no one knew a negro with a building large enough to hold a winter workshop and enough land to stage aeroplane trials in the spring. James Hood, the colored doctor, had died childless a few years earlier, leaving sizable acreage to his German-born second wife, who had sold the property within a year and gone back to Europe. The only other colored man with sufficient land lived in Lockport, too far away for what Will intended. Andrew only half seriously suggested the Driscoll property. Still, Will listened—as did Papa Joe—and considered the advantages of the location. Despite his brother's objections, he asked his grandfather to approach Sister Sophie for an introduction to Daniel Driscoll.

Now, watching the elder Driscoll out of the corner of one eye, Papa Joe wondered whether the man would try to claim Will's invention as his own, or his son's. His instinct told him no, that Captain Driscoll was an honorable man—a businessman, yes, who certainly enjoyed making money, but honorable enough to give credit to those who earned it. He was exactly the kind of white man Papa Joe had suspected from the beginning they would have to engage. Now he waited for Driscoll to finish his first glass, for liquor to unlock the silence that hung between them.

"You must be proud of your grandson," Driscoll said when his whiskey was gone. He stared ahead at one book-covered wall.

"I'm sinfully proud," Papa Joe said, "of both my grandsons. Because Will's larger and stronger, people sometimes overlook his brother. Both are special. Will is a builder who gives shape to his dreams. Gus keeps his thoughts tied in private bundles of paper. Perhaps he is a poet. I can't say for sure because he shares his writing with no one." Papa Joe took the last swallow of his own drink. "Yes, I am proud of them. They have learned in spite of hardship to carry themselves like men."

"No doubt your influence," Driscoll said, pouring each of them a second glass.

"I expect we've had our fair share of tragedies." Papa Joe did not look at Driscoll but kept his eyes fixed on the same wall of books. "Their mother died in childbirth with Gus, who was made sickly by some of the poisons of her passing and never grew as robust as he should have. Their father—my son Matthew—was killed working in my shop a year later. My wife and I raised them as our own, until her death when Will was ten and Gus was seven."

"I am sorry to hear of your many losses," Driscoll said. "My own Anna was taken from me not two years ago."

Papa Joe turned to Driscoll. "I'm sorry to hear that."

Facing each other, they gulped back more whiskey.

"I finished raising them alone," Papa Joe continued. "I tried to give them both a good Christian upbringing and a good American upbringing. I tried to teach them the importance of decency and learning and hard work."

Driscoll sighed. "I wish I could take as much pride in my boy as you do in yours."

Papa Joe shook his head in admonition. "Don't overlook

your son's importance in all this. He's a good judge of character and ability. If not for him, all the work done before my grandson set up shop in your barn would have been in vain. If Will has even the smallest chance of success now, Daniel gave it to him."

"Aren't you afraid for him, that he might be injured or killed in a flight?"

"Yes, I am." Papa Joe hesitated. "I am afraid for all of them—Will, Andrew, Daniel. They have agreed—the three of them—that Will must not fly until the aeroplane is a success. Daniel even threatened to end his support because if something happened to Will, who else could adjust his designs? The Driscoll investment, he says, would be lost. Gus tells me that Langley in Washington never pilots his fliers. He has a man for that. Here, that responsibility will fall to Andrew—and to Daniel too, if you do not object. It is a great risk, for both of them."

"If Daniel is willing to risk his life to become one of the first men to fly, he must have great faith in your grandson." Captain Driscoll was silent for a long time, rolling his empty glass between his hands. "Will is unusually keen—for a negro, I mean. He is not at all what one expects to find in the colored race."

"Do you know many negroes?" Papa Joe asked, gently.

"Most assuredly," Driscoll said. "I've known a great many negroes over the years. Even before the war—the big war, not this skirmish with Spain—I knew several in factories, dry goods stores, tanneries. I've employed many and find them to be reliable workers, honest and industrious—and quite devoted."

"Will is all those things," Papa Joe said. "What is it that makes him different from other negroes?"

Driscoll set down his glass hard, as if disbelieving the question, and gaped at Papa Joe. "What makes him different? By God, he's invented a *flying* machine! Not many colored men have done such as that, I'll wager."

"Nor many white men," Papa Joe said. Setting down his own empty glass, he rose and crossed the room to the books at which he'd been gazing. He withdrew a large volume from the left end of the shelf just above the midline of the wall. Paging through it, he turned to face Captain Driscoll. "'In disposition,'" he read aloud, "'the negro is, as a rule, cheerful, peaceable, and generally unconcerned for the future . . . negroes are inclined to live in colonies and are of emotionally religious instincts.'" He paused to gauge the effect of the words on his listener and found Driscoll's visible discomfort inspiring. "'As a rule, they are of a low order of intelligence, mechanical in their work, but capable of great endurance. They have a less nervous disposition than whites . . . are more frequently color-blind. They have smaller lungs and larger livers . . . and they are fond of music.'" Papa Joe snapped the book shut and returned it to its slot on the shelf. "I have this same reference work at home. I expect the author of that particular definition also knew many fine negroes."

Driscoll shifted in his seat.

"The fact is, he didn't know many negroes at all. He knew them from a distance. He knew them as he wanted to know them, as servants without feelings, laborers without ambitions, children without hope of growing up. He didn't truly know them as a man knows a friend or a neighbor. He didn't know what they thought or felt or talked about or wished for their children. He didn't the know the pain of being seen as inferior, depraved, mentally defective, less than human. Neither, Captain Driscoll, do you."

Driscoll's face flushed. "I trust, Mr. Lockhart, that you do not accuse me of being a racialist." He scooted forward, as if ready to rise. "Why, I fought to free the slaves!"

"I *was* a slave." Papa Joe felt the broad expanse of his back burn with memories and attempted to swallow his anger. He had to remind himself that a white man, especially a prosperous one, simply could not fathom the life of a slave.

Driscoll leaned back in his chair, as if afraid of being struck. "But your language, your bearing—I would have staked my property on your being freeborn."

"Joseph Lockhart was freeborn. How I came by his papers and stepped into his dead shoes was a story known only to a few trusted friends, all now dead themselves. No one living knows my whole history, not even my grandsons or Portius."

"I should like very much to hear your story," Driscoll said, "when you find me friend enough to be entrusted with it."

Papa Joe nodded, appreciating the sincerity in Driscoll's voice. "I would like very much to tell it, but it is a tale for another time." He took a deep breath. "Today we must talk not about the past but about the future for which I am supposed to have no concern." Smiling, he nodded toward the bookshelf. "I want books a hundred years from now to say something different about negroes. I want them to say we were a people like any other, with good, bad, and indifferent numbered among us. I want them to say we were a noble race that withstood suffering and adversity to find our true place in America. And I want them to remember Will Lockhart was the first man to conquer the air."

Driscoll stood and took a step toward Papa Joe. "If my son and I are to be a part of this rewriting of colored destiny, I'd like to know more about your plans."

Papa Joe fought the urge to smile. Newspapers had kept him apprised of Driscoll's disputes with Milburn and the Exposition organizers even before the meeting in the Vitascope Hall, even before Andrew suggested the Driscoll estate. "They're Will's plans, really. If all goes as expected, the first public demonstration of his aeroplane will take place sometime in late summer or early fall. He hopes to stage a flight over the Pan-American Exposition."

Only after Driscoll grinned did Papa Joe join him.

Three

Everything would have been perfect, Papa Joe thought.

The gilt-rimmed cup he held was perfect, as was the tea inside it—steam rising off the dark mirror of its surface like morning mist off a lake. The round ginger cake on the saucer in his left hand was perfect, and so was the house, wine-colored curtains matching the brocade sofa and settee in the parlor. The company was perfect, too. Seated on the sofa and settee and seven or eight wooden folding chairs were the most important negro leaders in Buffalo, among them Portius Banks of the Clinton Street African Church of the Ascension, Reverend J.E. Nash of the Michigan Avenue Baptist Church, Reverend Junius Ayler of the Vine Street A.M.E. Church, Mrs. Mary Talbert of the Phyllis Wheatley Club, and James Ross, publisher of the *Globe and Freeman* and leader of the Colored Masons. Presiding over the gathering was dry goods shopkeeper Louis Young, who had opened his Michigan Avenue home for this latest meeting of a group that first had come together last fall to promote negro involvement in the Pan-American Exposition.

Having come at the insistence of Reverend Banks, Papa Joe listened to one report after another on fruitless efforts to secure funding and space for an American negro exhibit. The more he heard, the more he understood why Portius was convinced that this was the perfect place to announce the existence of the aeroplane, which Gus had named the Blackbird.

Except Papa Joe had told Reverend Banks to say nothing.

First, the flying machine was still under construction and would not be ready for a flight attempt before summer. Second, there was no guarantee it would work. The aeroplane could roll down its rooftop track and smash straight into the ground. "The fewer people who know, the better," Papa Joe had said as they walked toward the meeting. He knew Reverend Banks did not understand. If three white men could be involved, then what was the harm in letting the negro leaders know? "We all swore an oath for a reason, Portius," Papa Joe said. "If word spreads, how soon before it reaches men who'd like to see us fail, or Captain Driscoll? The negro leaders don't need to know beforehand to benefit afterward. And if they are not a part of it, any failure is ours, not theirs." Reverend Banks remained unconvinced, but Papa Joe knew he would honor his oath.

Abner Tilson, a tanner, slid to the edge of the sofa but did not stand to give his report. "So far, very few colored have got Exposition jobs. We ain't allowed in the trade unions, so we got no part in buildin' it. That colored fella on the board, Gaius Bolin of Poughkeepsie, didn't answer my letter yet. Restaurants are hirin' waiters and cooks. A few companies with cleaning contracts need sweepers." He opened the leather case on his lap. "Past few weeks, I been going from office to office in the Ellicott Square. Some of the concessionaries and Midway shows say they're willin' to hire colored cleaners but not ticket sellers or hawkers or lemonade sellers. The souvenir company up on the fourth floor is lookin' for boys from ten to maybe fourteen to sell buttons and trinkets and playin' cards. They say they'll look at colored boys much as white." He extracted a folder full of papers from the case. "I made up lists of who'll hire colored." Starting with the person to his left, he passed them around the room.

Papa Joe received one of the last copies, studied it, and almost sighed. That there were openings in maintenance came as no surprise. There were always menial jobs, cleaning jobs, serving jobs for negroes, no matter how much education they had. Portius had told him that Essie's younger brother Ben, despite three years at Atlanta University, was a waiter in Saratoga and in a recent letter said he might be coming to Buffalo because his boss had gotten an Exposition food concession. Seven weeks ago, Ben's daughter Pearl, who lived with Portius and Essie, had gone into domestic service herself at the Delaware Avenue home of a doctor on the Exposition medical committee. And just yesterday Gus had been promised a sweeper's job by Captain Babcock, an Exposition official whose horses Papa Joe regularly shod. However great an opportunity it was for others, the Exposition was just another path to servitude for negroes.

Mary Talbert rose to speak, and Papa Joe remembered hearing that her eloquent call for a negro presence had been the highlight of the November meeting. A poised brown-skinned woman, she was clad in a dark blue dress with puffed sleeves and held several papers in her left hand. "I have here five more letters from prominent negroes who answered our call for support." She held up the first. "From New York, Will Cook, who wrote the musical show *Clorindy*, promises to compose a song for an American negro exhibit." She held up another. "Painter Henry O. Tanner, who won a medal at last year's Paris Expo, says his work *will* be on display at the Pan-American." The third letter, which she read aloud, was from W.E.B. DuBois, who praised their efforts to gain recognition. The color line would be the pivotal problem of the new century, he wrote. Only by organizing could negroes hope to confront the crises that lay ahead. "Writer Charles Chesnutt sends us his best wishes for success." As she produced the final letter, her smile widened. "And the young poet Paul Laurence Dunbar, who co-wrote *Clorindy*, promises to come stage a reading of his work, either at the Exposition or at one of our churches."

"Michigan Avenue would be honored to host him," Reverend Nash said.

From his seat across the room, Reverend Ayler spoke up. "I believe all three of our churches might like to take part. Maybe we can arrange something together." Reverend Ayler looked at Reverend Nash, then at Reverend Banks. Both nodded. Reverend Ayler continued, "Still nothing from Dr. Washington?"

Mrs. Talbert sighed and shook her head. "Not yet."

"He's very busy," Louis Young said as Mrs. Talbert sat.

Hezekiah Edwards, one of the Vine Street trustees, snorted. "Busy my foot! Ever since that speech at the Atlanta Cotton Expo, he thinks he's the one true negro leader. Who are we to him? We don't represent nobody official. We can't invite him to speak at the Pan-American, and even if we could, all he'd say is be happy cleaning up after the horses. All we are to Washington is another bunch of colored troublemakers that won't get in line behind him."

Several simultaneous discussions erupted, and Young needed nearly five minutes to regain control of the meeting. It occurred to Papa Joe that Will had received Dr. Washington's industrial education—though there seemed a world of difference between the carpentry he had studied at Tuskegee and the strange symbols he scratched on his drafting table. What would Washington say if he knew that one of his graduates was building an aeroplane?

Tugging at his beard in response to Young's call for the next report, James Ross stood and announced that Colored Freemasons would be plentiful at the Exposition's Masonic gathering in August. He would see to it that information reached the newspapers. "I have here the official description of the only exhibit about the American negro." He paused to let the last of the side conversations trail off. "As you know, there will be an African village with more than thirty tribes represented, making weapons, demonstrating music and dancing and silversmithing, though I've heard the Africans will not be allowed to leave their village, unlike villagers from Mexico, Japan, and the Philippines."

Hezekiah Edwards snorted and cleared his throat.

"But the only display of the *American* negro," Ross said, "will be every inch as backward as we feared." He adjusted his wire-rimmed spectacles and held the paper at arm's length. "This is about the Old Plantation, from a guidebook to be sold all over town: 'Presenting a veritable Old Southern Plantation, representing the "South be'fo de Wah," introducing 150 Southern darkies in their plantation songs and dances. Old Uncles and Aunties, formerly slaves, living in the genuine cabins in which Abraham Lincoln and Jefferson Davis were born . . .'"

"I've heard enough," Reverend Nash said. Others nodded or murmured their agreement.

"This doubles the importance of having a negro presence that shows our accomplishments as a people," Ross said. "Visitors will be here from all over the world. Surely we want foreigners to know the American negro is more than some bug-eyed dancing darky. Other expositions have had negro exhibits. Frederick Douglass spoke at the Columbian in Chicago in '93. The Cotton Exposition had a negro building as well as a negro soldier display. Even Paris had a negro exhibit from the U.S. government, charts and books and photographs. Reverend Nash and I have been corresponding with offices in Washington in an effort to bring that same exhibit here . . ."

When John Milburn wakes up black as my boot, Papa

Joe told himself, and then smiled. *Now that would be perfect.*

Later, Papa Joe breathed the crisp night air as he waited for Reverend Banks to complete his goodbyes. The air throbbed behind his eyes before it began to clear his head. He was glad to be done with the frustrating meeting, though if it helped convince Portius of the importance of keeping the Blackbird a secret, having come was worth it.

Presently, turning up the collar of his olive overcoat, Reverend Banks joined him. They began to walk toward Broadway. "What do you think of us?"

Momentarily, Papa Joe studied Reverend Banks. The colored leadership was important, to Portius and the whole negro community. Papa Joe did not want to disparage their work, however limited their influence with the Exposition board. "A good gathering," he said at last. "It has the makings of a strong colored association." He shook his head. "But the Exposition opens in less than a month. Our unfinished aeroplane won't do anything to bring a negro exhibit to Buffalo."

Reverend Banks drew in a deep breath, as if about to protest. Then he sighed and pressed his lips together and nodded grudgingly. "So, what should we do?"

"Keep trying to get an exhibit. History was built, one brick at a time, on the bones and backs of people like us. An exhibit will tell that story. But look past these six months to next year, to the future. Every parade, every letter, every achievement of our people, no matter how small, is another brick in the tomorrow we're building for ourselves."

*   *   *

Pearl Parker was tall, like her father, but had the delicate bones and facial structure of her late mother. Her mother had been petite—"too thin and too short," Rebecca Parker had often said of herself, for a husband who stood at least six and a half feet. But Pearl had never found anything odd about the sight of her parents together. Too often she had seen her gigantic father reduced to puppy-eyed silence in the face of her mother's angular beauty—or her slit-eyed anger, which made those high chocolate cheeks glow like black cherries in candlelight. Too often she had heard words of love come out of his mouth or the sounds of love come from behind the door of their room at the back of the small house in Atlanta. When her mother died— Pearl was eleven and already tall as most men—she feared more than anything that her father would die as well, that losing her mother would tear away his skin and melt the muscles away from his bones. She expected that within a week he would be as dead on his feet, in his shoes, as her mother was in the ground.

But in his grief he had sent her north, to live with his sister Essie and her minister husband Portius while he moved from city to city and job to job to find somewhere her mother would not haunt him. In the past six years, his travels had taken him to Savannah, Chicago, and Philadelphia. He'd worked as a mail carrier, Pullman porter, colored ward politician, and waiter. Unwritten in his letters but clear to the daughter who had grown up watching their love was the truth that he had found no place he could forget her mother.

Pearl thought of her father this particular spring afternoon because of his most recent letter to her. She thought of him as she stood in the Westbecks' backyard, wire-beating winter dirt out of the front hall carpet. She thought of him as she worked because the chance she might see him after two years lessened the ache in the arm she used to swing the rug beater. She had been at the Westbecks' since seven that morning. Already she had cranked enough coffee through the Enterprise grinder to hold the doctor's afternoon guests; silver-polished the tableware and the beverage service; washed the woodwork and brush-scrubbed the floors in the kitchen, pantry, front hall, and consulting room and surgery at the rear of the house; Bisselled every downstairs rug and oil-scrubbed the exposed floor; swept out the hearths in the front parlor and the dining room; cleaned the oil lamps that sat on the mantels and end tables; and dry-wiped the circular electric switches and thick cables that climbed the walls to ceiling light fixtures. Today was Monday. If not for the medical committee meeting, by now she would have put enough clothing through the Vandergrift Rotary Washer to keep the Westbecks in shirts and undergarments through next Sunday. With every swing she wished flapping laundry were on the lines in the yard instead of a heavy carpet.

The back door swung open and Pearl heard, "Child, ain't you done with that rug yet?" She turned and saw the other domestic gazing down at her from the back porch. Lorinda Coles was an old woman, small but solid, with coffee-colored skin and yellow eyes. Despite the audible creak of arthritis, she had the stamina of a younger woman and the strength of a man. She marched down the stairs, a scowl on her weathered face.

Pearl swung the braided wire rug beater again, with both hands, and said, "Almost done."

Lorinda leaned close to inspect the carpet. "You been sweepin' it like I told you?"

"Yes, ma'am. Twice a day."

"You been cleanin' the sweeper every time?"

"Yes, ma'am." Pearl could take the Bissell apart, dump the grit, and clean the roller brushes in her sleep.

"It'll do for now," Lorinda said finally. "Get it back down where it belong. The doctor's big meetin' gon' start in a hour, and we got a lots to do yet."

The meeting began promptly at four, most of the participants having arrived by quarter of the hour. In her dress uniform, Pearl held the door for them and hung their coats in the closet beneath the stairs as her mistress greeted them with a smile. A graceful woman with graying red hair and a pale green dress that matched her eyes, Mrs. Westbeck showed her husband's guests into the front parlor. When the grandfather clock beside the staircase chimed, she retreated to the kitchen to supervise preparation of the refreshment trays. Left alone to answer the door, Pearl peeked into the parlor.

The room was filled with men—white men in dark suits and wing collars and black ties, men with drooping jowls and drooping mustaches and gold-rimmed spectacles perched on veined noses, men with beards and pristine chins and hair that went from thick to thinning to forgotten. They were important men with important business, doctors mostly. She recognized some of them from their pictures in the newspapers—Mayor Conrad Diehl, John G. Milburn, president of the Pan-American Exposition, Dr. Roswell Park, chief of the medical committee. She recognized a few from prior visits to the house and knew she had heard others' names mentioned by Dr. Westbeck and his son Lucas, also a physician.

She saw Dr. Westbeck speaking to a tall, tired-looking man. "Good to see you, Herman. When this is over you must tell me about your trip." The reply came in a faint accent: "Good to be back, Mordecai. But Copenhagen at this time of year—"

"Surprised to see you here, Mr. Mayor," someone else said. "I was led to believe you gave up the practice of medicine for politics."

Mayor Diehl's mustache and gray beard parted as he grinned. "Somebody's got to check up on your bedside manner, Tom. Might as well be me. I haven't been away from my stethoscope and smelling salts as long as all that."

As Dr. Park called the meeting to order, Pearl answered Mrs. Westbeck's summons from the kitchen.

"My son isn't here yet, is he?"

"No, ma'am."

"Lucas is either on a call or just wishes to distinguish

himself by being late." She glanced at the wooden telephone box on the kitchen wall and frowned. "As usual, he's made no effort to contact us."

Lucas Westbeck let himself in the front door at four-fifty. He set down his black medical bag and leaned into the parlor to apologize for his tardiness. "An emergency," he said.

Pearl heard grunts of understanding as she moved down the corridor to take his coat. Before she reached him, he withdrew from the parlor and faced her. Tall and slender, he wore no hat, a state likelier than his lateness to have raised the eyebrows of the proper gentlemen in the next room. His auburn hair was parted in the middle, leaving his forehead bracketed by two large curls. His face was thin and Romanesque, his mustache narrow and waxed, his eyes a more vivid green than his mother's. He kept them fixed on Pearl as she drew near.

"Hello, Pearl," he said, shedding his coat and handing it to her. "Did they start on time?"

"Yes, Dr. Lucas."

"Good." As if sharing a secret, he leaned so close to her she could smell his hair oil. "Then I've missed the most boring parts but I'm in time for refreshments." Grinning, he turned and went into the parlor.

Soon the older Dr. Westbeck appeared in the kitchen, his broad face flushed. "Thomas Maybridge is such a fool," he said quietly. "He objects to having a fully functional surgery on the fairgrounds. Can you imagine? He says we won't need it to treat sprains and heat prostration." Crimson was visible beneath his white beard. "I don't care if the Exposition hospital really is nothing more than a clinic. The operating theater ought to be as well equipped as the new one in Buffalo General. Here we've gone and got new horseless ambulances—electrical ambulances. In case of serious injury, we can transport the patient with great speed to an operatory incapable of treating him." The whisper having left his voice, he threw up his hands.

Mrs. Westbeck had listened with the patient silence of a long-time wife, then patted his arm and said, "I believe the gentlemen are ready for refreshments."

Pearl wheeled the cart to the doorway of the parlor. Lorinda was at her heels with the first tray of sweetmeats and fruit slices. Mr. Milburn was standing in the center of the room, his big smooth face aglow as he congratulated the medical committee on their fine work. Thumbs in the watch pockets of his pin-striped waistcoat, he turned to Dr. Park: "And to our medical director we are so very deeply indebted. With you in charge, the other directors and I have been free to see to other details, confident visitors will receive the best health treatment available." A well-built man with sharp eyes and a neatly trimmed mustache, Dr. Park rose and shook Mr. Milburn's hand. Mayor Diehl joined them in the center of the room and clapped Dr. Park on the back. When Mr. Milburn and the mayor sat down, Dr. Park said, "It is my pleasure, then, to adjourn this meeting."

Pearl looked over her shoulder and saw both Lorinda and Mrs. Westbeck motioning her forward with their chins. She pushed the cart into the center of the room and began to offer coffee and tea to the medical men. Of all that happened the rest of the afternoon, the only two things she remembered with perfect clarity were the crumb of cake that remained caught in Mayor Diehl's beard and the heat of Lucas Westbeck's eyes on her back as he sipped his coffee.

Mr. J.B. Parker, Courtesy of University at Buffalo Libraries

Four

I am used to being unseen.

When we were children, it was Will who got the attention of people outside the family. It was always Will, or something he had made or done, that caused whispers of admiration and smiles of surprise. I was the small one, the sickly one. One of my earliest memories is being ill at four or five. I was trapped in bed, the four-poster I still share with Will, with a fever that left me so frail my grandparents believed I would die. I recall words spoken over me in a hushed voice that did not belong to either one of my grandparents: "At least he's the weak one. Better he die now than live a sickly life." I imagine it was Dr. Hood. Attending me in a later illness, he spoke to my grandparents as if I were not present: "I'm amazed the boy has lived this long." It seems my lungs were never quite right, nor my spine, nor even my brain after the many childhood fevers I suffered in my first few years.

But live I did.

My survival I owe to my family, especially to my grandmother, whose root teas and hot poultices were every drop the equal of Dr. Hood's bitter elixirs. It was my grandmother who slept beside me and bathed my forehead and face in cool water to draw the fever out of me. It was my grandmother who cleaned the crusts from my nose and eyes and forced soup into me when my lungs fluttered so thickly. She believed in my stubborn heart. And when she was too tired or too sick herself to care for me, my grandfather took her place. Even my brother helped, fetching tea or food, reading to me while our grandparents slept. I was fortunate to be a Lockhart.

Of all the scars my illnesses left on the family, none was worse than my grandmother's death. All I remember of her passing is that I was seven and sick again, that it was the only time I ever saw Papa Joe cry. Neither he nor Will has ever blamed me, but in later years I blamed myself. If she had spent less time nursing me, she might have seen to her own health. If she had left me to nature, as wolves leave an injured pup in the wild, she might still be alive. But in her absence, as if the small house behind the blacksmith shop could hold only three, I grew stronger. Without her care, I thrived on the memory of her love. Despite other illnesses, I grew to manhood—smaller, slower, weaker than other men, but manhood just the same.

It is my misfortune that the world does not see me as a man. First I am colored. Second, unlike Papa Joe, I'm too small to impose my manhood upon the eyes of those who cross my path. And I am quiet, so hesitant in speech that I try to avoid drawing attention to myself. Sometimes I wish I were like Reverend Banks, able to turn a phrase in the air instead of only on paper, or like Will, able to picture things in ways no one else can. But in the end I am only Gus—poor, feeble Gus. The world cannot see in me the man whose boyhood was lived in the pages of books, the writer whose notebooks are full of stories and sketches of city life. I am the younger grandson of a prominent blacksmith, the weaker brother of a carpenter, and I am invisible. More than most men, then, I must reach past the accident of my birth to carve out my own place in the world.

As much as they love me and as lost as they are in Will's dream, Papa Joe and my brother have given no thought to the unique contribution I might make to this invention. They have not paused long enough to consider what history will demand of whatever we accomplish. You just can't free man from the grip of the planet without some record of how it was done. As Will's first confidante, I have listened to his dream for years. I have studied his books and monographs, his drawings and calculations, until I could make sense of them. The others would be surprised to learn how much of the process of flight I understand. That understanding makes me the ideal chronicler of all we achieve. Unknown to anyone, then, from this date on, all my notebooks will be given over to such a purpose.

I am used to being unseen and unheard, but through this record the story of the Lockhart family and their Blackbird will be told.

*   *   *

Sunday April 14

Now that Reverend Banks is part of our endeavor he insists that we honor the Sabbath. After church today, instead of taking the buggy back out to the Driscoll place, we had dinner at the parsonage, along with Andrew and Mrs. Ridgewater. Mrs. Banks and Pearl served a fine meal of ham and salt potatoes, with beans and plenty of johnnycake. Afterward, we went into to the parlor, where Pearl played the piano and sang for nearly an hour. Her recital ranged from hymns to Stephen Foster songs, and when she finished with "Amazing Grace" her eyes were glistening. Whenever I closed my own eyes, it felt as if she were singing to me and only me. I could have listened for the entire evening without growing weary of her.

Afterward, of course, our conversation centered on flying.

Looking like a queen in her dark Sunday finery, Mrs. Ridgewater wanted to know when the Blackbird would be ready. "Seem like you been workin' on it long enough to try a little bit of flyin'," she said.

Will looked at his hands before replying, as if the answer lay between the knobs of his ashen knuckles. "Men have tried to fly for hundreds of years," he said at last. "The earliest tied feather-covered wax wings to their arms and tried to flap like birds, men who watched birds but did not see. They noticed only the general shape of the wing and the flapping, not its sequence of changes in flight. They ignored the convex top of the wing, the concave bottom. They looked at the up-and-down motion and decided that human flight was workable if the artificial wings were large enough and the flier's chest muscles strong enough. Men were so confident of this that they stepped off the nearest roof or mountain and died. Our work is built upon their mistakes. Nobody gets into the aeroplane until we're absolutely ready."

For the next half hour Will held us all spellbound with stories of men who tried to fly. The mechanicians of the Renaissance designed machines so heavy they would never have lifted off the ground. Others failed to study the wind and overlooked the importance of the kite. Gliderists and hot air balloonists gradually attached tails or rudders to control direction, but so many of those efforts failed because the air is an ocean of currents that requires adjustments on all sides at once. Modern gliderists have had to find new ways to steady their fliers, and the steam engine and the internal combustion engine hold promise for the dream of powered flight.

"Aeronauts have finally learned the importance of all the elements of flight," said Will. "Wings, wind, mathematics, and mechanics—from the smallest screw and cable to the curve of the wings, every element must work together perfectly if in a sustained flight. That's why every part of an aeroplane must be tested, slowly and repeatedly. Whoever makes every piece work in concert with every other piece will be the first to fly." Will was quiet as he studied our faces, one after another. Then he smiled and said, "This is the greatest of all races."

Will is asleep in our room as I sit at Papa Joe's desk to complete today's chronicle entry. Most nights Will sits in this very seat, or at the dining table, reworking drawings and calculations. For several nights in a row he has kept late hours, only to rise early the next morning and make the trip out to the Driscoll place. Once or twice a week he sleeps in the Driscolls' barn, though having spent two or three nights there with him I can say with authority that sleeping is hardly how he passes the time. Tonight, however, he looked tired when we came home and went directly to bed, as if his body had chosen to keep the Sabbath to spite his restless mind.

Papa Joe is across the parlor, beneath the painting of Jesus, slumped and snoring in his favorite chair, a book open in his lap. Soon I must pull off his spectacles and wake him, or else he will be so stiff in the morning that he will need help pulling on his boots. The sight of him there, his silver hair thinning, fills me with sadness. He has been so strong for so many people for so long that only Will and I see the true changes in him—the occasional frown of confusion, the pause to catch his breath, the sometimes slow climb from sitting to standing. To the world he is still Papa Joe Lockhart, taller than most men and twice as wide as life itself. But to us the smallest sign of frailty is cause to fear the passing of the one true rock in our lives.

Papa Joe has been our anchor in reality, our inspiration. If not for him, our studies would probably have ended with elementary school. It was from his passion for knowing that we learned the importance of our own minds, the worth of our own ideas. Without his example, I would never have begun keeping my journals, and Will's flying machine would have been stillborn in his brain. I expect Papa Joe does not realize his contribution to the idea of the Blackbird.

In fact, only I know how Will came to dream of sailing in the sky. When we were children and I went with him into the fields to fly kites or helped him feed the pigeons he kept behind the blacksmith shop, I did not yet realize he had been possessed by flight. Even after we graduated to small winged gliders which we tossed directly into the sky, I did not understand. Years later, only after he had shared with me his plans for a man-sized flying machine did I remember.

The time was soon after our grandmother died. It was a wet summer day when Papa Joe was out front working and I was sick in bed. Will was on his hands and knees in this same room, looking for a penny he had dropped and seen roll under one of Papa Joe's big bookcases. The gap between the bookcase and the floor was too narrow for Will's hand. He came to the bedroom and told me he would share the penny with me if I could get it back. The gap was tight for even my tiny hand, but I wriggled my fingers into it. Instead of the penny, I came upon what felt like old paper. I had to work it out one pluck at a time, until a corner was visible and Will could pull it free.

It was a dusty Harper's New Monthly from July 1869. Will blew off the dust, which made me sneeze, and began to leaf through the brittle pages. Almost at once he came to a piece entitled "Early Aeronautics." He read it aloud to me.

It was full of words I could not then understand—parachute, aeronaut, counterpoise, hydrogen—and names which made no sense. Will explained the words he knew and said many of the names were French. It was a history of attempted flight, with many illustrations. There were men who built devices to imitate birds or who leapt from prison walls while holding big umbrellas. One passage told of a balloonist's widow who became a balloonist herself, only to die when a Bengal fireworks display set her balloon afire. Saddest of all was the tale of an English aeronaut who leapt to his death to slow the descent of his leaking balloon and save the life of his fiancée. The illustration showed a man diving through the air as if into water, while the woman in the balloon's basket covered her eyes and swooned.

The penny forgotten, Will could not keep the excitement out of his voice as he read to me. It was the same excitement we heard when he told some of the same stories tonight. Of course, when we were children, I was too young to understand what was happening. I know now that Will became an aeronaut that day. That old magazine is still in his trunk, along with his aeroplane designs and his collection of flight materials: books like Progress in Flying Machines by Chanute, McClure's magazine articles about Maxim and Langley, and yearly technical reports from the Smithsonian.

All because Papa Joe lost a magazine many years ago.

Five

Hooves clattering on pavement, the cab lurched to a stop at the edge of a broad lawn that led to a dark red freestone castle with crenellated towers. Beneath the unfurled bonnet, Eustace Buttonwood gazed at the building as he waited for the driver to steady the restive horse. Then he climbed out, brown leather briefcase under his arm, and paid his fare. A small man with a prominent nose and neat mustache, he adjusted his black homburg and started up the tree-lined walkway. Ahead lay the most important repository of knowledge in the nation, the Smithsonian Institution, and awaiting him inside was the man charged with executing its mission—"the increase and diffusion of knowledge among men"—third Secretary Samuel Pierpont Langley.

It would be unwise to keep Professor Langley waiting.

Buttonwood had known the Secretary for nearly twenty years, since the latter's tenure as professor of astronomy and physics at the Western University in Pittsburgh. As a second year student who showed functional promise in the physical sciences but lacked the imagination that distinguished a great scientist from a pedestrian experimenter, he had been in one of Langley's classes, where his classmates had nicknamed him Useless Buttonwood. Still, for some reason, Langley had taken a liking to the quiet loner and invited him to participate in investigations of solar radiation and the measurement of time. It was inevitable that he should assist his famous professor in other work at the Allegheny Observatory. By the time he completed his studies, he had earned every kindness in the Langley letter of reference that he carried into the world.

That letter opened doors for Buttonwood. For a few years he worked as a teacher, first in a public school and then in a small Ohio college. Next he served as a project engineer for public construction efforts, most notably a town hall in Maryland and a prison in Georgia. Afterward, he drifted through a series of uninspired jobs—architectural assistant in Atlanta, apothecary assistant in Richmond, mortuary assistant in Baltimore. In 1887, when he was assistant curator of a Florida museum, his old professor became the Secretary of the Smithsonian. Buttonwood wrote to the new Secretary to ask for a position, enclosing the now yellow recommendation in Langley's own hand.

At first Washington was less than Buttonwood's salvation. Instead of becoming assistant to the Secretary as he had hoped, he was shunted into one department after another, where he worked with archivists, botanists, naturalists, historians, curators, and finally the head keeper of the Institution's zoo in Rock Creek Park. Buttonwood worked without complaint, seeing to his assigned duties with a steady compliance that earned him a reputation for reliability. Each evening he retired to his room four blocks north of the mall. There he enjoyed a meal, a book, a relaxing pipe, and an occasional glass of rye. All his relatives having long since died, he corresponded with few persons by mail and seldom traveled outside the city. Over time, his disappointment at not working directly under the man he considered his mentor faded, and he settled into the simplicity of his solitary existence.

One spring afternoon, three years after he had come to the Institution, he was surprised to see the Secretary at the zoo, throwing pieces of meat to the vultures and directing assistants to photograph them in flight. Buttonwood did not understand why such cold-eyed scavengers should be of interest to Langley when the zoo held more beautiful species of birds. But he knew enough from his academic days not to pose the question. After all, Langley was possessed of a genius that eluded most men. Never having attended college, he was entirely self-taught in both architecture and astronomy. If he deemed it necessary to take photographs of vultures, who was Buttonwood to second-guess his intentions, ornithological or otherwise?

The unexpected death of a Mr. Briggs afforded Buttonwood an opportunity to put himself in Langley's good graces. When Briggs failed to appear one Friday, it fell to Buttonwood to replace him in one of the observation towers near the vulture enclosure. The camera there was most unusual, electronically connected to its counterpart in the opposite tower. Its accordion lens telescoped farther outward than any he had ever seen. "Mr. Piper will work the shutter," Langley called up to Buttonwood. "Just train that lens on the bird's wings." Learning of Briggs's death, Langley named Buttonwood his temporary replacement. Later, pleased with the photographs, he made the appointment to his personal staff permanent.

It became clear to Buttonwood even before his first vulture session ended that Professor Langley was gathering data for an attempt to solve the problem of heavier-than-air flight. The Old Man called his work the study of aerodromics, Greek for "running across the air." Though he had done preliminary investigation back at the Allegheny Observatory, the inconclusive results had left his assistants, Buttonwood among them, unconvinced of the practicality of flight. Now, however, with the resources of the Institution behind him, he pursued the possibility with a singular sense of purpose. In addition to the vulture studies, his experiments included mounting dead birds on large, steam-powered turntables and the construction of vulture-sized flying machine prototypes driven by rubber bands. The former enabled him to examine the effect of moving air on wings. The latter helped him envision the type of craft that might one day carry a man into the sky.

Initially, Buttonwood cared nothing about the feasibility of flight. Happy to be working with Langley, he followed the Secretary's directives with clear devotion. Nevertheless, on the afternoon of May 6, 1896, Buttonwood became a believer. Atop a Potomac houseboat near Quantico, he waited for Langley's signal from the river's edge. At 3:05, Buttonwood triggered the catapult launch of Aerodrome No. 5. Then he watched the steam-powered thirteen-foot model fly more than 3,000 feet. A cheer went up from the gathering on the riverbank, where friends and associates shook Langley's hand and clapped him on the back. Armed with a camera, Langley's friend and fellow scientist, Alexander Graham Bell, took photographs of the launch and the flight. From that moment forward Buttonwood believed a Langley flier would be the first to carry a man aloft and felt thick with pride that he would be part of the accomplishment.

If only his former classmates could see old Useless now . . .

By the time he made it through the Great Hall and to the Secretary's private office, Buttonwood was several minutes late. Hat in hand, he eased the door open and entered quietly. The light flooding through the arched windows was such a change from the dimness of the corridor that he squinted against it and waited beside the door.

Langley sat behind his massive desk, fingers absently tugging his white beard, dark brow furrowed in thought. He nodded to acknowledge Buttonwood. Then he dropped his gaze to the papers and pictures spread across his desktop. Using a large round magnifying glass, he lowered his chiseled face to one of the photographs to examine it more closely. After a minute or two he sat up, pulled a pen from its inkstand, and scratched something onto a piece of paper. Then he leaned back in his padded chair, thumbing his gray lapels, and smiled.

"Please have a seat, Mr. Buttonwood," he said. "Mr. Manly will be with us shortly."

"Thank you, sir." Buttonwood sat in one of the two wooden armchairs opposite the desk and pulled his briefcase and hat onto his lap.

"I trust you have the engine and carburetor specifications from Ohio."

"Yes, sir." Buttonwood unfastened his briefcase and pulled out a tied bundle of papers, which he placed on the desk.

"Good." Langley sat forward and untied the string, paging through the first few sheets. He studied the mechanical drawings at length. "What did their engineers think of our intended use?"

Buttonwood shifted uncomfortably. "Mr. Stiers, the chief engineer, does not believe such an application is possible. The engine's weight is too great and its power output insufficient."

Langley smiled. "Stiers does not know Mr. Manly and most assuredly does not know me."

Presently, the door opened, and they were joined by Charles Manly, the Old Man's chief mechanical engineer. An even smaller man than Buttonwood, Manly was in his mid-twenties and clad in a tan suit. He had a narrow face, with round spectacles riding low on his nose, and a bushy brown mustache. Moving with the ease of his years, he flung his brown derby onto a coat tree behind the door and went straight to Buttonwood to shake his hand.

Buttonwood returned the greeting with equanimity, though he disliked Manly intensely. He understood fully that his feelings were rooted in jealousy. He had known the Secretary longer, had worked for him for more than a decade. He resented that Manly, however gifted an engineer, had reached a position of such high esteem after only a few years with Langley. Why should this boy be so close to the Old Man, move so freely in his presence? Yet Buttonwood knew enough of his own limitations to realize that he could never displace Manly. He lacked the creative talent.

"News from the workshop?" Langley said to Manly.

"The frame is complete and meets all specifications," Manly said. "So do the propellers and shafts. Regrettably, the engine and gear train tests thus far have been less than satisfactory."

"It's been nearly five years since No. 5 made its first flight," Langley said, "and three since President McKinley got the War Department to allot us money for a man-sized aerodrome. The President really hoped to use it as a weapon against Spain." Langley sighed. "An amiable man, the President, but he has no grasp of scientific processes. Give him a War Room full of telephones and telegraphs and let him become the first president to have direct contact with his generals . . ."

"And he expects an aerodrome overnight," Manly said.

"Precisely." Langley shut his eyes and massaged his temples with his fingertips. "Still, he is within his rights to expect some kind of product after three years and $50,000, especially since the Institution added another $20,000 to the pot." Opening his eyes, he sat back. "Gentlemen, are you aware of how many other men are working to achieve flight? Every year the Institution sends out information to hundreds of them. To be sure, many are simply collectors of information. But how many men are building aerodromes in their barns or testing them in their fields?"

"All with far less funding and scientific certainty," Manly said. "Like Otto Lilienthal, most are gliderists. They can hop off roofs and float fifty feet or so, but a flying machine is useless unless it can travel a great distance. Most of these men are poorly suited to the development of such a conveyance."

"Things have changed since I first saw Lilienthal back in '94," Langley said. "Even he left behind tables describing his work and the manner in which wind buoys a wing. Last September two men named Wright, who obtained much of their information from the Institution, flew an aerodromic glider in North Carolina. It will not be long before someone solves the problems of propulsion and control." He fixed Manly with his eyes. "I intend to be that someone. I intend to see you fly one of my aerodromes."

Manly smiled. "You will, sir."

Langley pushed the bundle of papers to the edge of the desk. Manly glanced through the top four or five pages. Then he sank into the empty chair, pulling the stack onto his lap. He read, uninterrupted, for nearly ten minutes.

"What do you make of it, Charles?" Langley asked finally.

Manly unhooked the wire stem from his left ear and pulled off his spectacles. He locked eyes with Langley. "I believe, sir, we have located a design we can modify to suit our needs."

"Excellent!" Langley's cheeks flushed with excitement, the pink incongruous with the steel-and-snow weave of his beard. His eyes sparkled. "I knew you would see the possibilities."

Buttonwood said nothing as the two men discussed the engine specifications he had brought back. Instead, he let his mind drift over other possibilities, ways that he could *personally* safeguard the Secretary's primacy among those who sought to fly.

* * *

There she is!

Lucas Westbeck felt something snag deep in his throat as he caught sight of Pearl. Bucket and scrub brush in hand, she had come to his father's surgery this Friday morning to clean both the empty waiting room and the operatory. Lucas was seated in the book-lined consulting room with his father and chanced to look up the instant she passed the open door. Momentarily, he could not speak. Even with her hair capped, her dark face unpainted, and her tall body hidden inside her simple servant's dress, Pearl was beautiful beyond her station.

"Lucas?" The elder Dr. Westbeck removed his spectacles and held them above the medical reference open on his desk and leaned back, desk chair squeaking. "Feeling all right, son?"

Lucas felt his cheeks flush and absently curled one end of his mustache. "Sorry." He did not know whether Dr. Westbeck had noticed his interest in Pearl. "I. . .I had a thought I wanted to share, but it seems to have fled my brain." In apology, he offered an awkward smile.

"Had it anything to do with treating Mrs. Bell's feminine inconveniences?" His delicacy was tinged with impatience.

"No, sir," Lucas admitted.

Dr. Westbeck sat forward. "Whatever the notion, it will return when you least expect it. In the meantime . . ." Replacing his spectacles, he bent over his desk and resumed reading.

Lucas exhaled slowly to hide his relief. It simply wouldn't do for his father to suspect that he felt so drawn to a servant girl—a colored one—that her proximity left him speechless. It was inappropriate that he should feel anything in the presence of this girl. Lately, however, he had been unable to help himself. Her appearance in any room, under any circumstance, invariably caused a stirring in his loins that left him filled with shame and regret.

Lucas slipped his jacket over his gray waistcoat and excused himself, promising to see his father at dinner. In the corridor, he stopped outside the open door of the white-walled operatory, where Pearl, on hands and knees, worked the bristles of the scrub brush into the seams of the flooring. Her back was to him. For nearly a minute, he watched her without speaking.

As a doctor, Lucas knew full well the dangers of racial mixing. Some mixed children were left unduly weakened by the combination of photosensitive European skin and diminished African lung capacity. Others, tragically, inherited white intelligence but the darker skin that precluded the successful application of that intelligence. The most unfortunate succumbed to the uninhibited thirst for pleasure that doomed the negro to subservience and with the keenest eye watched their own descent into hell. In any case, the mulatto walked a narrow road between the races, neither of which fully welcomed him into their number.

Better to die childless than to bring such a miserable creature into the world, he told himself. Still, there was something different about Pearl. She was unlike other negro women he had known. She moved with a self-assurance that belied her gender, race, and age. Studying her, he reflected upon the Southern racialist of the last century, who clung to his white supremacy by day but was helpless between negro breasts at night. However captivated such a man would have been by Pearl, he would have taken her treasures without preamble. That in another time and place Pearl might have been used cruelly instead of cherished brought a bitter taste into Lucas's mouth.

"Pearl," he said softly, stepping into the operatory.

Startled, she almost dropped her scrub brush and whipped her head around to look over her shoulder. "Oh, Dr. Lucas!" She stood, smoothing the front of her pale blue dress. "Yes, sir?"

For once she did not look away as his gaze sought hers. Lucas felt a surge of gratitude. Because of her height, her eyes were nearly level with his—intelligent eyes, almond-shaped and brown, deep beyond her years. Despite his comparatively short time practicing medicine, Lucas had come to believe that eyes were not only windows to the soul but also to the intellect. Pearl's were not the eyes of a woman who should spend her life scrubbing other people's floors.

He chewed his lip. "Pearl, I've been giving some consideration to establishing my own surgery." With the next tick of the clock, he confessed to himself, the thought would be two seconds old. "I was wondering if you might consider coming to work for me."

Pearl lowered her eyes, in spite of his mental plea that she continue to look at him. For a time she said nothing. Then she raised her eyes again and spoke, the discomfort in her words all the proof he needed that she was aware of his attraction to her. "Sir, I might have some trouble finishing all my duties here, but if Dr. and Mrs. Westbeck want me to spend a day or two each week cleaning your surgery—"

"No, no," Lucas interrupted. "That's not the sort of work I had in mind." She averted her face, lower lip quivering, and he realized he had frightened her. "Pearl . . . Miss Parker, please. I assure you I intend nothing unseemly or dishonorable with this suggestion." Trembling, he fought the desire to take hold of her hands, to comfort her with contact. His fingertips ached to feel her rich brown skin. But it would be better not to touch her at all. He kept his distance, fists clenched at his sides. "You seem to be an intelligent young woman," he said. "I wondered if perhaps you might find it more satisfying to work in a surgery in a . . . different capacity."

"In what capacity?"

He inhaled deeply. "I'd like you to be my nurse."

She looked at him, eyes wide in astonishment. "Me?"

He was surprised at the color deepening in her cheeks. He had never before given thought to whether negroes could blush. "I believe you'd be well suited to it," he said.

"But, Dr. Lucas, I don't know anything about being a nurse."

At last in a conversation with her, Lucas forced himself to seem more at ease. He hooked his thumbs in the watch pockets of his waistcoat. "Of course, you'd have to undergo appropriate training."

"I don't believe there's a hospital in Buffalo that trains colored nurses," she said. "There is one in Chicago . . . and maybe one in Atlanta."

"There must be a way a bright colored girl such as yourself can become a nurse right in this area," he said. "I could train you myself."

Pearl said nothing but looked doubtful.

"Other physicians train their nurses. Why shouldn't I?"

In the uncomfortable silence Lucas felt his own face burning with embarrassment, as if he were standing naked before not only Pearl but his parents and their entire social circle, before Cornelia Wilcox, who his mother had said more than once would make him a sterling wife. He wondered if he had let his impulses get the better of him this time. Establishing his own surgery would take money, certainly more than he had at this point in his career, with so many of his hospital cases *pro bono*. His father would advise him against it, reminding him that he still had much to learn over the shoulder of a more experienced physician before he could train a nurse himself. And when Dr. Westbeck and his medical colleagues learned that Pearl was to be his nurse—if she was to be his nurse . . .

He steadied his gaze at Pearl and swallowed involuntarily. His words came from deep within, betraying more emotion than he intended or considered proper. "I trust you will do me the honor of at least considering my proposal."

She waited several heartbeats. "Yes," she said finally, "I will consider it."

Nearly drawing blood from his upper lip, Lucas suppressed his smile with his teeth.

Six

From the Chronicles of Augustus Lockhart:
Friday April 19

This morning I caught the Michigan trolley to the Expo for my first day of work. Mr. Buckett's letter said to report to the Service Building near the West Amherst gate. All the way up Elmwood my stomach fluttered so with excitement that I could not read my newspaper. I have passed the grounds for months now, walking from the end of the trolley line to the Driscolls'. Through the bars of the fence I watched the Exposition take shape, workers and horse-drawn wagons slogging through the mud, turning piles of lumber into pavilions. Then bare wood and plaster disappeared beneath pastel paints, dirt paths became walkways, and pits became fountains guarded by dynamic statues. At last it was the Rainbow City promised by the newspapers, a magical burst of color beneath Buffalo's endless gray sky. Now I could hardly wait to show my letter and pass through the gate.

Mr. Buckett was waiting inside, with a dozen or so other boys, all of them white. I knew he was Mr. Buckett because he stood beside a gray trash barrel on wheels that said Buckett's Brigade, Sweepers. He is a round man, with gray whiskers curving up each cheek and stubby fingers with dirty nails. He was rocking on his heels when I went up to him.

"Mr. Buckett?" I said. "Sir, I'm Augustus Lockhart." I

held up the letter.

Without a glance at the letter, he told me to stand with the others. Then he pulled a silver watch from his waistcoat pocket and popped the lid.

Presently, other boys began to arrive. When there were about twenty of us, Mr. Buckett looked at his watch again, then faced us. "My good lads," he began in a loud voice, "my name is Edward Buckett. Welcome to the sweeper service that bears my name, Buckett's Brigade. Mine is one of the services hired to keep this here Exposition clean." He walked back and forth before us, reading our names off a paper he produced from his coat pocket. He explained our schedules and duties and wages, assigning most of us to three or four days of work. Mine are Monday, Tuesday, and Wednesday—which leaves me three full days to help Will and one to rest, as the Creator intended.

"Report here each day," said Mr. Buckett. He hooked a thumb over his shoulder toward the yellow building behind him, a mission style structure with bell towers flanking a center arch and a roof of red tiles. "Sweepers are not to disturb business by entering the Service Building or short-cutting through the inner courtyard. Go around to the sheds in back to get your rigs." His face reddened as he spoke, as if it took great effort to push the words between his lips. "I'll take you there myself today. Once you have your rigs, I'll lead you on a walk-through. Then I'll give each of you a map with your individual route." He wagged a finger at us. "Remember to stick to your own route. Won't do to have the whole Brigade in the northeast when the biggest mess is in the southwest. Now follow me. There's a lot to do before we open May first."

Maneuvering the heavy barrel took some practice, but the walk-through was even more exciting than I had imagined. Mr. Buckett rattled off names as we went—the Court of

Fountains, the Triumphal Bridge, the Esplanade, the Mirror Lakes. The buildings are generally pale—from green to blue to salmon to ivory—and reflect architectural styles that range from Greco-Roman to Spanish renaissance. Most have domes and arches and inscriptions in panels below their roofs. Some buildings represent states like New York and Ohio and countries like Mexico and Cuba. Others honor progress in science and industry, like Horticulture and Mines and Electricity. The Temple of Music is to be the scene of great performances. Watching over everything from a height of 400 feet is the Goddess of Light, a gold statue atop the Electric Tower to the north.

This is the most breathtaking place I've ever seen.

*　*　*

Papa Joe stood atop the hill opposite the barn. The Saturday sun hung high, unhindered by clouds, its threat to unmelted patches of snow down in the hollow diminished by the swirling morning winds. The wind was at his back and cut into his shoulders and spine, igniting memories of the lash before shifting its attack to his right, then his left. He was cold, coattails and sleeves and even trousers billowing like mainsails, but he did not care. This was exactly the kind of day Will had said they would need for their glider test. Inside his muddy boots, Papa Joe curled his toes to anchor himself in the wet ground, and he waited.

Soon the barn doors swung wide. Out stepped Captain Driscoll. He clamped his hat to his head with a hand and started down the hill at a brisk waddle, upturned lapels fluttering. In the hollow—below the point at which the twin launch rails fixed to the barn ended at an acute upward sweep—he slowed, as Papa Joe had done just minutes earlier, the soft earth sucking at his feet. By the time Driscoll had climbed the second hill to stand beside Papa Joe, he was breathing hard and fumbling with the top button of his heavy black frock coat.

"Mr. Lockhart," he said, "you must be freezing in so light a coat. May I offer you a stout topcoat from the house? Or a blanket? I must have something that will fit you."

"No, Captain Driscoll." Papa Joe smiled. "I am grateful for your kindness, but this is far too fine a day to worry about a little chill." Closing his eyes, he filled his lungs with the sharp air, then let it out slowly. "From time to time I need days like this to make this old body remember it's alive, that it can still feel the hand of God." He turned to Driscoll. "This is a day I want very much to feel the hand of God in our work."

Driscoll smiled.

Papa Joe was pleased that Captain Driscoll stood at his side. In the three weeks he had known him, he had developed a deepening affection for him. Sometimes, while the younger men worked, the Captain led him back to the house for food or drink. "We don't know enough about what they're doing to be more than a hindrance," he would say. "We're too old to help." So they would talk, two old men from different pasts in the same world, pasts which bound them to each other in ways the younger men would not understand. Separately, they had witnessed the nation's transition from slave federation to flawed republic, from farm commonwealth to industrial state. Together, in growing friendship, they would see it enter the age of the aeroplane.

In the beginning Papa Joe was content to let Captain Driscoll do most of the talking and found himself genuinely intrigued by the Captain's accounts of his business exploits. He'd always had some idea how a man obtained wealth; he had read such stories in the weeklies. But no one had ever illustrated for him in such detail the intricate toil that went into amassing even a small fortune. Later, Papa Joe made only cryptic references to his prior bondage but learned Driscoll had seen for himself the residual miseries of slavery as the Union army pushed farther south. Encouraged by the earnestness of Driscoll's Civil War experiences, he finally revealed how fifty years earlier a runaway named slave William MacAtley became blacksmith Joseph Lockhart. For the first time in a long while, he told the whole story—the killing of the slave catcher and the apprentice blacksmith, the release of the abolitionists when the slave catcher failed to return, the secret burial of the dead. "A slave catcher and a negro, companions in eternity. I still go to pray over them—for three souls, for the two who lie in unconsecrated ground and the one who put them there."

Captain Driscoll, who had listened that day without interrupting, said, "If freedom is one of the few ideas worth dying for, then it must also be one of the few worth killing for." Then he slid another glass of whiskey across the table.

One morning Driscoll invited him for a ride in the Packard, an offer Papa Joe eagerly accepted. As they bounced along Delaware Avenue, the Captain explained how Papa Joe might diversify his blacksmith business to accommodate the automobile. "The horseless carriage will need its metal parts reshaped and repaired as its horse-drawn ancestor does today. If you were a liveryman as well as a blacksmith, you could acquire your own automobiles. Think of the services you could offer— autos for hire, auto repair, autos for sale."

Nostrils filling with the smell of burning fuel, Papa Joe was quiet for a time and then shook his head. "I'm too old," he said over the rumble of the engine. "True, the automobile will make blacksmiths into relics, but I'm already relic enough not to worry about when I'll have to close up shop. The Good Lord will close it for me soon enough. I pray only that I live long enough to see Will in business with you and Daniel, and Gus with a job that doesn't exceed his physical limits."

"Gus is a good boy and hard worker," Captain Driscoll said. "I've watched how he does whatever he can to help his brother. I promise you, when this Exposition is finished, I will find Gus a job in one of my companies." He turned to Papa Joe. "Not as a sweeper or a bootblack."

Papa Joe swallowed. "Thank you."

Driscoll took a deep breath. "Now, I don't want you telling me you're too old. You have some years on me, true, but I know you're stronger than I am and could outrun me with your pockets full of scrap iron." He slowed, eased the Packard to the curb, and stopped. "The trouble with you, Mr. Lockhart, is that you have worked your entire life and never taken the time to play. In that respect you and I are very much alike. I, too, have spent my life working and caring for my family. After I lost Anna, then the Exposition, I left Buffalo last year, tired and defeated, feeling old. Someone once told me there is nothing like play to make a person feel young again. Going about the city in this, I have begun to see the truth in that." He climbed down out of the Packard. "Which is why you're going to drive us back."

Papa Joe's belly tightened. "I don't know how."

"Neither did I at first. You'll soon have the knack of it."

"This is hardly a plaything."

Captain Driscoll laughed. "It won't always be. There'll come a time when automobiles are as plentiful as horses. Right now, though, there is no finer toy in the world."

Minutes later, despite his protests that he was too old to remember how to work the tiller and the hand and foot brakes, Papa Joe lurched away from the curb and turned completely around in the street, much to the alarm of two carriage drivers forced to rein in their horses to avoid a collision. But after several wide swerves, he managed to bring the auto under control and was soon chugging north on Delaware, the wind plastering tears to his cheeks. He wondered if his exhilaration bore any resemblance to the feeling that would accompany flying. If so, whoever lay in the Blackbird's hammock was destined for a remarkable experience.

Presently, Will and the others emerged from the barn, coats buttoned to their necks. Andrew and Daniel each held a two-tiered wing and gripped one side of the tail as wind buffeted the miniature and tried to tear it out of their grasp. Will walked at the head of the procession, a thin rope coiled in one hand and Portius Banks beside him, carrying a camera attached to a tripod. Newcomb followed Daniel. Gus brought up the rear, arms enfolding one of Will's notebooks to his chest. Even from his spot atop the hill, Papa Joe could see that the other end of the rope was fixed to the bottom of the glider, which resembled nothing so much as a giant dragonfly.

"It will almost be like flying a kite," Papa Joe said.

When the men had put some distance between themselves and the barn, Will signaled them to stop. He pointed to an area of the sky, and Portius opened the tripod, angling the camera. Then Will indicated a spot just below the crest of the hill. Newcomb scuttled forward, producing a mallet and ring-topped spike from the folds of his gray ulster. He hammered the spike into the ground, leaving only the ring visible. Will knelt and tied his end of the rope to the ring. Then he stood, and Daniel released the tail. The glider bucked, like a horse kicking backward in its stall.

"It wants to go!" Driscoll said. "Damned if it doesn't!"

At such a distance and in such wind, Papa Joe could not hear what Will was saying but knew he was giving angling and release instructions to Andrew and Daniel. A few seconds later everyone stepped clear of the craft except the men holding it and Will, who unlooped several feet of rope and sank to his knees beneath the wings. Portius got into position behind the camera. Then, as if they had practiced the movement together all their lives, Andrew and Daniel took a step forward in unison and let go of the miniature with a gentle heave.

The glider nosed upward nine or ten feet and slammed into the palm of an invisible hand, the fingers of which closed round the wings and hurled it to the ground a few feet away from Will. The tether had not even tightened.

"Damn," Driscoll muttered.

Will knelt beside the fallen glider as if it were a comrade wounded in battle and examined the sateen and the frame and every fastener, then the entire tail assembly. Finally, gently, he cradled each wing and the tail, making fine adjustments with a small screwdriver he extracted from his coat pocket. When he was finished, he climbed to his feet and waved to his grandfather to indicate they were ready to try again.

Papa Joe waved back and looked over at Captain Driscoll, who nodded to reassure him.

The second trial failed also, as did the third, the fourth, and the fifth. On the sixth try, the glider hit the ground with such force that the frame of the lower left wing cracked apart. The look on Will's face was one Papa Joe had not seen since Augusta had been taken from them.

* * *

That evening Papa Joe convinced Will not to sleep in the barn. Tonight especially the boy needed the comfort of home, the security of family. With both his grandsons facing each other across the scarred kitchen table, Papa Joe moved back and forth between the larder and the ice box, chattering happily and firing up the old woodstove. Soon the air thickened with the smells of cooking as he produced a meal of pan-fried cheese bread, onions, beans, and sausage. Shoveling food onto plates with a spatula, he set one in front of Will and another in front of Gus, then returned to the sideboard for his own. He took his place at the head of the table, held hands with his grandsons as he led them in prayer, and picked up his fork.

Will held his tongue throughout the meal and merely picked at his food, despite Gus's best efforts to engage him. Instead of mentioning the glider trials, Gus talked about the Exposition. Much of what he said he had already told them, but Papa Joe made no attempt to interfere with his descriptions of the buildings and the grounds. The excitement in Gus's voice was a welcome antidote to Will's silence.

"There'll be a boat ride on a canal that goes all around it," Gus said between bites. "And the Midway has villages from the Philippines, Hawaii, and Japan. There's an upside down house and a thing called A Trip to the Moon. I can't wait to ride the Captive Balloon . . ." Gus's voice trailed off, and he looked at his brother as if he had said something wrong.

Will said nothing, letting his unfocused gaze speak for him.

"It's all right, Gus," Papa Joe said. "Why don't you leave the table, so Will and I can talk a spell. Maybe you've got some writing you'd like to do. Go on, take your plate with you."

Gus's face fell. He pushed back, chair legs scraping the floor, and climbed to his feet. "I'm sorry, Will." Then, plate in hand, he disappeared into their bedroom.

For a time Papa Joe said nothing. He simply stared at Will, who sat to his right, hands clasped above a barely touched plate of food. Papa Joe wanted to say something to him, knew he must, but despite the millions of words he had devoured in his lifelong hunger to learn, he could find none sharp enough to penetrate his grandson's profound desolation. Uncertain of a better response to the silence, he placed a hand on Will's shoulder.

"I remember when you used to keep pigeons out back of the shop," he said finally, "and how attentive you used to be when they'd eat right out of your hand, how sometimes you would stroke their backs or the edge of their wings."

Will turned to face him, brow knit in an unvoiced question.

"I don't have any answers for you, son, and I don't know why it wouldn't fly either." Papa Joe withdrew his hand, rested his forearm on the table. "But I do know Will Lockhart. He's the kind of man who won't separate himself from a problem until it is solved. I've always admired his patience and persistence, and I know he'll find the answer he's looking for."

Will smiled faintly. "Papa, I can't find it," he said.

The skin between Papa Joe's eyes knotted. "What do you mean you can't find it? You can't give up because of one setback—not a failure, mind you, a setback."

Will placed his fingers, lightly, on Papa Joe's forearm. "I don't believe in giving up," he said. "I haven't given anything up. I just don't understand how I understand what I understand."

Bewildered, Papa Joe sat up straight, lips parting.

"I don't find the answers," Will said. "They find me."

"I'm . . . lost. I don't know what you mean."

Will shook his head, as if doing so would clear Papa Joe's confusion. "I see something," he said, "notice some detail. It might be something big or something small, something everybody sees or something that catches only my eye. But when I see it, an idea springs into my head—just jumps in, uninvited and full of possibilities. It may solve a problem or create a new one, but it comes in all by itself. I can't force it."

Papa Joe sank back in his chair, studying his grandson with new insight. He had always known Will was special, had talents that others lacked. Will saw the world differently, saw it as a ball of clay to be shaped and reshaped, and Papa Joe had come to rely upon the certainty of that vision. He had accepted as an article of faith that it was based upon Will's own confidence in his innate abilities. Now it surprised him to learn that Will understood his own gifts no better than anyone else. "So you're waiting for the next idea—or answer—to find you?"

Will nodded. "It's the only thing I can do."

Papa Joe shook his head. "No, it's not the only thing you can do." He stood. "Get your coat, Will. We're gonna sit outside a bit. We're gonna sit there under the stars without talking and just look at the sky. When you want something to find you, it helps to wait out in the open. And when you're aiming to get somewhere, it's best to keep looking in that direction."

Temple of Music Colonnade
Courtesy of the University at Buffalo Libraries

Seven

From the Chronicles of Augustus Lockhart:
Sunday April 21

Today in church I felt unsteady and agitated, as if Will's grief at the loss of the first glider has settled into my bones. Much as I share Papa Joe's faith in Will, it occurred to me for the first time that the Blackbird might fail, that God might not have intended His pitiful children to fly. Then I saw Pearl enter the sanctuary and take her place at the piano. As always, her singing went deep inside me to a place I cannot reach alone. I felt the touch of God, the calming hand of the Almighty on my shoulder. How, I asked, could He let us fail? Our work is His work, larger than Will, larger than all of us together. This work is for our people, for those who toil in shadow, unseen by others who walk in the light. This work is the strength behind the smile the world finds weak and stupid. This work will elevate us, as a people.

How can we fail?

After church I asked Reverend Banks if I might walk with Pearl for a block or two. I had long wanted to join her for an afternoon stroll, but she is a head taller than I, and sometimes, in her presence, I feel the acute misfortune of my birth and my illnesses. With summer coming, I expect other young men from Ascension to call on her, hat in hand, on Sunday afternoons. Will she even see poor little Gus beside someone taller, stronger, and more handsome? Today, however, her music saved me from despair, gave me a new sense of purpose. If a colored voice can soar toward the angels, why not a colored man? She is privy to the Blackbird. Perhaps in that we will find a bond.

The walk lasted three blocks. The first passed without my saying a word. From a distance I imagine I looked proud. Pearl was so beautiful in her yellow spring dress and feathered hat that any man would have strutted like a cock to be with her. But anyone close enough to see my face would have seen my trembling lips and blinking eyes. I was too nervous to speak, too frightened of sounding foolish. I needed the first block to regain the courage I had found in approaching her uncle, the courage that abandoned me in sunlight.

However, it was Pearl who broke the silence.

"My uncle told me about yesterday," she said. "How's Will?"

I shrugged. "Discouraged, but by tomorrow he'll be reworking his figures and testing his last miniature in this device he calls a wind shaft." Then, suddenly, it struck me that if she asked after Will, quite possibly she had feelings for him. "Why do you ask?"

"It seemed a good place to start, since you were being so quiet." She smiled.

My heart stumbled and my cheeks went hot with embarrassment. I slowed to let her pass.

"I'm teasing," she said. "I hope I haven't offended you."

I told her she hadn't but I couldn't at once decide whether I was lying or simply incapable of annoyance in the face of her beauty. I had wanted to talk to her of poetry and flying and the Exposition, to impress her with all that I remember from reading, to intrigue her with descriptions of the Rainbow City. I had wanted to praise her singing, to let her see the man inside the boy's body. Now I was unsure I could.

We continued walking.

"I thought your playing today was . . . beautiful," I said, keeping my eyes focused straight ahead. My back teeth hurt as I clenched them. "And your singing."

"Thank you."

My heart was throwing itself against my rib cage, and I made fists at my sides to keep my fingers still. "I bet if you wanted to," I said, "you could be a . . . real singer—I mean, you could make your living at it. You could sing at Shea's Garden." It was easy to imagine her standing in the middle of that big stage on a warm summer night, as elegantly dressed gentlemen and ladies filed into their seats. The waiting audience would cool themselves with palm fans. Their voices would fade until the only sounds would be the whisper of paddle fans overhead and an infrequent cough from the back of the theater. Then the curtain would rise, and all eyes would be on Pearl, tall and smiling, her face and gown resplendent in the shimmering limelights. She would hold them spellbound with her singing, and afterward they would clap until their hands bled . . .

"I could never sing for a living," said Pearl, shaking her head.

"But you're so good," I said.

"Not good enough," she said. "Besides, I might become a nurse."

"A nurse?" The picture from the Garden melted into something white and indistinct. I had trouble imagining her—imagining any colored woman—in nurse's garb. Nurses are old and stern and lumpy, like sacks of potatoes. On streetcars and in passing carriages they wear pinched looks and strange hats. They are always white—but if Will can be first in flight, why shouldn't Pearl be first in nursing?

"I'm thinking about it," she said. "Dr. Lucas thinks I'd make a fine nurse. He'll train me himself if he can't convince a hospital to accept me."

I was confused. "I thought you worked for Dr. Westbeck."

"I do. Dr. Mordecai Westbeck. Lucas Westbeck is his son."

"He'll train you himself?"

"Yes. He'll need a nurse when he opens his own surgery."

Her voice held an unmistakable pride, and some other feeling I did not understand. What I did understand—even as we spoke of other matters and I offered to escort her to the Exposition and promised on the parsonage doorstep to accompany her to the market next Saturday—was the uneasiness creeping through my mind, the futility filling my heart. Should Pearl become a nurse, she will be lost to me forever. I do not believe nurses are permitted to marry.

*   *   *

Thursday April 25

Today's glider test was a great success.

Our procedure was the same, though I replaced Daniel on one side of the miniature so he could concentrate on keeping the tail steady. We practiced the launch steps for a long time in the barn. One-two-three, gently push away from the chest. Again and again we executed the motion, with Reverend Banks and Papa Joe carefully catching the released glider.

Finally, Will decided we were ready. We left the barn, with Danny holding the tail and the others bringing up the rear. Papa Joe and Captain Driscoll struck off down the first hill and up the second. Will made a quick calculation of wind direction and angled us accordingly, directing Jonas Newcomb where to drive his spike. Reverend Banks positioned the camera as Will tied the tether to the spike. Mrs. Banks stood back, with Will's notebooks in her arms. I held my breath and whispered a prayer. On Will's signal, Danny let go of the tail. The miniature strained to free itself of our hold.

One. Two. Three. Gently push . . .

It flew the first time, the coiled rope snapping to its full length as everyone cheered. It flew a second and third time, as Reverend Banks took photograph after photograph. It flew the fourth time, angling and dipping in the wind but righting itself after each light tug on the tether. Had it not been secured, the glider would have flown away.

The next glider will be the Blackbird itself, minus an engine. It will carry a man inside.

* * *

Saturday April 27

This morning, as I had promised, I caught the trolley to Dr. Westbeck's to accompany Pearl to the Chippewa Market. She was ready when I got there, wearing an everyday hat and a spring coat over her work uniform and carrying a large basket. I offered to carry her basket, and we strolled toward the streetcar stop. Before we could reach the corner, however, churning and popping noises from behind made us turn around. A topless black automobile with a high carriage seat sputtered to the curb, its tires and wheel spokes spattered with mud. Behind the tiller sat a hatless white man with dark red hair. He pushed his driving goggles up and looked down at us, calling Pearl by name. For barely an instant his eyes met mine, then focused on Pearl.

"Has my mother got you running to market today?" he asked.

"Yes," Pearl answered. She turned to me. "Dr. Lucas, this is Gus."

I went toward his automobile, my hand outstretched. Papa Joe has always taught us that the proper way to shake a man's hand is to move toward him, step into it, and gaze into his eyes. That way, he knows you are unafraid of him—even when he's looking down at you from the seat of a two-thousand-dollar automobile.

"Lucas Westbeck," he said, leaning down to take my hand. "You're Pearl's . . . brother?"

"My friend," she said before I could answer.

Dr. Lucas's hand was slender, the softness masking the strength of his grip. His topcoat was of fine wool, the top buttons undone to reveal a high wing collar and silk tie with jeweled stickpin. (I wondered if Pearl had starched that collar.) Something unsettling flashed in his eyes. This was the man who wanted Pearl to be his nurse, who would train her himself if necessary. I disliked him instantly and could see in his furrowed brow that he held me in equally low esteem.

Fascinated by the automobile, Pearl seemed unaware of the tension between us. "I didn't know you had this," she said, looking back and forth along its length.

"Just dragged it out of the carriage house," said Dr. Lucas. "This was the mystery object in the back, covered by a tarpaulin. But then I don't suppose going out there has been one of your duties, has it?"

"No, sir." Pearl pressed a gloved finger to the side of the automobile, as though curious about its composition.

"It's a Duryea Cosmopolitan," said Dr. Lucas. "My father bought it two years ago but tired of it rather quickly, so it passed to me." Then his face brightened. "Say, why don't you just climb aboard and let me drive you?" He slid away from the center of the seat to make room for Pearl, patting the black cushion to indicate where she should sit.

"What about Gus?" She looked from him to me and back. "He's helping me today."

For a moment there was no sound except the soft stutter of the automobile engine. Then Dr. Lucas pointed and said I could sit on the narrow flat surface behind the seat. "Might get a bit warm back there," he said, after I had helped Pearl mount the small iron step and settle into the carriage seat beside him. He pulled the goggles back down over his eyes. "And you'd better find something to hold on to," he added. "We wouldn't want you to fall off."

Holding Pearl's basket in my lap, I twisted to keep a grip on the decorative hand rail that framed the seat. Then we were off. I bounced with every bump we hit and feared I would tumble into the street. I must have been quite a sight. Several strollers pointed at me—a funny little negro clinging for life to the back of an automobile. But I was too concerned for my safety to count the smiles of the people we passed. I hung on. Besides not wanting Pearl to be alone with this man, I wanted to show him that a Lockhart is not so easily shaken loose.

At the market Dr. Lucas waited with his automobile while I went with Pearl to the stalls where farmers and butchers and bakers sold their goods. However much he wanted her to be his nurse, he seemed to hesitate when it was time to join us. Perhaps to his relief, a gang of admiring boys set upon him at once with questions about his automobile. How, I wondered, could he train Pearl if being seen with her made him so uncomfortable? Then it struck me that his interest in her might not be entirely proper. Suddenly, I felt the need to protect her, but how could I tell her that her dream of nursing had risen from an impure source?

Soon, however, my thoughts surrendered to the sights and sounds of the market. The long aisles formed by rows of boxy sheds were crammed with people, horses, and wagons, though things would be much more hectic in the fall, when local farmers brought in their harvests to sell. Despite the absence of fresh produce, there were plenty of cheeses and sausages, breads and cakes, and fresh pork and beef. Someone was frying bacon over a small fire in front of one of the sheds, offering samples to passers-by to get them to buy a slab. The air was thick with voices and scraping feet, the rasp of wooden scoops thrust into sacks of dried beans, the clucking of chickens crated for sale; thick with smells other than fried bacon—citrus that had come by rail from the South, coffee that had come by ship from South America, kerosene for lamps, and horse manure. Here and there amid the sellers of milk and eggs and flour were men hawking tins of meat, fish, beans, and stew. Several stalls were cluttered with household items—crockery, churns, kitchen tools, ice tongs, incomplete china sets. Others offered young potted plants ready for the home garden—tomatoes, assorted squashes, snap beans.

One stall in the fourth row was occupied by a seller of playthings—jacks, blocks, balls, ring toss—and dolls, from the floppy rag variety to delicate porcelain. I noticed Pearl admiring one of the porcelain dolls, but it cost more than I could afford. I went to the flower stall next to the toy seller and spent the trolley fare the automobile ride saved me on a bouquet of snowdrops.

The ride back was somehow less fearsome. Afraid I might lose sausages or break eggs, Pearl kept the basket on her lap. As I struggled to keep hold of the hand rail, I saw the snowdrops sitting atop the basket—for Dr. Lucas Westbeck, if not all the world, to see.

* * *

Wednesday May 1

Although some of the construction and several streets

remain unfinished, the Exposition opened its gates today. Dedication ceremonies have been postponed until May 20 because of the unusually cold weather and strikes among some of the workmen. (The carpenters struck just two days ago because they were forced to use inferior grades of lumber.) Still, the opening was most impressive. The first fairgoers were admitted at eight, as clouds threatened to stretch through the entire day. Unconcerned that no building was fully ready, well-dressed people strolled through the grounds in growing numbers, listening to military bands and trumpet fanfares. Children dragged their parents from one exhibit to another, until the benches along the Esplanade began to fill with the weary.

The size of the crowds doubled by noon, when the first buildings were dedicated, and then seemed to double again in the next few hours. Some people were drawn inside by the afternoon cannon salute, which must have been heard beyond the grounds. At three, with much ceremony and several bands playing "Home, Sweet Home" as loudly as possible, the Exposition's leaders released 3,000 homing pigeons, which rose in a great cloud over the Esplanade. The cloud hung in place no more than a second or two. Then it broke apart, its constituents dispersing in every direction to disappear into the brightening sky.

By early evening the clouds were gone and the gentle breeze had grown sharper. After my work ended, I remained behind to walk the grounds and imagine what this Exposition will mean to my family, my people. Just yesterday I read in the newspaper of a colored man in Lockport whose white neighbors burned down his horse shed to get the "darkeys" off Ohio Street. Such a story only makes me more determined to help Will see his dream become real. If what we do here before the world spares our children and their children from such cruelties, then this Exposition will be worth every cent of the five million dollars it cost to build and every instant of the dangers we are almost certain to face.

Finally tired, I sat on a bench near the Court of the Fountains and watched what had to be the most beautiful sunset of my life. Later, leaving through the Amherst gate, I overheard one ticket seller tell another that twenty thousand people had passed through the gates today. I had seen few colored among them.

"Soon," I whispered as I headed out to the streetcar terminal. "Soon."

Part Two

Proving the Wings

One of Papa Joe's favorite sayings for expressing his frustration with the limits placed on our race was "in another time and another skin." Sometimes he would shake his head and just say it, without qualification or explanation. He said more than once of my brother Will, who possessed an intellect and imagination second to none, "In another time and another skin, he would be a master engineer, a maker of bridges and buildings and machines." But Papa Joe said these things long before Will had seized upon the idea of flight. However big a dreamer he was himself, I don't think Papa Joe understood fully my brother's dreaming until two weeks after Will explained it to him over supper one hot summer evening in 1899.

"Everything changes," Will said, in a conversation whose beginning I cannot now precisely remember. "Consider what the electrical trolley has done to the horse-drawn car. How long before the automobile does the same to the horse and carriage? A few years ago, when the Ellicott Square opened, it was the world's largest office building. But buildings will continue to grow larger and taller. It will soon be dwarfed. And the telephone will be in every home—as will electricity, to power a good many devices not yet imagined." He spread his arms wide, a fork in one hand and a piece of bread in the other. "Everything changes. We must imagine those changes and be ready for them—or make them happen."

Two weeks after that, he showed us his first drawings of an aeroplane.

—From the unpublished manuscript Flight of the Blackbird *by Augustus Lockhart*

Eight

While his neighbors went out—couples to the theater, single ladies to quilting parties or reading groups, single gentlemen to nearby taverns—Eustace Buttonwood usually spent Friday evenings alone in his room. He had no use for tavern songs and romantic plays and frivolous intrigues. His natural inclination toward solitude had been reinforced over the years by memories of his classmates' reactions to his pedestrian approach to science and by the series of mundane jobs to which he had applied himself with singular diligence. No one in Washington— with the possible exception of the Secretary himself—knew Buttonwood's old college nickname, but he still bristled at the label Useless. He understood his own shortcomings well enough. He lacked the imagination of more adventurous thinkers, would never solve any problem facing society. But he was far from useless. It was his purpose in life not to be pivotal but to assist the pivotal. If given a task, he would complete it, competently and without question, even if he could not picture the grander design that encompassed his work. The eternal assistant, he stood ready to accept his next assignment, whether gathering laboratory materials or running errands. "There is a package waiting for me over at the Archives," Langley might say, or, "I need some research done at the Library of Congress on the migratory patterns of Monarch butterflies." Without further direction, Buttonwood would slip into his coat and put on his hat. Sometimes the Old Man simply had to think aloud to hand out Buttonwood's next task: "I wonder if those new lenses have arrived yet?"

Having no interests outside the Institution, he was content to surrender his evenings to quiet reflection. His room was a small corner affair on the top floor of a modest brick boarding house some blocks north of the mall. It was just large enough to hold a gentleman's four-poster bed, an oak wardrobe, a writing table and matching chair, a washstand, and a stuffed armchair. The most attractive feature, however, was a large bow window above a padded seat. Seated at the window, pipe in mouth, was how he usually spent most evenings. When he tired of reading but was still unready for sleep, or when the next day's suit was brushed and his shoes polished, he sometimes passed an hour sipping rye and puffing away as he watched the comings and goings of other Washingtonians, both glittering and grimy, four stories below. The detachment he felt from gentry and commonfolk alike infused his casual study of the people who passed below with a fascination—and sometimes an anger—that they could move so freely among each other. He had never quite felt at ease among people and did not understand the confidence with which so many approached life when they had so little to offer mankind.

But tonight was different. Tonight the bed, writing table, and window seat were covered with string-bound files. His pipe lay abandoned on the washstand as he paced the room, reading this or that document, occasionally sitting at the writing table to add information to his sheaves of notes. Tonight he had more than a casual interest in the confidence of others. He sought men of supreme confidence whose work would be of particular interest to Samuel Langley. Buttonwood was especially pleased with his own cleverness.

In the two weeks since his meeting with the Secretary, he had hit upon an idea inspired by Langley's claim that hundreds of men might be building aerodromes. What Langley needed—and Buttonwood was primed to undertake—was a reconnaissance mission to determine the readiness of other fliers. Taking advantage of his position as one of Langley's assistants, he had reviewed hundreds of requests for information on the progress of powered human flight. While many had come from the curious, he estimated there must be two dozen serious fliers. Some would push their machines off roofs only in the presence of a camera, but there must be others working in secrecy, waiting to prevail against the sky before announcing themselves to the world. It wasn't grand showmanship that threatened the Secretary's dominance of the sky but the quiet diligence of anonymous labor.

Buttonwood had worked his way through the correspondence slowly, seeking fliers with the best chance of success. It was his goal to compile a list of men to call upon, sites to inspect. Now he was willing to wager that the twenty or so names with five or more requests—the files strewn about his room—were the ones who warranted the closest scrutiny. On Monday, after returning the files, he would present his plan to the Secretary—who, doubtless, would endorse it and fund whatever travel he deemed necessary. Langley, he knew, would salivate at a chance to peer over the shoulders of his competitors.

Later, as Buttonwood settled into sleep, several names floated in his brain: Wright (the Secretary had mentioned them), Landry, Montrose, Weisskopf, Stoner, Whitehead, Billings, Lockhart . . .

*   *   *

From the Chronicles of Augustus Lockhart:
Saturday May 11

Today, in a dozen trials, we put Andrew up in the glider. We needed every hand present to help lift, angle, and push. On the first attempt I held my breath as the wind caught the wings. That glide was short and low, maybe twenty yards into the hollow from a starting height of about ten feet, but we cheered at how smoothly the Blackbird flew. Each glide thereafter was longer, as Andrew got the knack of working the cable and pulley controls. For the final trial of the day, he traveled nearly sixty yards. Will was most encouraged by Andrew's quick mastery of the controls. At this rate, he says, we will soon be ready for the next and most dangerous trial, launching the glider off the barn roof . . .

* * *

Sunday May 12

In church this morning Reverend Banks announced that there will be an American negro exhibit at the Exposition after all. It will be the exhibit from the Paris exposition—books, charts, photographs, and dioramas. It will occupy a rear corner of the Manufacturers and Liberal Arts Building, under the supervision of James Ross, the colored mason.

"They've put it where nobody will see it," said Papa Joe as we walked home after church. "It will be forgotten quickly, like everything else about us." He turned and looked down at me and wrinkled his brow. "You know how many patents are held by colored folk?"

"No, sir, I don't," I said, knowing he couldn't wait to tell me.

"Four hundred," he said proudly. "Four hundred! But most people believe the negro has never invented anything. Now, can you name me one negro invention? Just one?"

I couldn't.

"The first shoe pegger," he said, wagging a finger.

"Nobody remembers it was invented by a negro because people forget what we do. Even we forget what we do. The things we build, forgotten. The books we write, forgotten. The wars we fight, forgotten. Sometimes it seems all we're good at is being forgotten." His shoulders had sagged as he recounted the sad state of the race, but then they rose again, and he seemed even taller as he smiled. "But an aeroplane that flies! Nobody will ever forget who made that."

*   *   *

Thursday May 16

While Will and Andrew prepared for Saturday's trial, the rest of us did no aeroplane work today. I spent my afternoon at the Exposition, a fairgoer instead of a sweeper. The attractions I wished to see most were along the Midway, which is closed Sundays, the day I am most likely to accompany Pearl, if she accepts my invitation. Many Midway exhibits and cycloramas are not yet open to the public, like the House Upside Down or A Trip to the Moon. But I did accomplish my deepest Midway desires by riding the Aerio-Cycle and the Captive Balloon.

The Aerio-Cycle has two wheels that revolve slowly, one at either end of a long steel seesaw balanced atop an A-frame tower. Each wheel seats several passengers, while the tower acts as a fulcrum, lowering one wheel as it raises the other two hundred feet in the air, giving riders a view of the entire Exposition, with its fountains and pastels and red tile roofs.

The view was even more splendid from the Captive Balloon, which rises higher than the Electric Tower and looks out over the whole city. I feared my stomach would lurch into sickness but nothing of the kind happened. People, houses, carriages—everything looked so small from the sky. To my right Elmwood stretched toward downtown, to my left Delaware. Each street had a long canopy of trees whose leaves glistened green in the sunlight. In the distance, beyond rooftops and chimneys, I could see the Prudential Building and downtown clock towers. In the other direction I could see the Driscoll estate and wondered how preparations for the next trial were going. I stared for a long time at the barn and sloping hills, hardly noticing how much the balloon shifted in the wind or the sharpness of the breeze on my cheeks.

I was flying.

Nine

It is late and I am seated at the kitchen table as I attempt to write. The scratched-through lines at the top of this page are witness to my distress. New doubts about our undertaking have arisen because Andrew Ridgewater was almost killed this morning.

Today began as any other this May, unusually chilly and cloudy but with a distant promise of sun. Will rose earlier than I and was ready to go when the first hint of light pulled me from sleep. After breakfast we squeezed into the buggy, Will and I sideways, almost standing, on either side of Papa Joe, who urged Mac forward with a gentle snap of the reins. The trip took longer than it would have by streetcar or with a younger horse and a lighter load. Poor Mac moves with a labored, lopsided gait, from the onset of ringbone a year ago. Papa Joe must sit through the night with him now and again, applying mercurial blisters to shrink swelling in his hoof. I know how deeply my grandfather cares for that old horse, and so must my brother. He did not ask that the stanhope move faster, despite the excitement building inside him.

By the time we reached the estate, the sky had begun to brighten. Will was the first one out of the carriage. He hurried up the hill toward the barn, where the others were already waiting. I followed him, as Papa Joe tied Mac to the carriage post. Reverend Banks and the Captain came toward us first, followed by Danny and Andrew. Captain Driscoll looked pale to the ends of his mustache hairs. I looked back to see Papa Joe and Mrs. Ridgewater on their way up the hill, with Jonas several paces behind them. Reverend Banks announced that the camera was positioned and ready. Danny, flushed and smiling, asked if we would try to fly today.

Will looked at the sky, then gazed into the faces nearest him. "Today," he said.

Andrew stepped in front of Will and for an instant neither said a word. Then both started to speak at once but each gave ground. In the heartbeat of silence that followed, Will took the lead by placing a hand on Andrew's shoulder. Their eyes met, and something I could not name passed between them. Perhaps it was an understanding born of a friendship begun in childhood, or silent reassurance that all would be well. Maybe it was even a love like that shared by brothers. Whatever it was, I felt a twinge of jealousy, for I would have given anything to have my brother look at me as he looked at Andrew, with a mixture of confidence and admiration. After a few seconds, both smiled broadly, and Will withdrew his hand.

Papa Joe reached the gathering. "How should we start, son?" He paused to catch his breath. "Tell us what to do."

In truth, we had attached and detached the wingwork so often in the past few weeks that we needed no guidance in bringing the aeroplane out of the barn and fixing the sateen-covered spans in place. But today we had to hoist the center frame to the top of the barn first and slot its wheel-bearing sledge runners between the launch rails. Next we used wooden wedges to block the wheels. Finally, we hoisted and affixed the wings.

I had not been atop the barn before and concentrated on keeping my footing on the weather-worn shingles. Papa Joe had cautioned me against such a climb because of my history of illness. He feared that sudden vertigo might make me fall. But the Aerio-Cycle and the Captive Balloon have lessened any uneasiness about heights. If I am to be the chronicler of our work, I must have as close a view as possible of our efforts.

Andrew arranged himself on his stomach in the piloting hammock. Will attached the control cables as Danny crouched beside the glider. Will looked down at Reverend Banks, who took his Bible from a coat pocket and opened it to a marked page. Just then the wind snatched the hat from Reverend Banks's head. He made no move to chase it, no effort to follow its flight with his eyes. Instead, he gazed up at the work on the roof. Then he lowered his head. As eyes closed and chins sank, the wind snapped the corners of the thin Bible pages. Reverend Banks began to read from the Psalms in a shaking voice, full, I suspect, of wonder and more than a little fear.

"Why leap ye, ye high hills? This is the hill which God desireth to dwell in; yea, the LORD will dwell in it for ever. The chariots of God are twenty thousand, even thousands of angels. The LORD is among them . . ."

The longer he read, the stronger his voice grew. As it rose above the wind, I cracked an eye to make a mental photograph of the scene for inclusion in this account. Papa Joe's hands were locked together at his waist, Captain Driscoll's clasped behind his back. Mrs. Ridgewater moved her head from side to side in a slow rhythm that matched the cadence of Reverend Banks's voice. Jonas stood still, bowed head slightly twitching. Atop the barn, everyone's eyes were lowered or closed but mine.

"To him that rideth upon the heaven of heavens, which

were of old; lo, he doth send out his voice, and that a mighty voice. Ascribe ye strength unto God: his excellency is over Israel, and his strength is in the clouds."

Reverend Banks shut his Bible and raised his own closed eyes to the clouds. "Dear Lord, we beseech You to bless this endeavor by Your humble servants to serve Your people. Smite us not, for we seek not to challenge Your strength in the clouds. This work is born not of arrogant flesh but of faith in the Holy Spirit, that what we may here accomplish will lift those of Your people who have languished at the bottom for so long. You have blessed these common men with uncommon wisdom, and we seek permission that they may soar above the earth. This we ask in the name of Your Son, our Lord, Jesus Christ. Amen."

Eyes opened. The seconds that followed were lengthened by silence. Reverend Banks returned the Bible to his pocket and went to fetch his hat, which he jammed down on his head. Hands still folded, Mrs. Ridgewater looked up at her son. I turned my gaze from Papa Joe and the others on the ground to my companions on the roof. Will knelt beside Andrew and broke the silence with a whisper so faint I could not tell whether it was instruction or encouragement. Then he asked if Andrew was ready.

Andrew took a deep breath and nodded.

Together, Will and Danny removed the wedges from beneath the wheels and flattened themselves on opposite sides of the roof to permit the wings to pass over them. I caught my breath—as everyone else must have—when the Blackbird squeaked and groaned forward. Within seconds the glider was rattling down the rails, speed growing as our eyes followed it. Andrew bounced in the hammock as the rig reached the end of the roof and began the sharp descent that would carry it up the rise at the end of the launch track. The wings fell below my line of sight. Then, before we could let out our breath, the Blackbird was in the air.

For a moment it seemed to float in place, perhaps forty feet above the ground, the gray sateen taut in the wind. Then Andrew performed a wing buckling adjustment that caused the craft to angle to the right. He repeated his action for the left wing, which returned the Blackbird to its initial course and set it on a path I could imagine clearly. If Andrew maintained height, the glider would soar beyond the hill across from the barn! Here I must confess that I was so in awe of my brother's invention that I was completely unaware of the others, unaware even that I was standing atop a roof. The rest of the world fled my mind as animals flee a fire in the forest. I simply stared at the glider, willing it forward, forward.

Then the unthinkable happened. The glider nosed upward, as its smaller predecessor had done a month ago, and I expected it to point downward abruptly, then plunge without ceremony to the ground. Andrew, however, was equal to the challenge and regained control before the Blackbird could drop. Even so, the front was angled toward the rolling grass beyond the hill and the tail was too high as Andrew began his descent. He inclined the glider to the left, then to the right sharply, then to the left again. The tail dropped a bit below the nose. At a height I guessed must be forty feet, it appeared that the Blackbird would alight gently, that Andrew would crawl out of the center frame unscathed. But at that instant, for reasons Will has yet to discover, the hammock assembly came apart, and Andrew slid backward, out of the glider. Half turning in the air, and tangled amid canvas and cables, he dropped behind the rise of the second hill.

As if possessed by an intelligence of its own, the Blackbird floated effortlessly to the earth, thirty yards past the accident. For a second, Will stood motionless, transfixed by the sight. Then, like the rest of us, he began to move.

Even now I cannot recall how I got down from the roof. From the instant Andrew disappeared behind the hill, all our actions were fueled by our inability to see him and the terrible pictures our imaginations conjured. I must have run to the scene of the mishap because I recall that I was breathless when I reached it. The only sound I remember before getting to Andrew is Mrs. Ridgewater's scream, the only image her running halfway down the first hill before the rest of us could start toward her son.

He had landed on his arms and neck and lay like a discarded doll near the bottom of the hill, head turned to his right, arms and legs entangled with the hammock and positioned at odd angles. There was very little blood, which I took to be a good sign, though a point of bone was visible through a tear in one of his sleeves and his breaths came in ragged gasps. Then a bloody froth appeared upon his lips. Reverend Banks and Papa Joe knelt beside him. Meanwhile, Captain Driscoll took hold of Mrs. Ridgewater to soothe her and to keep her from interfering. He eased her back, calling for his old army stretcher, in the milk shed behind the barn. "Somebody crank up the Packard!" he shouted. "We must get him to the hospital!"

Danny disappeared into the hollow to intercept Jonas, who had not yet made it to the top of the second hill.

Will sank to one knee and opened Andrew's left eyelid. The eye looked wild and filmy. It was streaked with red. Andrew moved his lips but managed no sound through the bursting bubbles of blood. "Say something, Andrew," said Will. "Please say something."

Reverend Banks wiped Andrew's lips with his handkerchief and placed Papa Joe's folded coat beneath his head.

Then he directed me to disentangle Andrew's legs from the canvas and cables. "Gently," he said. "Very gently."

I worked slowly and gingerly, Mrs. Ridgewater's sobs filling my ears. I unhooked the control stirrups from his feet and undid the fasteners that connected them to their cables. Then I went to work on the cables themselves, unwinding and unkinking until I could pull them free without causing him additional pain. Presently, Danny returned with the stretcher.

Will continued to comfort his old friend with words and the touch of fingertips to his forehead. Andrew blinked, tried repeatedly to speak, finally forced out a hoarse "Sorry." Will shook his head violently. "No, I'm sorry. This is my fault."

Danny unfolded the stretcher beside Andrew. Papa Joe bent to grip Andrew under the armpits and Danny tenderly arranged his legs to get a better hold under his knees. "This'll hurt," said Papa Joe. "But we have to do it to help you." Together, they lifted Andrew an inch or two off the ground to shift him onto the stretcher. When he neither moaned nor howled with pain, Papa Joe and Captain Driscoll exchanged grave looks.

Papa Joe and Danny crouched between the stretcher poles, took hold of them, and stood.

"We'll get him to the hospital as quickly as we can," said the Captain to Mrs. Ridgewater.

Jonas already had the Packard out of the carriage shed, rumbling in wait. The automobile was too near Mac, who snorted and stamped the ground. I reached the yard before the others and tried to steady the horse. Captain Driscoll and Mrs. Ridgewater arrived next. "Thanks, sergeant," he said to Jonas, who climbed down from the seat with some difficulty and returned to the shed. "Gus, the horse is tied. Jonas needs your help." There was no rebuke in the Captain's voice, only the calm authority of a man accustomed to being obeyed.

Jonas had brought two wooden planks out of the carriage shed and laid them on the grass. He was now trying to unfasten the automobile's carriage top. I went to the opposite side to help, and after a moment we set the top aside. Then we lashed the two planks together and placed them lengthwise over the seat back, securing them with rope to the seat frame and the right head lamp. When Papa Joe and Danny arrived, with Will walking beside the now unconscious Andrew, we placed the stretcher on the planks and tied down the corners. Everyone saw at once that the arrangement left barely enough room for a driver to squeeze into the seat and twist the tiller.

"I want to ride with my boy!" sobbed Mrs. Ridgewater.

Captain Driscoll gripped her shoulders and held her at arm's length. "You can't. There's no room. I need a man on the back to steady the stretcher and one on the side to brace Andrew." He led her to Papa Joe's stanhope. "I know Mr. Lockhart will be right behind me." He helped her inside. "I will see you there." Then he said something I could not hear to Papa Joe.

Will insisted that he be the one to ride on the side of the Packard. He stood with one boot inside and one on the step, leaning over the stretcher and bracing Andrew's body with his own. Papa Joe was already seated beside Mrs. Ridgewater in the carriage when I climbed onto the back of the Packard and took hold of a stretcher pole. Papa Joe and Mrs. Ridgewater are both large. No small man himself, Reverend Banks could not fit in the stanhope with them. He uttered a brief prayer to get us under way. Then I felt the frame grumble beneath me, and for the second time in less than a month I found myself clinging to the back of a moving motor car.

*   *   *

Sunday May 19

Last evening I wrote as much and as late as I could before an agitated sleep overtook me. Now, before church and traveling to the hospital to see Andrew, I must resume my narrative of the previous day's events.

The excursion to the hospital was frightening. Neither Will nor I had a truly satisfying hold on Andrew or the Packard. In his haste, Captain Driscoll seemed to find every bump and hole in the macadam, each jolt threatening to throw us off. He announced that we were going all the way downtown to Emergency Hospital instead of somewhere closer. I tightened my grip for the longer ride. A glance over my shoulder told me that Papa Joe's buggy would soon fall far behind, but I was certain he already knew our destination.

At the hospital, Captain Driscoll ordered me inside for help and said to use his name if I faced difficulty. That directive proved especially effective, for the nurse at the front desk seemed inclined to dismiss me as a ranting negro until I mentioned the Captain's name. "Captain Driscoll is right outside," I said, "with my injured friend." Then, after listening to my brief account of how Andrew had fallen from the roof of the Driscoll barn while laying shingles, she summoned a pair of burly hospital attendants to follow me with a rolling stretcher. I pointed toward the Packard at the curb, and the attendants went to it at once. Carefully, they transferred Andrew to the padded stretcher. Then they strapped him in place, inviting Captain Driscoll to follow them. Will walked beside the stretcher, promising Andrew that everything would be all right. Andrew opened his eyes briefly, but I cannot say whether he heard Will, or believed him.

Joined by another nurse, the attendants and Andrew disappeared behind a pair of wide swinging doors. We were shown into a spacious waiting room with hardback benches and tall windows through which streamed bright sunlight incapable of lightening our mood. A large clock on the north wall said it was five of eleven. Despite the shadow that had fallen over our efforts and interminably lengthened the passing of each minute, it was still only morning. Fifteen minutes later, the front desk nurse showed Mrs. Ridgewater into the waiting room. Papa Joe strode in behind them and helped Mrs. Ridgewater into a seat. Thus began our vigil.

I sat beside my brother on a bench across the room from the others. I knew he must feel responsible and could use a comforting word himself. He didn't look at me when I put my hand on his shoulder and whispered that he shouldn't blame himself. He startled me when he asked— quietly, so the others would not hear—"Don't you have doubts about what we are trying to do?" I confessed that I did, that I had begun to wonder whether flight was worth the risk. Will said, "If Andrew dies, part of me will die with him, and the part that lives will always bear the burden of his death. I'm the one who got him into this." He looked down at his hands, clasped tight in his lap. "Friendship is sometimes a greater punishment than it is a gift." Then he raised his face and his eyes bore into me. "But I have no doubts." He shook his head emphatically. "None." His whisper intensified. "Papa Joe and Reverend Banks are the ones who made this into something bigger than it had any right to be. It was a simple dream—my dream—but in their hands it became this great racial quest." The bitterness in my brother's voice surprised me. "I don't care so much about that part of it. I just want to make a flier that works. Even if . . .even if. . ." He turned away from me with tears in his eyes and gazed across the room at our grandfather, who sat with an arm draped over Mrs. Ridgewater's shoulders. Captain Driscoll sat on her other side, holding one of her hands.

For a time Will and I said nothing. Then, still whispering, he asked what he'd dared not ask until we had done what we could for Andrew: "Did you see it land?"

I said simply, "Yes."

"Then you know that it works. It flies."

Another thirty minutes passed before Captain Driscoll was summoned into the corridor. After a minute or two, he returned and reassured Mrs. Ridgewater that Andrew was alive and being given the best possible attention. Then he asked me to join him in the corridor. "You saw all that happened," he said. "I have faith in your powers of observation." Puzzled, I followed him out and came face to face with Dr. Lucas Westbeck, in banded shirtsleeves and surgical apron.

At first he seemed not to recognize that I had held onto the back of his automobile just a few weeks ago. I imagined all negroes must look the same to him—all except Pearl. But then the light of remembrance flickered in his eyes, and before Captain Driscoll could introduce us, Dr. Lucas offered his hand.

"Hello, Gus," he said. "How have you been?"

"Fine, sir. How's Andrew?"

Captain Driscoll looked confused. "You know each other?"

"We've met," said Dr. Lucas. "As for your friend, both arms have compound fractures. His collarbone is broken. His back doesn't appear to be broken, but I am concerned about spinal compression. There may be internal injuries that will yet require surgery. For now he's splinted and we've given him morphia. But there are some secondary injuries I can't yet understand . . ."

"As I was saying, Gus works for me," said Captain Driscoll. "I myself didn't . . . see the accident, but he did." He prodded me with his eyes. "Maybe he can shed light on what happened."

Then I understood. I had told the nurse at the desk that Andrew had fallen from the roof while laying shingles. Now I was being asked to supply details Captain Driscoll dared not chance, lest he contradict my story and raise questions that might lead to the exposure of our work.

"So, Gus," began Dr. Lucas, "tell me what happened."

"We were on the barn roof laying shingles." I hesitated. "And Andrew fell."

"He just fell off the roof."

"Must have slipped on something, maybe a loose shingle."

"Did you hear him slip, perhaps make a scraping sound?"

"No, sir. He just went over the edge, backwards."

"He just went over? He wasn't working from a scaffold?"

I shook my head.

Dr. Lucas frowned. "Then I'm at a loss to explain the marks on his arms and legs."

"Marks?" asked Captain Driscoll.

Dr. Lucas turned to him. "Rope burns."

The cables, I realized. Andrew had been tangled in them.

Dr. Lucas said, "When I cut away his shirts, I was surprised to find abrasions on his arms, such as those that might result from a rope suddenly tightening against his clothing. Similar marks were on his legs. If he didn't get caught up in the ropes of some kind of scaffolding . . ."

The Captain looked from Dr. Lucas to me. "Gus, were you boys using rope for anything?"

I thought for a moment, then said, "The block and tackle, Captain, sir." Having hit upon a good lie, I ventured forth with confidence. "We were hauling up crates of shingles and boxes of tools and . . . well, Andrew was doing the hauling. I'm not much help with the heavy work." I lowered my eyes, as if ashamed of my size and lack of strength. "It was just the two of us. He must've been using his arms and legs on the pulley rope . . . but that was long before he fell."

Dr. Lucas studied me as he considered my explanation. I tried to remove any trace of deceit from my face. At last he nodded. "I wanted to clear that up before I saw his mother."

"How long will he have to stay here?" I asked.

"The next day or so will be the most critical," replied Dr. Lucas. "If he survives, we can look forward to the healing of his bones, though future arm motion and strength may both be impaired. But remember there is still the possibility of some injury we have not yet seen, as well as paralysis."

Captain Driscoll swallowed. "Whatever he needs, whatever it takes to heal him, expense is not a consideration. Now please speak with his mother. Promise her you will do all that you can."

"Of course, Mr. Driscoll."

When Dr. Lucas was gone, Captain Driscoll smiled grimly and shook his head before he put his arm around my shoulders. "Not much help with the heavy work indeed."

The Old Plantation and Pickaninnies Playing Dice
Courtesy of Peggy Brooks-Bertram,
Barbara Seals Nevergold,
and *The Uncrowned Queens Institute*

Ten

Monday May 20

"There he is!"

The excitement of the crowd wrenched me out of my daydream and deposited me on Main Street near Chippewa. Despite trumpet fanfares, policemen on horseback and bicycles, marching bands, and the tramp of foot soldiers, I had withdrawn deep inside myself. I had begun what felt like my hundredth reliving of the accident, a good measure of my faith plummeting to the ground with Andrew. Then people around me were stabbing the air with their fingers and jostling me and my trash barrel to get a look at the approaching carriage. It was a shiny black victoria, top down, drawn by a pair of mammoth black horses. In it were two men in dark frock coats and high silk hats. Even from a distance, I recognized the trademark grin of the man on his feet, waving to the crowd. The most famous smile in America belongs to Vice President Theodore Roosevelt.

Amid the cheering there were shouts of "Teddy!" and "Hurrah for the Rough Riders!"

I was on special assignment outside the Exposition grounds, to clean the Dedication Day parade route after the celebration. I did not want to come today, but Papa Joe insisted. He would be at the hospital with Mrs. Ridgewater, he said, and there was nothing I could do. Still, my heart was at Andrew's bedside, and my mind was elsewhere with Will, caught up in a quest that had begun to feel impossible, as futile as it was dangerous.

The carriage passed slowly. Mr. Roosevelt shook hands with the various men who pushed past police lines to reach him. Veterans of various wars, in full or partial uniform, threaded their way to the front to salute him. He returned these salutes sharply, each snap of his hand producing louder cheering and more applause, especially when he bowed to a gathering of older veterans. Then the carriage was past. In its wake clattered victorias and broughams and rockaways with other dignitaries.

The Midway parade filled the street behind the carriages, a river of color and sound stretching as far back as the eye could see—Indians in warpaint, horse-drawn floats and displays representing the Aerio-Cycle, the House Upside Down, and other Midway attractions. A woman near me shrieked when the Wild Animal Show went past, for it held not one but two lions, a male and a female, in a cage with a helmeted tamer. The float labeled A Trip to the Moon carried two men as tall as Papa Joe and half a dozen shorter than I, all wearing sickly-green outfits. The float was shaped like a winged boat. Despite my turmoil, I couldn't help smiling at the silliness of a design that had no hope of flying. And in that instant I began to realize how much of Will's work I had come to understand.

Floats, marchers, and performers continued past. Soon the float carrying the pickaninny band creaked into view. Old-looking horses wore even older-looking straw hats. Barefoot banjo players and jug-blowers lounged about on bales of cotton, picking and tooting, while a grinning washboard-brusher in one corner and a stomping harmonica player in another kept time. Other members of the Old Plantation cast pretended to pick cotton as spiky-headed children danced among them. The dough-faced man beside me burst into laughter and pointed at the pickaninnies and made monkey sounds. My hands gripped my broom handle so tight I thought it would snap. I turned to glare at him, to will him quiet. It was then, from memory or desire I cannot say, that I heard the whisper of God: "If ye have faith as a grain of mustard seed, ye shall say unto this mountain, Remove hence to yonder place; and it shall remove: and nothing shall be impossible unto you."

The man looked at me, blinked, and fell silent. Perhaps the whisper saved both our lives.

*   *   *

Lucas Westbeck was restless. His father, sitting beside him, was clearly disturbed by his periodic sighs. Twice he whispered shushing noises and let out his own faint hiss of exasperation. Fingers silently drumming one side of the high silk hat that rested in his lap, Lucas chewed his lip. Already sick of the pomp and pageantry, he did not look forward to the speeches and the poetic drivel. He wished he were anywhere but here in the Temple of Music, waiting to hear Theodore Roosevelt.

The lavish interior, with its mammoth pipe organ and statues and starburst windows beneath a high gilt-edged dome, did nothing to ease Lucas's discomfort. He had wanted no part of Dedication Day, but the elder Dr. Westbeck had left him no choice. Since they both belonged to the medical committee, his father explained, Lucas's absence from the parade and the Temple speeches would be a discredit to the Westbeck name and their practice. Moreover, the automobile would remain in the carriage house and they would ride in the same respectable brougham. "And like any true gentleman," his father had concluded, "you will wear a proper hat in the presence of the Vice President of the United States."

Lucas had sat opposite his father during the slow ride along the parade route, bored and sullen. He was still bitter about the curt reaction the old man had given his proposal to establish his own surgery. "Out of the question," his father had said over the top of his morning *Express* two weeks earlier. "You can't afford to do this on your own, and I can't afford to do it on your behalf." Before Lucas could protest, his father fixed him with a reproving stare. "Besides, you already stand to inherit a well-established practice. Is this in some way insufficient?" Without answering, Lucas shook his head and left the room—like a scolded schoolboy, he thought now. He had not yet broached the subject of training Pearl to be his nurse. He wondered what *that* would do for the Westbeck name and felt the corners of his mouth pull into a vicious little smile.

They were at the back of the main gallery. An ocean of brilliantine, with scattered islands of baldness and millinery sea monsters, separated them from the vast stage. On stage, large potted plants flanked the rows of speakers' chairs. Front and center stood a pair of lecterns draped with American flags. Applause began when the speakers filed in and Vice President Roosevelt crossed the stage. He sat beside John Milburn in the center of the first row, which left him hidden by one of the lecterns. Milburn and two other men sprang to their feet and slid the lectern aside, which brought a cheer and louder applause from the audience.

It was going to be a long afternoon, Lucas reflected.

Mayor Diehl was in the second sentence of his address when Lucas felt a numbness begin in his buttocks. By the time the first poem was read, he was bored and ready to bolt from his chair. However estimable the Exposition itself, the men taking bows for it were the same old self-important prigs whose company he had avoided since finishing medical school. His father appeared to thrive in their presence, as if their friendship were a dividend of his medical practice. Even if social order and obligation were important, Lucas cared little about politicians and money men. And he would much rather be outside on so fine a day. Decorum demanded that he hear Roosevelt, but at the first opportunity after that he would slip away.

Finally, after more speeches and tiresome poetry and a long orchestral selection, John Milburn stepped up to a lectern and introduced the Vice President.

The audience rose to greet Roosevelt, clapping and waving hats and kerchiefs. Amid the applause, someone shouted, "Three cheers for Teddy! Hip, hip—" Roosevelt shook his head and raised a hand to call for quiet, but his gesture produced only prolonged applause. He smiled at the crowd and bowed, then bowed a second time, and a third. Then he extracted a thick wad of paper from the inside pocket of his cutaway coat, unfolded it, and smoothed it out atop the lectern. When the audience sat, he adjusted his pince-nez, studied his text for a moment, then gazed out at the crowd and cleared his throat. "Today we formally open this great Exposition, by the shores of the mighty inland seas of the north, where all the peoples of the Western hemisphere have joined to show what they have done in art, science and industrial invention . . ."

The speech lasted over half an hour. Lucas's numbness had spread into his legs by the time the Vice President closed: ". . . and we must keep ever bright the love of justice, the spirit of strong brotherly friendship for one's fellows, which we hope and believe will hereafter stand as typical of the men who make up this, the mightiest republic upon which the sun has ever shone." During the standing ovation, Lucas clutched the back of the chair in front of him as the blood returned to his legs. Then he whispered an excuse to his father and made his way outside.

People thronged the Esplanade. Despite their Sunday clothes Lucas had no difficulty distinguishing laborers from landholders and common folk from their betters. Even when the quality of the clothing was high, suit coats on poorer backs bore the dust and nap of careless brushings. Dresses were ill-fitting or frayed, sure signs they had been passed down to the wearers. Shoes, with their scuffs and worn heels and mud residues, always betrayed the station of the feet they encased. Representatives of every class trod the paths around the Fountain of Abundance, shuffled toward the music that came from the bandstands, and rested on benches.

Reflecting upon the Vice President's speech, Lucas pondered the notion of brotherhood Roosevelt had mentioned repeatedly. Was it possible, he wondered, to be true brothers with inferior nationalities and weaker races, with common men? Through no fault of their own, Italians, negroes, Jews, and the like had been deprived by their Creator of talents and abilities necessary for the construction and maintenance of modern industrial civilization. Such gifts had been bestowed in greater measure upon the upper classes of Germany, England, and America. These were the nations whose practices would chart the course of this new century. Still, like the ablest brothers in a family, they were obliged to look after their less fortunate siblings. It was the duty of the stronger to secure the place of the weaker.

Such was the philosophy followed by many a generous employer of menial men. Like Captain Hayward Driscoll, who had brought in his injured boy and remained beside his mother. Lucas made a mental note to return to the hospital this evening to see if there had been a change in the boy's inability to move. It had been apparent, even before his pledge to cover medical expenses, that Driscoll had a deeper than casual attachment to the Ridgewaters and the other negroes who worked for him— that old black giant and little Gus, Pearl's friend.

Then Lucas's mind turned to Pearl, to the intelligent glow in her eyes and the weakness he felt in her presence. Neither of them had spoken again of his offer to train her. He knew it must be he who spoke first; it would be unseemly for her to do so. Yet he was no closer to establishing a surgery and was ashamed that he had even raised the subject. He had been foolish to hope to deliver her from domestic service, to have her near him if he could not have her with him. Now he wondered if his silence disappointed her, or was she so accustomed to the limitations of her color that she had never seriously considered his offer?

Lucas strolled across the Esplanade to where a rough-coated man with heavy boots helped one fairgoer after another—many of them children, for school was closed today—launch a kite. Gradually, the sky filled with multicolored diamonds and boxes, floating, dipping, swooping. Here and there one became entangled with another and both crashed. But most remained aloft, paper or fabric skins rippling in the wind. Lucas watched the kite-fliers' faces, envious of their smiles and dreamy glee. Their laughter rose above the din of footsteps, chatter, and music from the nearest band shell. Lucas could not recall if he had ever heard Pearl laugh. Domestic service forbade the deep, prolonged laughter that signaled joy. He ached to hear such a sound from Pearl, to be privy to such joy. In this time and in this place, however, he might as well be a kite-flier, tugging his string and hopelessly wishing he were no longer earthbound.

* * *

Papa Joe had counted Tobias Ridgewater among his closest friends. Like Papa Joe, he had been one of the founding members of the African Church of the Ascension in the autumn of 1883. He had served as a deacon until his death from a stomach ailment in 1895. A dozen years younger than Papa

Joe—and a foot shorter and fifty pounds lighter—Tobias had been the stable man at the old Farnham Hotel, a quiet fishing companion, and the best horseshoe partner anyone could ever want at a church picnic. One of the saddest duties of Papa Joe's life had been his service as a pallbearer at Tobias Ridgewater's funeral. Now, as he stood with his arm around Tobias's widow, he wondered if she would ask him to perform the same service for Tobias's son.

They were standing just outside the ward where Andrew's body lay covered by a sheet. Sister Ridgewater wept into Papa Joe's coat—quietly now, her loudest wailing and most violent trembling having come a few minutes earlier, when her son's ragged breathing ceased as she held his limp hand. Papa Joe had tried immediately to lead her away from the body, softly urging her to come with him as nurses unfolded screens around Andrew's bed to isolate him from other patients in the ward. Only after she had pulled free and planted a kiss on her son's forehead did she permit herself to be helped into the corridor.

Presently, Papa Joe felt the weight of Sister Ridgewater's breasts against his chest, the heaviness of the tears soaking into the fabric of his coat. If her tears could solidify, he thought, they would anchor him to this spot, in this moment. His belly contracted with a mixture of grief and guilt, the former because one of their number had passed on, the latter because for just an instant he had allowed himself a breath of relief that death had not claimed one of his grandsons. His jaw tightened in anticipation of what would happen when her numbness gave way to sharper reflections, when she told herself that his grandson was responsible for her son's death.

His wait was brief.

Her tears slowed, and she wrenched herself away from him. She moved a few paces away, keeping her back to him as she hugged herself. For a time she was silent. Papa Joe said nothing to inspire her to talk. Then she spoke in an over-the-shoulder whisper: "I can't hate him, Joe. Jesus won't let me hate him. Maybe this is the Lord's way of testin' me, to see if I can hold my faith when I lose the one I love most in the world." Then she sniffed and swallowed loudly. "But I wish everything was different. I wish I was the one lettin' you cry on my shoulder 'stead of the other way 'round. God forgive me, but I wish it was Will in there under that sheet." She shook her head. "I can't hate him but I wish it was Will, dead from his own handiwork, not my Andrew." Then she began to cry again.

Quietly, Papa Joe crossed the corridor and placed his hands on her shoulders. "I'll take you wherever you need to go, Sister." Mac and the stanhope were outside. "Portius would be a good place to start." He offered her the handkerchief from his inside coat pocket, but she waved it aside and pulled away again. She moved to the nearest window—to gaze out, he imagined, at the world her son would never see again.

"No, Joe. I got to start doin' things on my own. Been me and Andrew for so long . . ." She turned to face him. "When Tobias passed I thought, least I still got our son. Least I still got somebody to look after—'course, even then Andrew said it was his job to look after me." She sniffed. "Now I got nobody, 'cept my sister in Charleston."

"You got your church family."

"Ain't the same as your own flesh and blood."

"Let me help."

"You can't."

At that moment Dr. Lucas Westbeck appeared, some distance behind her, in the archway at the far end of the corridor. He was dressed in a frock coat and high silk hat. He stopped, as if wary of intruding. Papa Joe wondered if someone had told him of Andrew's death. Then he recognized the concern in the doctor's eyes and was certain he knew.

"If Will'd never made his flyin' machine, Andrew'd be here now." Sister Ridgewater's voice quavered. She was unaware of the doctor behind her. "This is God's punishment, Joe. God didn't intend nobody to fly," she said, with more bitterness than he had ever heard in all the years he had known her, "'specially no colored folks." Then she turned and saw the doctor coming near and wiped her eyes as she pushed past him on the way out.

Eleven

The remainder of May and all of June passed slowly. The emptiness which had deepened within Papa Joe after Andrew's death lingered in the weeks following the funeral.

For a time his greatest concern had been Sister Ridgewater. It was difficult to face her, but he went to her home often, did Andrew's chopping, hauling, and lifting. He was there when her friends and neighbors stopped by to offer condolences and food. He was there to help maintain the fiction that Andrew had fallen from the roof. He had always prided himself on his honesty, but he knew—as did Reverend Banks, who prevailed upon Sister Ridgewater to keep secret the cause of her son's death—that if word spread Andrew had died in an aeroplane of negro design, the Blackbird would have no chance of success. Captain Driscoll's business rivals would find a way to force him out of the project and destroy whatever Will had accomplished. Should his dream of flight become known only among the Ascension congregation, Papa Joe still feared what might befall his grandson. It was painful enough for a dream to die in private. A public death—even witnessed only by friends—was a humiliation few dreamers could endure without scars.

However great the burden of deceit for Papa Joe, it was worse for Reverend Banks. He had, miraculously, convinced Sister Ridgewater that her son was a martyr to a great cause, the advancement of the race. Anything that impeded such advancement would strip away the meaning of his death. But Papa Joe knew Portius well enough to see the misgivings in the minister's face, to watch the guilt that blossomed behind his eyes when he preached a funeral sermon laced with half-truths to mask both the nature of the accident and his own self-disgust.

The deception only compounded Sister Ridgewater's grief. Her face bore the stigmata of unreached sleep—wrinkles, slackened cheeks, bags beneath the eyes. She tolerated Papa Joe's visits but made him pay for the privilege of helping her with cold hard stares. She had little use for the other men and eventually found scant comfort in the company of Essie and Pearl. Early in June she announced she was moving to her sister's in South Carolina. Papa Joe felt a surge of relief so strong he'd have been ashamed to admit it.

After her departure, Papa Joe busied himself in his shop. With the rise in tourists, demand for horseshoes was increasing among liverymen. Forging left him few opportunities to speculate when aeroplane tests might resume or who might replace Andrew. Still, he was concerned about Will, who spent most of his time at the Driscoll estate. Despite earlier setbacks, he had never truly believed his grandson capable of failure. Will solved problems because he believed in his ability to do so. What if a deep conviction that he had killed his best friend was unraveling that faith?

Papa Joe was struck by the irony of his concern. He was worried about Will, who until this aeroplane business had never given him a minute's anxiety. Meanwhile Gus, over whom he had passed many a sleepless night, divided his time between his job and the Driscoll estate and seemed fine. The few times during June that Will did come home, he would discuss neither the accident nor his progress. Instead, he insisted on helping in the shop, as did Gus, and Papa Joe was grateful for the extra hands. On such days, when they worked together and ate together, they were a family again, but Papa Joe felt enough tension in the air to choke. Sadly, he realized that the fellowship which had underscored the whole Blackbird enterprise might be another casualty of the accident.

He saw Portius and his family only on Sundays and knew from brief exchanges that he had not returned to the estate since the mishap either. Captain Driscoll had come back some time ago from having escorted Sister Ridgewater to Charleston, but Papa Joe had not seen him since the funeral. One day, in the Walbridge store on Main, he had spotted Jonas Newcomb's unmistakable bowlegged scuttle on the other side of the hardware and tool department. He considered walking over to greet Jonas but decided against it. If the Blackbird circle was truly broken, Jonas was just as likely as Papa Joe to feel the shame of their necessary silence.

There was another whose silence puzzled him. For more than a week he had wondered how much the young doctor had overheard in the hospital corridor. Enough to piece together what had really happened to Andrew? Did those strange rope burns finally make sense? How long before someone made the trip out to Captain Driscoll's to investigate? But neither Gus nor Will reported anything out of the ordinary. No one had come around asking questions, officially or otherwise. Papa Joe did not understand—unless the doctor had dismissed what he heard as some kind of absurd fantasy: *Colored men and flying machines indeed!* Instead of feeling relief at such a prospect, he felt furious that someone could so casually disregard negro potential. Gradually, however, the doctor receded from his thoughts and by the end of June was completely forgotten.

* * *

On the first Monday in July, Papa Joe dropped his nickel

in the coin box on the dark red Michigan car, took a seat, and gazed out the window. As the trolley clacked along, he marveled at the changes the city had undergone in the half century since he had sought sanctuary in the Quaker abolitionist's cellar. By the river that night, a bullet burning in his shoulder, he could not have imagined that he would live fifty more years, let alone spend them in Buffalo. Nor would he have guessed that the town to which love bound him would grow into a pivotal North American city. After he had been found and his wound had been dressed and his fever had broken, he had known his survival was no accident. He had been spared for a purpose, one he believed would reveal itself to him over time. Through the years he had watched buildings rise and streets thicken with people of every stripe. He had given no special thought to why God had placed him among them—until the evening Will came to him, nearly a year ago, with a drawing and an idea.

Now he was on his way to an Exposition that might hold the key to all their destinies.

The streetcar switched tracks at Forest, then rattled north up Elmwood. Papa Joe stood and moved to the front to gaze at the Rainbow City as it came into view. Despite his years, he was the first man off the car, having let several ladies disembark ahead of him. He crossed the street and paid his fifty cents admission. Once he was past the turnstiles he waved aside the hawkers who tried to sell him guide books, programs, and souvenirs. In his right-hand coat pocket, he already had a dark green guide book, courtesy of Gus, but there was no need to consult it for the first thing he intended to see. A quarter of a mile away, to his left, the cream white Electric Tower rose into the morning sky.

* * *

At half past one he purchased a bottle of orangeade from a vendor in the East Esplanade. Then he sat on a bench facing the Court of Fountains, close to one of the geysers in the hope that the mist would cool him. But the air was unusually still; there was no breeze to carry the spray to him as he took from his coat pocket bread and cheese wrapped in baker's paper and a small apple.

He had ridden the elevator to the Electric Tower observation deck, from which most people looked south at the Exposition and the city beyond. Papa Joe, however, gazed north, past the Plaza and rail station toward unpaved roads and undeveloped tracts, many of which were still farms. The Driscoll property was the largest among them, less than a mile away. At this height anyone could see a test of the Blackbird—if he looked at the right moment and recognized the shape above the treetops as an aeroplane and not some kind of kite. Papa Joe stared for a long time, hoping Will's invention would rise from amid the summer foliage. It did not.

The remainder of the morning he had spent walking at random through various exhibits. He was fascinated by the devices on display in the Electricity Building and in one of the chocolate pavilions sampled fudge that made his back teeth hurt. He entered the Ethnology Building only after making a complete circuit around its exterior to read the quotations set into panels beneath its dome: "And hath made of one blood all nations," from the New Testament; "What a piece of work is man!" from Shakespeare; "All are needed by each one" from Emerson. Inside he found the beneficial products of human ingenuity— tools for growing and hunting food, art, pottery, resins, fibers, aromatics, medicines—and all kinds of weapons, from clubs to spears, from slings to longbows, from battle-axes to firearms. He wondered if swords would ever be beaten into ploughshares, if notions of equality and one blood would ever come down from temple walls and up from Bible pages to reside in the hearts of the living. Later, as he walked past paintings of rivet-laden steam fliers in a Machinery and Transportation exhibit devoted to the future, it struck him that flight might be the achievement that made lasting peace possible. One day the Blackbird might be exhibited as the one of the most important moments in human history, and beside it would be a plaque with his grandson's name. The idea made him dizzy.

After lunch he walked south through the Esplanade and down to the East Mirror Lake. At a landing for the canal ride, he got in line behind a young woman in a yellow lawn dress who held the hand of a girl about four or five. They were speaking a language he thought must be German. The girl stared up at him, the ringlets beneath her bonnet glistening gold. Papa Joe smiled at her and tipped his hat, then turned his attention to the electric launches and gondolas in the canal.

An empty gondola glided to a stop beside the platform. The smooth-cheeked gondolier looked as if he had just entered manhood, but the rolled-up sleeves of his dark boatman's costume revealed the corded forearms of someone accustomed to heavy labor. Papa Joe centered himself in the last seat, directly in front of the standing boatman. The woman and her daughter sat on the middle bench. At the prow was a pale man in a gray summer suit and straw skimmer.

The gondolier pushed off with his long-handled oar and moved them forward with a deft combination of paddling and poling.

Papa Joe settled back as the gondola moved out toward the middle of the man-made lake. The sun-dappled surface was dotted with other gondolas and electric launches, navigating in so many directions that collision was a certainty if any boatman attempted to go faster. Most of the passengers were couples, the women twirling parasols that shimmered in the afternoon brightness. Papa Joe's gondola entered the Grand Canal, and the boatman explained the statuary and exhibits and flowers they passed. Gently rocking, they slid under one bridge after another until they came to one that was enclosed, with latticework covering the windows. The gondolier announced they had entered Venice in America.

Ahead was a small man clad in a furry costume and garish red and black face paint. To Papa Joe he looked like a cross between a monkey and a muskrat. The man had climbed the rail separating the water from the walkway and Renaissance facades. Holding the rail with one hand, he leaned out over the canal, head bobbing like a cork on the surface of a pond. He grunted and snarled and sang as he shook a feather-covered stick at the passing gondola. The little girl tugged her mother's sleeve and pointed, frightened and excited. *"Der Troll! Der Troll!"*

The gondolier chuckled. "That was no troll," he said when the painted man was behind them. "That was KiKi, the House Upside Down spieler. He just wants you to see his show."

The girl's mother explained at length. Papa Joe caught the words *Vater* and Alt Nurnberg and surmised they were meeting the child's father at the Midway's German restaurant.

The gondola went under two more bridges. After the first, the gondolier stopped to discharge the German woman and her daughter. The girl looked back as she was led away by the wrist, and Papa Joe tipped his hat again. She giggled and covered her face with her hand. When the gondola emerged from beneath the second bridge, Papa Joe saw DARKEST AFRICA in huge letters on a stockade fence straight ahead. Unlike other Midway villagers, he recalled, the Africans were not permitted to leave the Exposition to see the host city. He had read a newspaper article about one chieftain's acceptance of Christianity. Now he shook his head at the irony of such a conversion in the absence of Christian hospitality.

Then they rounded the corner and passed a long wall with STREETS OF MEXICO in bold letters. Papa Joe was surprised to see Gus pushing his trash barrel past a line of trees.

"Where can I get off?" he asked the gondolier.

"Right up ahead."

They came to a landing just before the arch that led into the Electric Tower Basin. Papa Joe thanked the boatman and left the gondola. Then he climbed the steps, sidling past a smartly dressed couple on their way down to the landing, and walked back to meet Gus.

Gus looked hot and tired, and his overalls were dusty. His face brightened at the sight of Papa Joe. "Hi, Papa," he said. "Wondered if I'd see you today. Enjoying yourself?"

"Very much." Papa Joe squinted past Gus, as if inspecting the walkway he had just swept. "And your work, how is it coming?"

"Just fine." Tugging his tam down on his head, he smiled up at Papa Joe as if challenging him to find a shred of trash on the path behind him. "I'm on my way over there, to the other side." He nodded toward the Electric Tower. "Come with me. I want to show you something."

As they walked, Papa Joe gave his grandson a wide berth to maneuver his big gray barrel, which held a push broom and long-handled dust pan. From time to time, Gus stopped to sweep up debris. Papa Joe recounted his morning and the canal ride. But Gus seemed distracted and paid only token attention. They had gone around the back of the Tower and nearly crossed the Plaza before Papa Joe asked what the matter was.

"I want to show you something," Gus said and pointed to the Captive Balloon ride on the rim of the Plaza. An easel-mounted sign said CLOSED. Gus headed toward the ride anyway.

The balloon itself was cordoned off from the adjacent path. Four men in shirt sleeves stood inside the red velvet barrier, in the great oval shadow of the shiny silk balloon. A pair of large equipment cases lay open on the grass, the upper edge of each bearing a white stencil that read EDISON MANUFACTURING COMPANY. Two of the men seemed to be lashing some kind of wooden box to the huge wicker basket suspended from the balloon. One of them turned, saw Gus and Papa Joe approaching, and waved. Gus waved back and wheeled his barrel to the edge of the walkway. He left it there and threw a leg over the barrier, motioning for Papa Joe to follow.

"How are you doing, Gus?" The man who had waved came forward, wiping his hands with a red kerchief. He had sparkling eyes set in a wide, friendly face flushed with excitement.

"Just fine, Mr. Porter," Gus said. "This is my grandfather, the one I told you about, Joseph Lockhart."

Porter looked up at him, and Papa Joe heard a slight intake of breath as the man registered his size. But Porter hesitated only an instant before stuffing his kerchief into a front trouser pocket and sticking out his hand. "Ed Porter, Mr. Lockhart. Pleased to make your acquaintance." He pushed up his brown felt hat and put his hands on his hips. "Gus tells me you're interested in the motion picture, curious about how everything works."

Papa Joe realized the wooden box was a camera, but he could not recall having expressed any particular interest in motion pictures. He turned to Gus.

"He's interested in the future," Gus said quickly.

Porter grinned beneath his unwaxed mustache. "The motion picture is the future."

"Mr. Porter works for Thomas Edison," Gus explained. "He makes films of things. I got curious when I saw him one day and started asking questions."

"When I first got into this business I called myself Edison, Junior," Porter said. "Then I met the real Edison and he hired me. Part of my job is to come up with new things to film and new ways to do it." He looked back at the balloon. "Today I'm going to make a motion picture from the basket of the balloon ride." He went to the camera and began to polish the lens with his kerchief. Papa Joe noticed that on one side *Thomas A Edison* had been burned into the wood and painted white. "This is the finest kinetograph made," Porter said with pride.

Papa Joe was still uncertain why Gus had brought him to meet this man. He was certain his bewilderment must be apparent, for Porter narrowed his eyes at him.

"Mr. Lockhart, have you been to the Midway Cineograph?"

Papa Joe shook his head. He had been to a few nickelodeons and also had seen a few films projected onto a larger screen at the Vitascope Hall in Ellicott Square, which he hadn't visited since going with Portius to that meeting last autumn. Both viewing experiences had left him feeling little else but sore in the neck, the former from bending to align his eyes with the view shaft and the latter from tilting his head back to gaze up at the screen. In neither case had the images been much more than fleeting scenes with little relationship to each other— animals on parade, a train chugging into a station, well-dressed ladies hiding behind parasols as gentlemen tipped their hats, scenes from a prize fight—and, of course, that nearly obscene reproduction of a man and a woman kissing! Papa Joe had read of the wealthy buying Edison kinetoscopes for their homes but saw no point. The motion picture was a minor amusement in a world beginning to clutter with amusements.

"There was a film at the Cineograph last week," Porter went on. "It was a French thing called Conquest of the Air and showed a flying machine soaring over Paris."

That caught Papa Joe's attention. He felt air seep out of his chest as if from a balloon. His stomach knotted, and he swallowed hard. "Someone has made a working flying machine?"

"No," Gus said quickly, placing a reassuring hand on Papa Joe's forearm. "Not yet."

"This Zecca fellow, who shot the film, made his camera do a trick," Porter said. "He covered the bottom of his lens and made pictures of a man riding a bicycle with bat wings. Next he rewound the film and covered the top half of the lens. Then he went up in the Eiffel Tower and made pictures of Paris down below. When he showed his film the man appeared to be flying over the city. French fakery, I call it. Zecca's probably another stage magician with a kinetograph, like Georges Melies. Personally, I like realism. The illusion can't be too obvious."

"I don't understand," Papa Joe said. "What does this have to do with the future?"

"The motion picture is going to link the past to the future. Film will be the window people look through at the past. It will record history as history is made, and nobody will be able to argue about what happened because it will be there for everybody to see. Film may even make history with stories that never happened. Imagine filming one of Shakespeare's plays so . . . Listen—Mr. Lockhart—what kind of work do you do?"

"I'm a blacksmith."

"Hmm." Porter pinched his chin thoughtfully. "Maybe I could come film you sometime, on our next trip back here."

"Me?"

"Sure. Mr. Edison likes me to get films of people doing what they do." Porter shrugged. "Who knows? A hundred years from now there may be no such thing as a blacksmith. Somebody'll look at that film, see you working at your anvil, and know what blacksmiths did. You could make something right in front of the camera—no tricks—and people would see forever what you'd done. The moment of creation would be preserved for all time."

Preserved for all time . . .

Papa Joe looked at the balloon, at the camera fixed between two of the cables that held the basket. For a moment he let his mind drift on the winds of imagination. He saw the Blackbird in flight in the grainy flicker of a motion picture image, gliding and circling, its conquest of the air documented for all eternity. He saw it land and discharge its pilot. Even from a distance there was no mistaking that the pilot was a black man. A motion picture record of Will's achievement would be history that could not be stolen.

Now that he finally understood, Papa Joe grinned at Gus with admiration—and mild astonishment, at how much he had underestimated his grandson. Already he knew of—but had said nothing about—Gus's written accounts. And now there was the possibility of film. What other surprises, he wondered, would this boy spring on him before their enterprise was completed? Then Papa Joe turned to face the motion picture maker with awakened interest. "Mr. Porter," he said quietly, "would you mind if I watched you make the future?"

* * *

"Sweet Jesus, it's flying!"

It was Saturday, ten days after his visit to the Exposition, and Papa Joe was beside Captain Driscoll as the Packard bounced into the yard. But Papa Joe was half out of the automobile, his mouth open and his heart drumming in his chest. Ahead, having just left its rooftop track, the Blackbird climbed into the distance and made a sharp right turn, followed by a wide left, before gliding out of sight beyond the second hill.

Papa Joe turned to Captain Driscoll, who shrugged and said, "They told me to pick you up but not tell you what was going to happen. Looks like they waited till they saw us drive up before they let it go. Your boys wanted it to be a surprise."

A surprise . . .

Papa Joe barely heard these last words because he was out of the Packard and running up the hill as fast as his old legs could carry him. His mind restaged the moment he had just witnessed in vivid color, not the black and gray tones of a motion picture. By God, Will had done it! The pilot had soared and turned and landed—or appeared to land—behind the far hill. Puffing hard, Papa Joe reached the barn. He saw Daniel shouting and laughing as he climbed down from the roof, Will behind him. On the ground Daniel hugged Jonas. Will reached the ground, serious as ever, smiling only slightly, and shook both men's hands.

Papa Joe looked from one to the other, blinked, and said, "But who . . .?" When the answer came to him, he whispered, "Oh my God!" Then he was running again, unconcerned about the protest of his heart or the arthritis that flared in his knees with every pound of his boots on the ground. He knew only his fear, a fear unlike any he had felt since his time as a bondsman. Halfway down the hill he stumbled and plunged arms first into a fall that should have knocked the wind out of him but didn't. Aware only of the loss he dreaded, he scrambled to his feet. He charged up the second hill as if into battle but stopped at the crest to look down at the glider, which had settled undamaged on the grass. The pilot was already out and waving as he trudged up the hill toward him.

Unaware of the tears of relief welling in his eyes, Papa Joe smiled as he waved back. Even in a pair of Captain Driscoll's oversized driving goggles, Gus had never looked better.

\

Canal Scene
Courtesy of University at Buffalo Libraries

Twelve

It was Sunday, and fortune smiled on Eustace Buttonwood—or, rather, FORTUNE, the name on the iron padlock hanging unclosed on the door of this particular barn. Someone in the Montrose family had forgotten to lock it, which meant Buttonwood did not have to use the small crowbar he had tied to the cross bar of his rented bicycle. All he had to do was pull the lock from the hasp, open the barn door, and slip inside.

Morning sunlight flooded the interior, washed over the contraption in the center of the straw-covered floor. Was this Ned Montrose's idea of a flying machine? An ungainly-looking creation with large rubber tires, uneven bat wings, and a dirty cloth canopy? Attached to the back was an engine, likely from the same automobile that had surrendered two of its wheels. Buttonwood approached the flier slowly, walking completely around it one way, then the other. He studied it for a long time, comparing it to his memory of the Secretary's designs. The wings were smaller and stubbier. From what Manly had said of the limits of automobile engines, it was improbable that this heap of rubbish would ever fly.

Still, it was better to be sure . . . .

Turning to go back outside to the bicycle and loosen the crowbar he had brought, he spotted an ax in a worm-eaten stump just inside the barn. The handle was long and pitted, the blade rusted and buried deep. It would take a little spit and vinegar, but he was certain he could free it. Yes, fortune had favored him. An ax could do so much more than a crowbar. He peeled off his striped suit coat, folded it, and laid it on a nearby stool before taking hold of the handle. The blade came out on the third twist, and Buttonwood walked around to the right side of the flying machine. He raised the ax and brought it down on one wing, again and again, until he had reduced it to a pile of sticks and shredded sail cloth. Then he repeated his actions on the other wing. Afterward he hacked through both tires to make splinters of the wooden spokes and chopped the pilot's bench into kindling. Finally he turned his attention to the engine's hoses and cables and valves, the ax blade clanging and sparking as he lopped off one fixture after another.

When he was finished, he stood back to consider whether he had done enough. However close it had been to success, this aerodrome had no chance of taking to the sky now and scarce possibility of being rebuilt any time soon. Buttonwood was about to leave the barn when he noticed two wooden propellers leaning against the far wall. Pulling his watch from his waistcoat pocket, he checked the time. The Montrose family would still be in church, but he wanted to quit the premises early enough to avoid encountering them on the road as he pedaled his rented bicycle back to Scranton. And he did have a train to catch. But there was more than enough time for him to make the aerodrome's destruction complete. Holding the ax at waist level, he moved toward the propellers.

*   *   *

"It was my hope," Captain Driscoll said softly to his son, "that with Andrew's death you would become the Blackbird pilot."

The two men were seated across from each other at the small circular table in the library. Sabbath or not, Captain

Driscoll had decided to enjoy a glass of his best whiskey and, surprising even himself, had invited Daniel to join him. His long-standing disappointment in his son was no secret but had seldom surfaced in the months following his return home. Now his words came in the wake of his third whiskey, when his belly was warm and his tongue loose. But then why shouldn't he have hopes for his son's immortality? The first man to fly would live forever, right next to the man who invented the flying machine. Despite a dreaminess born of drink, he studied Daniel's thoughtful face and waited for a reaction, some indication he felt the hunger necessary for success. But Daniel was silent for a long time, his first drink still untouched. Captain Driscoll sensed in him only a mixture of sadness and contempt.

He thought, *My God! What have I done to make him thus? Is this the outgrowth of my hope for him, my impatience with him?*

Running a hand through his red hair, Daniel leveled his eyes at him. "Father, I am not afraid to fly, and perhaps I will eventually, but for the first flight, I have no right."

Captain Driscoll furrowed his brow. "I don't understand."

"I've worked with these men and come to respect them," Daniel said. "The first pilot must be colored. Frankly, I'm glad it's Gus. It's fitting that Will's brother be at the controls."

"But we've provided so much for these men, for this flying machine. We've given them space to work, materials, food . . ." Even as he spoke, Captain Driscoll felt repulsed by his own empty reasoning. He knew very well why he'd agreed to support this effort, but he too had developed great respect for the negroes.

"We've done so to profit from their work." Daniel rotated his glass between his thumb and forefinger, gazing into it as if contemplating whether to bring it to his lips. His voice was steady. "For us the aeroplane is a business investment, one I knew would meet your approval. For them it is so much more." He paused, looking expectantly at his father.

Captain Driscoll said nothing.

"I did not understand Will's explanation of the principles of flight," Daniel continued. "But I looked into his eyes and knew that he understood. Suddenly, I realized I had never looked deep into a negro's eyes before. I remember the shock I felt when it struck me that a colored man had the answer to the problem of flight. He understood what few white men ever would and I knew he could make the aeroplane a reality." He raised his glass. "If the aeroplane succeeds, you will manufacture it and sell it and make more money than you thought possible." At last he took a hefty swallow and gasped as it went down. "But for Will and Gus and the others, the Blackbird is a tool that will do nothing less than change how we whites look at them and treat their people."

Captain Driscoll closed his eyes and nodded. "Believe it or not, son, I am proud of your initiative and grateful you linked us to the negroes. You can't fault an old man for wishing his son a bigger share of the glory." He smiled sadly. Papa Joe had spoken the truth. Danny's hunger was there, all right, but the appetite was different. His talent lay not in business but in his ability to see into others and recognize their worth, to look through another man's eyes. *His mother's child*, Captain Driscoll reflected. If through Daniel's efforts people came to see the negro in a different light, he would have made his mark upon the world after all.

What more could a father ask?

* * *

Pearl kept her father's latest letter in the pocket of her

apron for nearly a week and took it out to reread it whenever Lorinda made her sit for a cup of tea. "Mr. Bailey says he can't spare me here just yet and won't need me at his Expo restaurant until the end of next month," her father had written. "I'll be there sometime the last week of August." She hadn't seen him in over two years. The news that he was finally coming, even if his arrival was a month away, lightened her movements and helped her glide through her chores.

On the last Thursday in July, as she was on her knees wire-brushing the cookstove, Pearl heard footsteps behind her. She did not need to look over her shoulder to know that Dr. Lucas had come into the kitchen. She recognized him from his soft footfall and the scent of his hair oil; from his silence, punctuated only by the slight acceleration of his breathing. Why, she wondered, must he sneak up behind her when she was working? Her own heart quickened, not with gladness but with dread. She was not blind to his feelings for her. They didn't quite seem to be the lust Uncle Portius sermonized against from his pulpit every fifth or sixth Sunday. She knew Dr. Lucas was a gentle and sincere man and did not fear that he would attempt to ravish her. But no matter how earnest his gazes felt, he was still a white man of some importance and she was still a colored maid. Every time he drew near, she was afraid that this would be the occasion she must tell him his desire for her was hopeless.

She sat back on her haunches and dragged a sleeve across her forehead as she let out a long breath. Beside her was a wooden pail with a mixture of water and a cleaning compound. She stuck the wire brush into the pail and swirled it through the solution. Then she opened a tin of pungent stove black and scooped some out with a thick rag.

"Dirty business, that stove," he said. Managing a smile, he crouched beside her and picked up the tin, bringing it to his nose. He winced. "This'd turn even an iron stomach. How does one manage?"

She looked at him, in his newly chemically cleaned suit and freshly waxed mustache. He held the tin gingerly, as though the contents would smudge his delicate medical fingers. She looked down at her own hands. Already the polish was soaking through the rag to stain her fingertips and outline her nails. Before she was finished, her palms would be black. She raised her eyes to Dr. Lucas again and felt anger rising in her throat, sour as a half-digested dinner. Of course the stove was a dirty business. Such seemed the lot to which she and her people had been assigned in the grand scheme of creation.

"One just does it," she said, making no effort to hide her irritation as she applied the paste in tight, overlapping circles.

"Miss Parker, I meant no offense." He put a hand on her shoulder. "Please."

She stopped, gazed at his hand. It looked odd where it lay, scrubbed-soft pinkness against the coarse blue of her workdress, a forest of tiny red hairs erect from his knuckles to his cuff. And before panic could follow her realization that today was the day she would have to smother his longing for her, everything poured out of him with surprising urgency: his love for her, the love he had fought and tried to deny, the love that now consumed his waking hours as fire consumed paper, the love for which he would toss aside his world and his family and all he had ever known. He took hold of her hands, staining his own fingers and cuffs, and stared into her eyes. "There's Canada, Pearl. We'll set up a practice there. You'll be my nurse."

Then he leaned forward to kiss her just once, lightly, his dry lips and moistened mustache tickling more than arousing her. He pulled back to look at her, perhaps expecting her to initiate a second kiss.

She searched his eyes, his wide green eyes, and detected no guile. The anger drained out of her. Far from being afraid, she wanted to cry, not out of desire or happiness, but out of pity. Poor Dr. Lucas. There were things he did not understand, despite the seven or eight years he had on her. There was no place for him in her heart, no pocket into which he could crawl and find shelter from a bruising world. The bruises dealt in his world differed from the slashes delivered by hers. That contrast in injuries would be an impassable gulf between them. She could not love him.

She had given more than fleeting consideration to the type of man she would eventually love. She was taller than most men she knew and sensed their discomfort beside her. Too many considered her unapproachable because her uncle was a preacher, as if courting her would bring down the fist of God. Others in search of simple wives were put off by the education apparent in her speech or by the joy in her voice when she sang. She had long known that the man who married her would have to accept her as she was, to love himself enough to love her. Ironically, here was a man willing to be the kind of man she wanted, yet she did not want him, was unwilling to abandon all she had known to live with him in exile.

On his knees beside her and still holding her hands, Dr. Lucas had watched her face as these thoughts ran their course. Now he closed his eyes and lowered his head. "Your hesitation tells me I have said too much." He exhaled thickly, as if his lungs had taken on cold fluid. "Serves me right, I guess. First I offer to make you my nurse, then I say nothing more for months, and suddenly I'm on my knees begging you to run away with me. If that isn't madness . . ." He released her hands and climbed to his feet. He took a cloth from the back of a chair and began to wipe the black off his fingers.

"Dr. Lucas . . ."

"You needn't say anything, Pearl. I see the sad truth in your eyes. You love another."

The only suitor who had come close to what she wanted in a husband was so short she feared *he* would sense *her* discomfort. But Gus was sympathetic and kind and had a way of putting her at ease. Given time, she believed she could love him. "I'm sorry."

Dr. Lucas bit his lower lip. "You have no reason to be sorry. I'm the one who behaved badly. I'm the one who should be sorry." Now he rubbed more furiously at the stains on his hands, but instead of cleaning them he worked the coloring deeper into his skin. "I believe I will need alcohol to remove this . . . this residue of our meeting." Face reddening, he backed toward the door that led to the front. "Pearl, I hope my indiscretion won't prove unforgivable. I would hate to drive you away from this house. I would never forgive myself for that."

"No, sir."

"I will say nothing of this to anyone. I hope you will find it in your heart to keep silent as well." He smiled bitterly. "Anyway, who could I tell? Certainly not my parents. Mother would discharge you in a flash, for my stupidity. Father would disinherit me at the hint of a suggestion there might be something between us. I couldn't ruin both our lives, unless we had another life. . .to share. But since that seems never to be. . . "

"Please don't think harshly of me, Dr. Lucas."

"Pearl, all that I have said remains unchanged. My life is yours for the asking. If ever you reconsider my proposal . . ." His unfinished sentence hung between them for a heartbeat. "Or if you should ever find yourself in trouble and in need of help, I would consider it my privilege if you called upon me."

Before she could thank him, he turned and was gone.

*   *   *

From the Chronicles of Augustus Lockhart:
Monday August 12

My entries continue to be brief. At the end of my work days I engage in lengthy sessions with Will, who reviews with me the subtleties of flight as he continues construction of the engine. On my days away from the Exposition I spend so much time gliding and refining my control of the craft that I am exhausted in the evening and unable to set down more than a paragraph or two before sleep claims me. Even in sleep, however, I fly and fully appreciate God's gift of wings to Will's mind and Will's gift of wings to my body.

All of this has made me a better flier but a less reliable chronicler. Today's entry will be no exception to my brevity of late, but today's news does have some bearing on our work. We learned that next month William McKinley is coming to the Pan-American Exposition. Will assured everyone that if we work on Sundays (Reverend Banks has given his blessing!) and continue to progress at our present pace, we will be ready in two weeks' time for the first engine test.

If all goes well then, I could soon be the first man to fly an aeroplane. Shortly thereafter, it is possible I will do so for the President of the United States.

The American Negro Exhibit,
With Rev. J. E. Nash (standing) and James Ross
Courtesy of Susan J. Eck and *Doing the Pan*
and Peggy Brooks-Bertram, Barbara Seals Nevergold,
and *The Uncrowned Queens Institute*

Thirteen

From the Chronicles of Augustus Lockhart:
Sunday August 18

Today we met the poet laureate of the negro race, the author of Lyrics of Lowly Life, Paul Laurence Dunbar. Mr. Dunbar and his wife arrived early Friday, at the invitation of the leadership association. They spent their first night in the home of Reverend Nash and all of Saturday at the Exposition. Last night they stayed at Reverend Ayler's parsonage and worshiped at the A.M.E. Church this morning. Tonight they are with Reverend and Mrs. Banks.

This afternoon Mr. Dunbar gave a public recital at Ascension. The sanctuary was filled to bursting. The warm air was heavy with perfume and hair oil. Scattered among colored faces were a dozen or so white men—from the newspapers and the university, someone said—and a few white women from a poetry society. Except for the infirm, nearly every man stood because there were so many ladies, who fanned themselves and chatted as they waited for the program to begin.

Papa Joe and I stood beside Reverend Banks at the end of the front pew. Seated there between Mrs. Talbert of the leadership group and Mrs. Banks and Pearl were the Dunbars.

Mrs. Dunbar sat beside Pearl. I was amazed at the resemblance. Though Pearl is taller, both women have softly sloping shoulders, long, graceful necks, and deeply attentive eyes set in delicate faces. Even their dresses were similar—cream-colored with frills and puffed sleeves. They might have been sisters.

Mrs. Talbert went to the podium before the altar and raised a hand for quiet. She called for the gentlemen along the walls to make sure all the windows were open, as well as the doors at the back, so no one suffered a heat stroke. Then she read a list of the speaker's accomplishments, pausing to praise his latest book, The Fanatics. When at last she said, "I give you Paul Laurence Dunbar," the sanctuary erupted in applause.

Mr. Dunbar is not a large man. He is dark and slight of build, with narrow shoulders and a face as sensitive as any woman's. On his way to the podium he somehow looked older than his twenty-nine years. He covered his mouth and coughed as he laid out on the reader's stand three books with several places marked. Then he pulled on a pair of small gold-rimmed spectacles. By the time he covered his mouth again, the clapping had stopped and his grating cough echoed through the church. It seemed the cough of an unwell man.

"Excuse me," said Mr. Dunbar, clearing his throat. "My dear wife and I have spent much of this summer confined by illness. I have had to cancel several appearances around the country." Even with sickness vibrating behind it, Mr. Dunbar's voice has a musical quality, a poetic rhythm laced into his everyday speech. "Once we were well enough to travel, however, I knew there were two places we must go—Kentucky, toward which we start tomorrow, and where my cousin Ella Burton is performing the title role in Clorindy, and Buffalo, whose good people of color had sent so gracious an invitation."

When the second outbreak of applause had died away, the poet glanced inside one of his books and positioned himself beside the stand. "My father was a soldier," he said. "But before he was a soldier he was a Canadian, and before he was a Canadian he was a slave. If not for the War Between the States, he would never have returned to this country and joined the 55th Regiment Massachusetts Volunteers to fight deep in the South he had fled. Nor would he ever have met my mother, and I would not be standing here today. It is to my father's memory, then, that I dedicate this poem, 'The Colored Soldiers' . . ."

For the next hour Mr. Dunbar held us all spellbound as he recited one piece after another, alternating between his colored dialect poems and his work in the style of the English Romantics. His voice rang with strength and passion that belied the severity of his periodic coughing. The conclusion of each poem was met with enthusiastic applause. Each time he smiled his thanks and gave a slight bow, then stood back, his face full of patience as he waited to resume. He ended the reading with his well-known poem "We Wear the Mask," which brought the colored audience to their feet, cheering and clapping and stomping so heavily the floorboards beneath us felt unsafe.

Later Papa Joe and I joined the Dunbars at the Banks home for supper. The discussion around the table was lively and exciting. In a lighter mood than usual, Reverend Banks recounted various boyhood misadventures he had shared with my father, including the hiding my grandfather gave them both the day they slipped out of school to swim in the river. No one laughed at that story more than Papa Joe himself. In fact, he got on so well with the Dunbars, discussing books and politics and famous negroes, that he even spoke briefly of his bondage, something he does rarely. "I share a special kinship with your father," he said to Mr. Dunbar, "but I never reached Canada." (I have always thought it romantic that he chose to risk capture by remaining in Buffalo with my grandmother. Maybe one day he'll tell me the whole story.)

The Dunbars talked of their travels, of New York and Denver and their life in Washington. Mr. Dunbar once worked for the Library of Congress, and Mrs. Dunbar is an author herself, having published two books of short stories. I was surprised to learn that Mr. Dunbar sometimes faces difficulty publishing his romantic poetry. Magazine editors are more interested in his dialect pieces. "They get excited about a negro writer only when he sounds like their idea of a negro," Mrs. Dunbar said. The irony, of course, is that in their own speech Mr. and Mrs. Dunbar bear no trace of the colored dialect their editors prefer. A gracious and fascinating couple, they appear devoted to each other, but Mrs. Dunbar seemed unusually protective of her husband, responding with concern whenever he cleared his throat and urging him to drink more tea for the congestion in his chest.

"I understand you were part of the President's inaugural parade in March," said Reverend Banks at one point, "with the honorary rank of colonel."

"Yes," said Mr. Dunbar, "though sometimes when I sit I have a most painful recollection of my experience astride a horse."

Mrs. Dunbar laughed. "You see, my husband had never ridden a horse before. The saddle lacked the padding of a good carriage seat." She squeezed Mr. Dunbar's left hand and smiled. "Still, he sat in that saddle with more dignity than any soldier there."

Mr. Dunbar said, "It wouldn't do for the only negro for miles around to fall off his horse in front of the President."

When the subsequent laughter died away, Reverend Banks narrowed his eyes and leaned forward. "What kind of man is McKinley?" he asked. "I mean, in terms of colored concerns."

Seated at the opposite end of the table, his wife to his left, Mr. Dunbar thought for a moment before answering. "He's a good man, I believe. A fair man, though he advises the negro to keep his house in order and have patience as his lot unfolds on the American landscape. That's hardly a surprise. He's patient himself and believes the future of the nation lies in the expansion of American business interests around the world." Now Mr. Dunbar narrowed his eyes. "Why, sir, do you ask?"

Reverend Banks glanced to his left, where Pearl sat between Papa Joe and me, then to his right, where Mrs. Banks sat beside Mrs. Dunbar. He studied his wife for a moment. "Papa Joe and I have already discussed this . . ."

"Yes, Portius," said Mrs. Banks. "Tell them."

"Pearl? Gus?"

Pearl and I nodded, almost in unison.

"Mr. Dunbar, Mrs. Dunbar," said Reverend Banks, "what I am about to reveal must not leave this room. Some months ago I wanted to tell members of the negro committee, but Papa Joe warned me against it in case we failed. Now that success is within reach, you, Mr. Dunbar, may have insights that could be of some benefit to our enterprise . . ."

The Dunbars looked at each other with puzzled expressions.

"Each of us at this table has sworn an oath." Reverend Banks took the Bible from his coat pocket. "I ask you to swear it now, for the good of our people."

Mr. Dunbar studied Reverend Banks with uneasiness.

"It involves nothing immoral or illegal." Reverend Banks offered the Dunbars a reassuring smile. "It promises only a great leap forward for the race."

The Dunbars seemed to confer silently, with their eyes, then agreed to swear. When they had done so, Reverend Banks and Papa Joe took turns telling them about the Blackbird, from the genesis of Will's ideas to the Driscolls' support to Andrew's death to the recent glider flights. When he was finished, the

Dunbars looked at each other and then at the rest of us, from one to the other. No one spoke for a long time.

Finally, Mr. Dunbar ended the silence. "May the Lord rest the Ridgewater boy's soul," he said, with his eyes closed. After an amen had circled the table, he opened his eyes and drew in a deep breath. "Fantastic. Apart from the tragedy, this is wonderful news."

Papa Joe shook his head. "It is not yet news." He gestured toward me with his fork. "It won't be news until Gus here flies over the Exposition—during President McKinley's visit."

All eyes turned to me, and I lowered my own in embarrassment. The Dunbars had not imagined that quiet little Gus might pilot the flying machine Reverend Banks described. Sudden fear grew heavy in me, fear that the entire undertaking was doomed to fail, that all I would do is join Andrew in the churchyard. Seated to my right, Pearl laid her hand atop mine and encircled my fingers with hers. Mr. Dunbar gave my left shoulder a gentle squeeze. I shuddered once, for a breathless instant, despite their touch.

"Reverend, I believe I understand your question now," said Mr. Dunbar. "If the first man to fly is colored—the grandson of a slave—President McKinley will be suitably impressed. The real question, of course, is how this accomplishment will benefit the negro." He sat forward, elbows on the table and hands clasped as if in prayer. "Your aeroplane will prove the negro is capable of purposeful industry and scientific creativity, that he possesses a brain and not just a back. Unfortunately, it will not remedy a host of colored concerns." He pulled off his spectacles. "It will not inspire the Congress to pass new anti-lynching laws or enforce those already on the books. It will not make jobs or schooling available to those who have neither. It will not free the sharecropper from indenture to land he does not own." Mr. Dunbar shook his head. "Your flying machine will do none of these—unless you make surrender of the design dependent upon changes in policy."

Papa Joe nodded. "No one gets the Blackbird until, say, lynch laws are changed."

"Exactly," said Mr. Dunbar, smiling.

For the next half hour we listened as the poet suggested one strategy after another for presentation of the Blackbird to the world. Once the President is interested, he said, we must offer a bill of particulars about the mistreatment of the negro, along with a demand that such particulars be addressed with all due speed before the aeroplane is put into the service of the nation. We must use the newspapers to make our case, letting the story of our achievement become known only in small degrees. In such a manner would we keep our triumph current and slowly accustom the public to the idea of negro accomplishment and changes in negro treatment. But first we must safeguard our interests.

"You're not the only Americans trying to fly," said Mr. Dunbar. "Two of my schoolmates from Central High in Dayton are conducting similar experiments. Your Will sounds a lot like my friends, by nature builders of machines. Orville and Wilbur used to go from repairing one device to making another. They built a printing press from scratch when Orville was in school with me, and we worked together on two newspapers. Now they own a bicycle shop, but they go south every year to fly gliders. Men like them, like Will, don't think about protecting themselves. Get a lawyer, for everyone's sake, but especially for Will's."

Directly across the table from me, Mrs. Dunbar noticed that I had produced pencil and notebook and was dutifully recording her husband's ideas. She pressed a finger to his forearm and when he turned to her indicated me with a slight nod. Mr. Dunbar said, "And I hope someone is keeping an account of your progress, a written record."

"We've taken many photographs," Reverend Banks said. "We have Will's papers . . ." He spread his hands apart.

Papa Joe leaned forward to look past Pearl, to look at me, as if he had known all along the content of my nightly writing. His eyes urged me to speak.

"Excuse me," I said, "but almost since the start I've been keeping a chronicle." I passed this very notebook to Mr. Dunbar. He paged through it, eyes snapping back and forth over my words. I said, "I believed somebody ought to write a book about the aeroplane."

"Your writing shows much promise," Mr. Dunbar said finally, passing the notebook to his wife. "I would like to read more of it." He took a small leather-backed notebook from his own inside pocket, tore off a sheet, and with a stub of pencil scratched in his address. "Please send me some of your writing. It would be my pleasure to comment upon it, perhaps even endorse it to my publisher when you are ready to reveal your aeroplane."

Pearl squeezed my hand, and my head swam. Past thanking Mr. Dunbar, I had no idea what to say.

Before long Papa Joe climbed to his feet and said it was time for us to take our leave. Mr. Dunbar rose and edged behind my chair and Pearl's to reach Papa Joe and shake his hand. "Mr. Lockhart, meeting you truly was a pleasure." Then Reverend Banks and his wife stood, followed by Mrs. Dunbar, who excused herself from the room.

Both Pearl and I pushed back our chairs at the same instant and got to our feet, as we had been taught, only after all our elders were standing. During the exchange of farewells, she bent close to my ear long enough to whisper, "Gus Lockhart, you once offered to escort me to the Pan-American. I'm still waiting." Before I could swallow my heart and free my throat for a reply, Papa Joe was urging me toward the front door and laughing at something Reverend Banks had said. I looked back at Pearl once, and felt my legs weaken at the sight of her smile.

Outside, before we had gotten more than a few steps away, the door was flung open. Mr. Dunbar emerged. "Gus," he called, "I have something for you." I went back to him. "My wife and I thought this was a fitting token of our hope for your success." He pressed a folded paper into my hand. "Know that you are in our prayers."

It was a page neatly torn from a book. I affix it now to the bottom of this entry because it bears the author's signature:

Preparation

The little bird sits in the nest and sings
A shy, soft song to the morning light;
And it flutters a little and prunes its wings.
The song is halting and poor and brief,
And the fluttering wings scarce stir a leaf;
But the note is a prelude to sweeter things,
And the busy bill and the flutter slight
Are proving the wings for a bolder flight!

Paul Lawrence Dunbar

---

* * *

Saturday August 24

Will's gasoline engine works!

It is smaller and lighter than the engine in an automobile but much more powerful, according to Will. We mounted it on a special platform inside the barn. At Will's signal Danny spun the crank until the engine sputtered, then thundered into life as threads of bluish smoke curled into the air. The sound was deafening, soon painful. If I am to lie beside it in flight, I'll need some kind of ear covering to tolerate the roar.

At last we are ready to consider where the Blackbird should fly so that it may catch the greatest number of eyes. The most populated area is the Esplanade, the magnificent open space between the Triumphal Bridge and the Court of the Fountains near the southern end of the grounds. It can hold a quarter million people. With the Temple of Music and the Ethnology Building in opposite corners, foot traffic in this area is always heavy. An aeroplane would be quite a spectacle. But if the engine consumes fuel too rapidly, there may not be enough time to reach the Esplanade and return to the Driscolls'. A fall from the sky might kill innocent fairgoers. While the northern half of the grounds may seem safer, the Plaza, the Propylaea, and the sunken gardens are always teeming. The Electric Tower and the Captive Balloon ride could be dangerous as well, should the Blackbird prove hard to control at great heights. If anyone else is killed or injured in a mishap witnessed by thousands, the struggle of our race will be set back years.

If the aeroplane loses power or cannot hold its course, I must guide it to where the only life lost will be my own.

*　　*　　*

Thursday August 29

Will has modified the Blackbird since my last glider flight. He has added a crossbar to the front framework just beneath the edge of the upper wings. To this he has affixed the propellers, which are connected to the engine's gear wheels by means of elongated bicycle-type chains. He has also lengthened both the upper and lower wing tips on either side by about a foot, leaving the right side a few inches longer than the left, to compensate, he says, for the disparity between my weight and that of the engine which must share the center of the internal framework. Danny has added thick wads of batting to the inside of a large riding helmet to cover my ears and shield them from the noise of the engine.

In headgear and goggles, I must have looked an ungodly sight as I crawled into the pilot's hammock at four this afternoon.

Will had spent the morning and the first part of the afternoon making final calculations and adjustments for my first powered flight. My heart was pounding and my belly twitching as I slid my hands and feet into the controls. Danny cranked the engine, and the propellers spun so fast in opposite directions they seemed to disappear. The noise filled my ears even through my protective headgear. When the wheel wedges were removed, I eased the lever forward and felt my stomach pulled back to my feet as I shot toward the edge of the roof. Wind threatened to peel the clothes from my back as I rattled down the track at great speed. I bit my tongue too hard and hurtled into the air.

Danny told me later the flight lasted more than half a minute, but there was a wonderful endlessness to staying aloft, a sense that my weight, my connection to the earth, had disappeared. I was skirting the heavens, offering myself up to God. I felt far from angelic, however. Working the controls and shifting myself to cut through the air took effort, much more effort than riding the winds. With the taste of my own blood on my tongue, and being able to draw in only shallow breaths, I ought to have been terrified of suffering Andrew's fate, of plunging earthward even faster and not surviving long enough to reach the hospital. Yet however graceless it must have appeared, free flight was so exhilarating, so intoxicating, so unlike anything I had ever before done, that I was not afraid, even when my height exceeded what I knew must be forty feet.

Gazing down, I saw that I was beyond the second hill and skimming trees that marked the boundary of Captain Driscoll's property. However, not even the prospect of coming down among them and destroying myself and my brother's wonderful creation frightened me. I had a strange sense that I belonged to the sky. Calmly and gradually, as I had practiced so often, I angled the right wing and began the wide circle that would direct me back toward the barn. Below, in the distance, I saw the others in the hollow, waving their arms and working their mouths in what could only have been cheers. When the moment felt right, I eased the lever back and brought the Blackbird in low, angling the wings simultaneously to slow down enough to glide to earth on a long stretch of grass.

I was down. I felt more alive than ever before, as if I had pressed my fingertips against the face of God.

Before I could free myself, Will and some of the others surrounded the Blackbird, dancing and screaming as they tried to pull me out. When they had done so and torn off the helmet and goggles, Will, Papa Joe, and Danny hoisted me onto their shoulders and marched toward the barn. Jostled, nearly dropped, I looked down and saw Captain Driscoll and Jonas Newcomb coming toward us, laughing and clapping. Reverend Banks trailed them, shouting, "I got pictures, good pictures!" With another cheer, Will and the others tossed me a foot or two into the air and caught me. Again. And again.

After my third descent into this rough cradle, I felt a rush of lightheadedness. Everything about me began to spin, until one sense blended into another—until the blue and white of the sky, the laughter and shouting, the green and brown smell of the earth, and the taste of the johnnycake and eggs I'd eaten four hours earlier became one sickening swirl—and I passed out in their arms.

Fourteen

At the Terrace Street station, Eustace Buttonwood hailed a cab and settled back in the stuffed leather seat as the driver cracked the whip above his horse. It was a sunny afternoon, the last Friday in August. Buttonwood had never been to Buffalo before. Though he knew there was an Exposition going on, he had not known what to expect. For several blocks he gazed about like a tourist adjusting to the look and feel of the city. The architecture was a mix of old brick—with striped awnings and hammered copper sheeting beneath upper bow windows—and new terra cotta and stone. The streets teemed with pedestrians, cyclists, carriages, and trolleys. There were few automobiles. The concentration of electric wires overhead suggested that downtown was dazzling at night, glowing with its own hunger for growth. He wondered if power lines went as far out as his destination, if electricity had any role in the aerodrome he had come to investigate.

Just then the carriage creaked to a stop. The driver turned to Buttonwood and said, "Here y'are, sir."

Buttonwood blinked and sat forward, not understanding.

"The address you give me, sir." The cabby was an old man with a clean blue cap and a neat gray mustache. He jerked his head toward a building. "This is it."

"But we've gone no more than nine or ten blocks," Buttonwood said. "We're still in the city. The place I want must be farther out, with open spaces around it."

The driver repeated the address. "This here's Broadway and that there's the number."

It was a simple enough wood-frame building, with a barnlike front and a small house and horse stall in the rear. Buttonwood read the black inscription in an arc above the wagon-wide double doors: Jos. Lockhart, Blacksmith. He slumped back in the seat, pushed up his homburg to think. The name was right but the location was all wrong. Though the shop looked large enough to hold an aerodrome, there was no room for flight trials amid these buildings and such traffic. He opened his valise, on the seat beside him, and riffled through papers until he came to the one he wanted. *William* Lockhart, not Joseph. Who was William? Maybe Joseph's brother or grown son, who collected his mail here and worked on aerodromes elsewhere. Or maybe he was just another of the numberless boys who requested aerodromics monographs from the Smithsonian because they were dreamers with too much spare time on their hands. Most likely, William was a stripling with an overactive imagination.

Still, it was better to be sure . . . .

The small door beside the wagon entrance of the blacksmith shop opened. An old negro stepped out—one of the tallest men Buttonwood had ever seen. He produced a long key and inserted it in the keyhole. Turning it, he gave the door a shake to make sure it was locked. Then, pocketing the key, he saw the cab and came near.

He was in his late sixties or early seventies but appeared powerfully built, with broad shoulders that threatened to split the uppermost seams of his suit coat and a face chiseled as much by circumstance as time. He greeted the driver, lifting his cap with a hand huge enough to crush a skull. "Horse throw a shoe?"

The driver shook his head.

"Figured I'd ask before I left," the negro said. "We'll be

closed the rest of the day."

His pouched eyes met Buttonwood's, held them for a second, just long enough for dread to take root in Buttonwood's mind. Then, touching his brim, the giant negro strolled off and began to whistle when he was a few feet past the cab. Watching him, Buttonwood knew that he was no employee. His eyes and his walk were those of a man who had worked for no one but himself for a long time. He was Joseph Lockhart—far too old to have a child gathering flight literature. No, this man had a son, or even a grandson, old enough to attempt the unimaginable.

"Someplace else, sir?" the cabby asked.

Is it possible a colored man is building an aerodrome? A flying dinge! Wouldn't that make a laughingstock of Langley?

"Sir, beggin' your pardon—"

"Is there a hotel nearby?"

"One right around the corner, sir. The Clinton is a gentleman's hotel and rents rooms for a dollar a day."

"Take me there," Buttonwood said.

* * *

Ordinarily Pearl worked until two every Saturday, but today Mrs. Westbeck had given her the day off so she could meet her father's noon train at the Exchange Street station. She had spent the morning hot-combing her hair, cleansing the hem of her best summer skirt with a damp cloth, ironing her new white blouse, and searching the yard for a daisy to slip into the band of her best straw hat. Now, flanked by her aunt and uncle, she stood at the edge of the railway station platform, gazing down the track at the locomotive, which slowed as it hissed toward the terminal.

Her father was easy to spy amid the disembarking passengers. At more than six and a half feet he towered over almost everyone. He saw her and waved. Pearl worked her way to the side of the platform and down the stairs. She stepped off the gravel path and lifted her hem as she hurried through the sparse brush.

Face split by a broad smile, he disentangled himself from the crowd and met her halfway. Dropping his carpetbag, he caught her in his arms, lifted her off the ground, and twirled her around twice. "Pearl!" he cried. "My beautiful, beautiful Pearl!"

He set her down and stepped back, grinning. His cheek lines were deeper. Gray speckled the hair visible beneath his cocked slouch hat. But to her relief, despite the wife who lay in the shallow grave of his memory, his eyes still glittered with his gentle sense of humor. He was still a man who inspired laughter. Her father would be the perfect remedy for Uncle Portius and Aunt Essie's steadfast seriousness.

"Girl, you are a sight," he said. "About as grown as you can be and looking mighty fine."

"You look mighty fine yourself, Papa," she said. And he did. She saw he was still fussy about his appearance, from his close shave to his wing collar. Eyes moistening, she took his big hand in hers and squeezed it hard. She had plenty she wanted to tell him about—singing in church, her job, the idea that she might go away to a colored nursing school, Gus and their plan to take him to the Exposition tomorrow. And at her uncle's urging, the others had already agreed that it would be easier to bring him into the Blackbird covenant than to hide it from him. So many words spun madly in her brain—but her throat tightened so much she was unable to utter a sound. Her father understood and simply pulled her head to his chest, knocking her hat askew and then laughing as he caught hold if its edge to keep it from falling.

By this time her aunt and uncle had made their way through the crowd and joined them. Aunt Essie waited for her brother to release Pearl, then hugged him herself. "It's been too long, Ben." Uncle Portius shook his hand. "Welcome back to Buffalo. You won't believe what's happened since you were last here."

Looking up at her father, James Benjamin Parker, Pearl felt the warmth of his crooked grin and laughed when he said, "Shoot! Now that I'm back, it's time for the real party to start."

*   *   *

From the Chronicles of Augustus Lockhart:
Sunday September 1

Papa Joe once told me that you can judge a man by how easily laughter comes to him. A man who cannot laugh at the surprises that add texture to his day, the peculiarities of his fellow men, and particularly his own failings is a man who suffers from an impoverishment of character. If Papa Joe is correct, Pearl's father is a good man with a wealth of character. His is the effortless laughter of a genuinely kind man, the deep laughter that comes only from men of ponderous size. In the shadow of my grandfather, I have come to believe men so big tend to be gentle and unthreatening, as if they are obliged to put those around them at ease. Joking his way through the Exposition today, Mr. Parker only confirmed that belief. I had feared meeting him, believing he would find me an inadequate suitor for Pearl. He seemed to like me, though, and I had no trouble liking him.

When we had seen the principal exhibits and the restaurant where he will be working, a fancy-looking eatery in the Plaza, Mr. Parker, Pearl, and I walked through the quiet Midway. Curious about some of the closed attractions, Mr. Parker asked about Esau, the Missing Link. I told him that though Esau wears clothes, eats with a fork, drinks from a cup, and smokes cigars, he is just a chimpanzee. Then Mr. Parker seemed fascinated by the exterior of A Trip to the Moon. When I told him I'd already taken the moon journey after work one evening, he pressed me for details.

The entire trip is an electrical illusion. Passengers board

a huge winged ship called Luna. It is green and white and full of steamer chairs. The wings groan up and down as music fills the interior and lights blink outside the portholes. The whole thing rocks from side to side to give the illusion of flying. Outside, the Exposition grounds fall away, as does the nation, until the earth disappears. After a series of lightning flashes, the moon slides past the portholes. Luna drops through sunlit clouds to settle in a volcanic crater. The passengers are then conducted through an underground city with green rocks, red lava pilings, and twisting yellow streets. Moon dwellers — gnomes, Selenites, and giants—wander about in odd costumes and headgear. Finally, in the throne room of the Man in the Moon, visitors watch the dance of the Moon Maidens.

"Sounds clever," said Pearl, and her father nodded.

I agreed, though I did not say that all the electrical ingenuity in Creation was no substitute for flying itself. Still, because his family had told him of the aeroplane last night, I expected Mr. Parker to ask how the moon ride compared to real flight. But he said nothing as we made our way to the gate, leaving me to wonder if he truly believed what Reverend Banks had shared with him. Until he saw it for himself, I realized, Mr. Parker likely would find the very idea of a flying machine too fantastic to take seriously. Before we left, I looked back at the interior of the Exposition. I had left my resignation letter in Mr. Buckett's box in the Service Building. Fantastic or not, my next glimpse into the heart of the Rainbow City will be from the sky.

We walked up Elmwood, crossing the railroad beltline and continuing north through knee-high grass until we reached the wagon road that ran past the Driscoll place. We started up the road to the house. It was late afternoon, past time for Sunday dinner but we knew they were waiting for us. Jonas has done most of the cooking at Captain Driscoll's since Mrs. Ridgewater left. While no one who's eaten his fried potato, bean, and meat concoctions has complained, we are all grateful for Sundays, when Mrs. Banks prepares a proper feast. She met us at the kitchen door and embraced her brother.

"How was the fair, Ben?" she asked.

"Oh, we had a fine time," said Mr. Parker. "But Portius was right. They had next to nothing about colored folk." From his pocket he took out a yellow souvenir booklet with a blue-tone photograph of two men—Reverend Nash and Mr. Ross—flanked by charts and books. "Just this, a book exhibit."

"That will all change next week." Mrs. Banks smiled. "The men are out in the barn right now." She turned to me. "Gus, would you take Ben out there?" Then she turned to Pearl. "I could use some help here in the kitchen." She looked up at her brother again. "We're having corn and chicken and rice and red-eye gravy."

Still making faint pleasure noises in his throat, Mr. Parker followed me out back to the barn, where everyone was gathered around the wingless Blackbird. Reverend Banks introduced his wife's brother. After circling the aeroplane to shake hands with everyone, Mr. Parker turned his attention to the Blackbird itself, asking how it worked.

As always, Will's face lit up like a lantern when he came forward to recite his explanation: how air gathers beneath the wings, how the wings buckle to adjust to currents, how the small rear wings and forward leveling panels stabilize the aeroplane in flight. He reminded me of a preacher reciting cherished Bible verses, retelling favorite homilies, possessed of a godly joy he must share with the world. As he had shown me in his flash of anger at the hospital, he could no more give up flight than he could give up breath. I found myself wondering how the Almighty chooses to bestow His gifts, why He gave Will sight, insight, and foresight that detach him from the rest of us. Even I, who have slept beside him since childhood, know him only so well. But perhaps my meditations are backward. Maybe it is not Will who was given God's gift. Maybe he is God's gift to us.

After Will had finished, Reverend Banks took Mr. Parker to the wall opposite the door, which bore all the photographs he had taken of the aeroplane's development and flight. I hung back, near the Blackbird. Despite having made dozens of glides and half a dozen flights, I have no desire to see myself severed from the earth. Indeed, I have been photographed only a few times in my life and pleased with none of the results. In pictures I seem too scrawny to be of much use to anyone, too weak to accomplish any feat worthy of recognition. When next I lie in the pilot's hammock, I do not wish to remember myself as looking puny and out of place there.

Presently, the meeting resumed, led by Will. We reviewed our plans for the week. Monday, Tuesday, and Wednesday we will put the Blackbird through its final trials for control, distance, and time. I will fly low, sometimes north, sometimes east—away from the Exposition, to avoid being seen. I must pay special attention to the lever that controls the flow of fuel to the engine and thus the speed of the aeroplane. Should I fail to push the lever far enough forward, the propellers will not spin at sufficient speed to lift the Blackbird into the air and keep it there. On the other hand, pushing the lever far enough to reach maximum speed will consume the fuel too quickly, forcing me to the ground too soon and jeopardizing the lives of fairgoers below.

Will has calculated that I will need perhaps five minutes to reach the Esplanade and return. So far the longest I have been able to stay aloft before the fuel reservoir begins to sputter is about ten seconds shy of six minutes. Will has fixed a modified Waterbury timepiece inside a small padded case, which he attached to the framework of the Blackbird at eye level. Thus can I keep watch on the passage of time while I am in the air. "When two and a half minutes have passed, you must turn around," said Will, "no matter where you are, or you won't make it back."

Of necessity, then, I must strike a balance between the engine and the winds, between the aeroplane and my body. To stay aloft as long as necessary, I must feel my way through the flight with the instincts of something that flies.

I pray that I am ready.

If I cannot be ready, I pray that God is merciful.

On Wednesday evening the President's train arrives at the Amherst terminal on the fairgrounds. Captain Driscoll, who knew the President when they were both young Union officers, will try to pass a letter to Mr. McKinley or someone in his company. The letter, already written in the Captain's hand, briefly describes our aeroplane work and promises that the craft will soar overhead during the President's Esplanade speech the next day. Papa Joe, armed with a similar letter from me, is to locate Mr. Porter on the day of the speech. The Edison cameraman already told me he would be there to film that event. We hope he can capture the aeroplane in full flight, moving across the sky. Both letters invite the recipients to the Driscoll estate to learn more of the Blackbird's particulars. Should neither letter reach its destination, the Blackbird will still appear before the fifty thousand spectators expected to attend the speech. If sudden rain or some other unforeseen circumstance stops Thursday's flight, there will be a second opportunity. The President is scheduled to hold a public reception Friday afternoon in the Temple of Music.

One way or another, this week holds our moment in the sun.

Bird's Eye View of the Pan-American Exposition
Courtesy of Susan J. Eck and *Doing the Pan*

Part Three

Flight of the Blackbird

What you must understand above all else is that our beliefs were interdependent, self-sustaining, roused by the divine. We became inextricably linked, a family of many colors. You see, we believed in God and hoped that we could inspire God to believe in us. Flight was not our challenge to Him but our observance of Him, of the gifts and talents He saw fit to bestow upon each of us and which together gave us a purpose larger and more meaningful than any of us would have discovered alone.

Papa Joe had been given freedom and had used it to give Will and me the foundation upon which to dream. The Driscoll household had given us money and friendship and a place to work. Reverend Banks and his family had become our spiritual center, keeping us anchored in godly purpose even after Andrew gave his life and his mother gave up her peace. As far as I know, Mrs. Ridgewater never told a soul the truth of how her son died. I believe she kept the secret because, through everything, Will had given all of us the substance of a dream in which we could place our faith, even amidst necessary sacrifice and loss.

Every time I lay in the Blackbird's hammock or picked up a pencil to chronicle the events in this book, I celebrated what I saw in the face of each member of our endeavor, a boundless belief that nothing is more powerful than a dream meeting an idea in an age of possibility . . .

—From the unpublished manuscript Flight of the Blackbird *by Augustus Lockhart*

The Electric Tower
Courtesy of Susan J. Eck and *Doing the Pan*

Fifteen

The last person Pearl expected to find standing on the Westbecks' front porch when she answered the door chime was Gus. Cap in hand and a package tucked under one arm, he smiled at her. At the curb, amid the lengthening late afternoon shadows of trees, sat Papa Joe's carriage.

"Gus, what are you doing here?" she said in a sharp whisper. "Shouldn't you be at the Captain's?"

"We're on our way," he said. "We'll be there all night."

"Who's at the door?" came Lorinda's voice from the kitchen.

Pearl hesitated. "I can't talk now. I'm working."

"Didn't come to talk," Gus said. "Came to give you this, in case I don't get another chance." He put on his cap and held out the package with both hands. "I got this a while back. Guess I was waiting for the right time . . . or maybe to get my nerve up."

She took the bundle, fingertips telling her what it was even through the heavy brown paper. "Oh, Gus . . ." She felt her eyes moisten.

"Pray for me tomorrow," he said. Turning, he went down the steps and walked out to the stanhope. Before climbing in, he waved once. Then Papa Joe snapped the reins, and Mac snorted as he clopped away from the curb.

Lorinda appeared at Pearl's elbow, making no effort to hide her irritation. "You answer me when I talk to you, child!" She pointed toward the buggy turning around in the middle of

Delaware Avenue to head north. "Who was that?"

"A friend," Pearl said, wiping her eyes with the back of her hand. "He wanted to bring me something before he went away."

Lorinda frowned. "Girl, this ain't no place to be receivin' menfolk! This where you work! Now you'd best get back to it 'fore Mrs. Westbeck have a fit." She gestured toward the package. "And you can put your thing there in the mud room with your wrap."

Pearl went through the kitchen and pantry to the cold gray mud room. There she laid the package on the bench, beneath the hook that held her shawl. Glancing back to make sure Lorinda was not watching, she sat and began to untie it. She had known from the feel, from the arms and legs and hard head that it was a porcelain doll. Gus must have remembered her fondness for dolls from their trip to the market. He must have gone back to buy one for her. She unfolded the paper and caught her breath.

The doll was not black the way most negro dolls were—with glistening coal skin, empty minstrel eyes, and huge red lips. This doll's complexion was a deep, delicate brown, not unlike Pearl's own, and stood in sharp contrast to the cream-colored dress. Her eyes were black dots beneath upswept lashes, her tiny mouth rosebud pink. Doubtless she had begun her existence as a white doll, but she had been painted skillfully, with loving care. Pearl lifted her out of her paper bedding and saw that she had been lying upon a stiff-backed card with the emblem of the Exposition: two women swathed in fabric arranged to depict North and South America clasping hands over Central America. Beneath the emblem was a penned inscription:

Custom Made For Pearl Parker
By The Artisans Of
The Pan-American Doll Works

Closing her eyes, Pearl whispered the first of many prayers she would offer heavenward for Gus Lockhart before morning.

*   *   *

Captain Driscoll reached the railway terminal well in advance of the President's expected six o'clock arrival. Already plentiful, spectators had not yet congealed into an impenetrable mass. Gradually he made his way toward the banner-draped platform beside which the President's train would stop. Two open victorias waited nearby, several simpler carriages and an automobile lined up behind them. Captain Driscoll knew the lead victoria must be for the McKinleys, so he edged as close to it as possible. There he remained, two sealed copies of his letter to the President in the inside pocket of his frock coat.

During the next hour and a half the crowd thickened, stretched through the Propylaea, and spilled into the Plaza. Fathers hoisted children onto their shoulders. Young men and boys stood atop benches or climbed lampposts and statues for better vantage points. Mounted guardsmen flanked the platform, their fiery helmet plumes stirring in the evening breeze. Policemen stood alongside the cordons at intervals of five or six feet, and plainclothes detectives clustered near the turnstiles. Looking about, Captain Driscoll was glad he had come early enough to have even a slim chance of passing his letter to Mr. McKinley. Out of the corner of one eye he noticed a man with a shock of dark blond hair beneath his brown hat, edging toward the gate. His right hand was in the pocket of his gray suit coat. There was something furtive, almost guilty, about the way he moved, slipping past one guard and then another. Captain Driscoll suddenly felt he should call out a warning. Before he could do so, an Exposition policeman stepped in front of the intruder and clamped a hand on his shoulder, hurling him to the ground when he turned to run. The copper took a step toward the cringing man, hand outstretched as if to seize him by the scruff of his neck.

At that instant, however, the shriek of a train whistle sliced through the din. The bands gathered at the mouth of the Midway began to blare a cacophony of welcome songs. The copper turned to gaze toward the tracks, as did nearly everyone else. Captain Driscoll blinked in disbelief. It seemed no one but he was paying attention to the wretch seated in the dust. The forgotten man struggled to his feet and vanished into the crowd.

Presently, brakes squealing and funnel belching smoke, the Presidential Special rolled to a stop. John Milburn and Director General William Buchanan emerged from the train first. Captain Driscoll bit his lip to keep from smiling. These were two of the men whose wheeling and dealing had kept him out of both the Exposition and the coming steel mill. Now it was his turn to surprise them with something that would eclipse any money magic they were accustomed to performing. Tomorrow the whole world would change. Before long, these men and their associates would beg him for a stake in the most profitable venture of all time.

"A roller chair!" Buchanan called. From inside the station came a boy pushing a wicker wheelchair up the platform ramp.

Then President McKinley stepped onto the platform, doffing his high silk hat and nodding as the crowd applauded and whistled. A man of average height and uncommon circumference, his thinning hair gone gray-white, he was different from the officer Driscoll remembered, the dashing second lieutenant who had made major by the end of the war. A frail-looking woman in black appeared behind him on the steps of the Pullman car. The President gathered her in his arms and eased her down to the platform. Like most Americans, Captain Driscoll had followed the lengthy newspaper accounts of Mrs.

McKinley's illness all summer. Now, when Milburn and Buchanan removed their hats, he did likewise and was pleased to see thousands of men following suit. An astonishing silence settled over the crowd.

Mrs. McKinley waved aside the wheelchair and clung to her husband's arm to walk to the victoria. A deep-throated cheer came from somewhere in the thick of the crowd. Other cheers followed and soon reached a deafening crescendo. Once he had helped his wife into the carriage, the President turned to the crowd and bowed before climbing in beside her. Milburn hauled himself into the front seat and sat facing the McKinleys. The driver cracked his whip over the double span of roan horses.

Captain Driscoll, still too far away to put his missive into the President's hand, cried, "Major McKinley!" He held aloft the first of his two letters. His heart began to hammer because he saw that despite all the nods and salutes and noise, his greeting had caught the President's ear. Their eyes locked— and he prayed McKinley would remember him from their long ago wartime service together. Then he saw the President smile in recognition. Relieved, he waved his letter madly, even as he was jostled into a nearby policeman. He tried to thrust his arm out far enough and high enough to make the envelope seen amid the fluttering handkerchiefs and waving hats. But the policeman planted his feet and spread his own arms to keep the crowd from surging too far forward. When the victoria rocked past, McKinley simply waved back and called out, "Hello, Hayward! It's been a very long time!"

Then the carriage was out of earshot, the President's eyes were elsewhere, and Captain Driscoll's letter was torn from his hand and lost when he tried to lower his arm.

* * *

It was ten when Eustace Buttonwood stepped into the smoke and noise of the Clinton Hotel tavern. He went to the bar, put his foot on the brass rail, and pushed back his homburg. "Do you have Hunter's Baltimore rye?" The barkeep, a jowly Irishman with oily red hair, nodded and produced a dark bottle from a shelf behind him. Buttonwood took the bottle and a shot glass to a corner table. For the next hour he alternated between sips of fire and pulls on his pipe. He gazed around at the men puffing cigars and playing cards and shooting pool. Untroubled, they laughed and drank and ate with a freedom he envied. None of them knew what he knew, that a colored man named William Lockhart had solved the problem of heavier-than-air flight, that at this very moment his aerodrome was housed in a barn on the property of a wealthy white sponsor. And none could imagine that tomorrow, during an address by the President of the United States, a dinge would fly overhead and capture the eyes of the world.

But he could imagine only too well. Having followed Joseph Lockhart's buggy past the fair the previous Saturday morning, he had left his cab and worked his way through a wooded area to hide in a thicket at the edge of the trees. He'd counted six men—some colored, some white—but only four worked to assemble the aerodrome and hoist it up to some kind of rooftop launch ramp. He'd studied the machine through his brass spyglass. With long wings and gleaming blades, it bore little resemblance to the Secretary's cumbersome creations. This looked light and graceful as a bird.

Then, to his dismay, he had watched it fly.

Lying in the brush some distance away, fingers gripping the tube of his spyglass, he suddenly understood the significance of what he had read in the newspaper the evening before. President McKinley was coming to this city next week, the same McKinley who'd given Secretary Langley a small fortune to develop a flying weapon for the Spanish war. He was going to visit the fair, give a speech expected to draw thousands. If by some chance the President or one of his party saw the Lockhart aerodrome in flight . . .

Langley was a great man, had done much for his country as Secretary of the Smithsonian. But in his unswerving and very public quest for flight he had not realized that placing second in such a race would mark him as a pathetic failure. Buttonwood shuddered. He could not let that happen to the Old Man.

He had gone back to that same thicket for the past three days, in sporting clothes he had got from the Walbridge Company on Main Street. On Sunday he had hoped the negroes would go to church. Instead, a colored man in a minister's frock came to them—along with two women, and a negro he had not seen before who was just as tall as Joseph Lockhart. For much of the afternoon there were seven or eight men in the barn, and Buttonwood began to wonder just how many people knew of this aerodrome. He felt his hopes rise when one of the women stepped onto the back porch to call the men to dinner. But the youngest white man padlocked the barn.

On Monday and Tuesday they had practiced flying all day. Buttonwood remained in the thicket until dark, praying the aerodrome would be left alone and the barn unlocked. It would be best if he burned the barn, he thought, and the aerodrome with it. If he could get inside, soak the aerodrome with kerosene from the lanterns . . . but first he would like to gather the design papers he had seen one man—William Lockhart, he presumed—consulting during the flight trials. Those would be an added treat, something he could take back to Langley. If Buttonwood was lucky, the men would go somewhere and leave one behind to watch over everything—that bowlegged old man, he hoped, who would be easier to overcome than one of those bucks.

But no such opportunity developed.

Today McKinley had come to town. Time was running out—in fact, had run out. There would be little sleep for

Buttonwood tonight, perhaps just a nap in the uncomfortable wing chair in his room. He would stir long before morning light. Then there would be a cab ride in darkness. Next would come a foot journey past the fairground, concealment in a stand of trees . . .

Draining his whiskey and steeling his nerve, Buttonwood was keenly aware of the weight of the hammerless .32 in the right hand pocket of his jacket.

Sixteen

Buttonwood was back on his belly in the thicket before dawn, his teeth hard at work on the cube of sour pepsin gum he hoped would settle his stomach.

Earlier, attempting to get closer to the barn, he'd been startled by the sudden appearance of the blacksmith's horse, tied behind the house. The huge beast began to whicker and stamp as though trying to alert the occupants of the house to his approach. Buttonwood scuttled backward through the grass, tumbling into the thicket seconds before a night-shirted figure with a bull's-eye lantern appeared on the back porch. A shotgun barrel glinted in the soft lantern light. A coarse voice stretched out across the clearing: "Who's there? Come out and show yourself!" Then one of the giant negroes was on the porch. The barn door swung open on four or five figures silhouetted in the light of additional lanterns. Buttonwood kept himself pressed to the ground, squinting as if his eyes might betray him by glowing catlike in the dark. His heart beat in his throat, like a fist clenching in his windpipe, blocking his air.

But no one ventured into the darkness to search for him.

Now, dawn light seeping into the sky and dew soaking into his clothes, he pondered his predicament. He was outnumbered. Even if he were an expert shot, the pistol in his pocket would be useless at this distance, especially against a shotgun. Worse, there were likely other guns in the house. With the horse already spooked, it would be hard to reach the barn before they knew he was coming. Perhaps he could circle around to the far side and get close to an outside wall. Then maybe he could slip inside, find the plans, and damage enough of the aerodrome to stop today's demonstration.

By half past eight, when the two old men drove away in the buggy, Buttonwood was soaked to the skin and his gum had long since lost its bite. He spat it into the grass, his stomach still churning, and waited for his chance.

*   *   *

The morning air was warm, and the absence of clouds held the promise of relentless sun. Papa Joe and Captain Driscoll left the stanhope in a line of carriages outside the Elmwood gate. They crossed the Triumphal Bridge and separated as they walked toward the speaker's platform, which faced the Esplanade near the northeast pylon of the bridge. Festooned with star-spangled bunting, the stand had a central balcony with a broad wing on either side. It was crammed with chairs, some already occupied by summer-suited gentlemen and pastel-clad ladies. On one side a woman photographer positioned her boxy camera atop a tripod. The east wing held a red-jacketed military band, their brass gleaming in the sun.

Papa Joe consulted the President's Day program he had bought for a nickel at the gate. McKinley was due at the grandstand at 10:25, more than an hour and a half from now. Papa Joe watched the Captain work his way closer to the plain rope barrier near the platform. There was plenty of time for him to get there—and for Papa Joe to complete his own task. He opened the envelope and read Gus's note one last time.

Dear Mr. Porter,

We are a group of negro men who have built an aeroplane. We have tested it repeatedly on the nearby property of our host and sponsor, Captain H. Driscoll. We assure you our machine can fly. If all goes well, you will see it in the air, either today during Mr. McKinley's speech or tomorrow after his reception. Afterward it will be available for inspection on the Driscoll estate. We hope this news will be of interest to you.

Truthfully yours,
Gus Lockhart

He returned the envelope to his pocket and began to look about for the Edison man. He saw four or five cameras mounted on tripods, but none had cranks like the device Gus had taken him to see. Where would be the best spot to put a motion picture camera amid such confusion? The Esplanade was filling steadily. Already, thousands had raised parasols and umbrellas to shield themselves from the brutal sun. Despite his height, Papa Joe had trouble seeing over the bobbing umbrellas and knew Porter's camera would have the same difficulty. Weaving among them and fending off the points of their ribs with his hands, he spotted another stand by the Court of the Fountains—a low platform less than a hundred feet from where the President would speak. He did not know whether the Edison man was there, but thanks to Gus he knew a motion picture camera when he saw one.

Mr. Porter looked surprised to hear his own name surface in the maelstrom of words that swirled around him. When he saw Papa Joe, a moment passed before he smiled and raised a hand. "Mr. Lockhart," he said, as if suddenly remembering the name. "Beautiful day, isn't it?"

"Yes, Mr. Porter, it is. A glorious and wonderful day." From inside his suit coat Papa Joe produced the envelope, which he held up to Porter. "For you, sir."

Porter opened the envelope, drew out the single sheet, and began to read.

Moving back into the crowd, Papa Joe heard him say,

"My God! A film like this will blow old Tom Edison right out of his boots!"

* * *

Captain Driscoll had squeezed in sideways and was barely able to move, but he had reached the cordon—and just in time, for the first cannon report boomed from the south. The reverberation lingered a moment, to be followed by a second, then a third. The 21-gun salute that signaled the President's arrival thundered across the Park Lake from the encampment near the Lincoln Parkway gate. Voices fell and hats came off. When, finally, the cannonade faded into the wind, it was replaced by the sound of hoofbeats and jangling scabbards. Then a big black victoria rolled into view on the Triumphal Bridge and stopped. The President stood, gazed at the buildings and the people, and tipped his hat. As the crowd began to cheer, the horsemen peeled off, and the victoria eased into a lane formed by helmeted soldiers.

When it stopped beside the speaker's stand, John Milburn climbed out and held the door for the President. McKinley tipped his hat again, then stepped down and assisted his wife from the carriage. Arm in arm, they moved toward the stand.

Captain Driscoll was about ten feet away from where the McKinleys and Milburn would pass. He took out his second letter. Swallowing his pride, he called to Milburn, who walked ahead of the President and First Lady as if clearing a path. "John!" *Look this way—at me, you scheming bastard!* "John!" He reached over the cordon and waved the letter. "Major McKinley!" Milburn and McKinley both looked at him just as a guardsman pushed his arm down. McKinley smiled, directly at him. The soldier had seen the President's smile, the recognition in his eyes. Driscoll was sure of it and used his sternest military voice: "This is a message of vital importance. It must be given to the President at once." The guardsman hesitated only an instant before answering, "Yes, sir."

Thus, Captain Driscoll watched his letter passed first to one officer and then another, until it reached the free hand of William McKinley just before he guided his wife up the platform steps and the Marine band struck up "The Star Spangled Banner."

*   *   *

Eustace Buttonwood saw his chance. The old bowlegged man had gone into the house, the aerodrome was on the roof, and the other men were in the barn. It was now or never. He clambered to his feet and started across the clearing. The swish of his boots through the sun-dried grass sounded dangerously loud to him. By the time he made it to the carriage shed between the barn and the house his belly was knotted with fear. He prayed the door was unlocked, the hinges oiled. Luck was with him on both counts, and he slipped inside, unseen and unheard.

It was sweltering in the shed, and dark. The only light, a narrow band filtering through a small, dust-laden window, fell upon the automobile that occupied most of the space. Buttonwood stood still, listening. Sweat gathered beneath his homburg, on his forehead and temples, trickled into his eyes. He took out his handkerchief and wiped his face and eyes. Thick dust settled behind his tongue, and he worked his throat muscles in a silent cough to bring it up in a wad of phlegm. He spat toward a corner and sidled past the automobile, admiring the feel of its smooth body, the faint glimmer of its brass lanterns in the dimness. He had paid scarce attention to the horseless carriages in Washington but now he wished he knew how to operate one; he would have liked to use this to get away when his work was done.

Stuffing his handkerchief into a back pocket, he looked through the window at the barn. His time, he knew, was limited. At any moment now the men might come out of the barn. He would find himself trapped in a shaft of light if someone threw open the door of the shed. Or they might just go up to the roof. Once they were there and cranking the propellers there would be no stopping the aerodrome. Fire still seemed his best option, a ravenous blaze that would consume the barn and the men and machine atop it. But all he had was a book of Diamond matches in one pocket. He would need some kind of agent if the flames were to spread quickly enough.

He edged along the automobile to the back wall and ran his hands along a high shelf. His fingertips scraped through deep accretions of dirt and dust, and he winced when something sharp slivered into the ball of his thumb. He jerked his hand down and fumbled for his handkerchief. When he tried to wrap his thumb, pain shot through it, and he hissed. The injury was doubly frustrating because he had found nothing with which to start a fire—no kerosene, no lantern, no tin of oil to which he could put a match. He felt along the other walls, discovering only a disused harness hanging on a spike. He scraped his feet along the edges of the packed earth floor and stubbed a toe on an old carriage spring. Of all the damnable luck! There was nothing in this shed but a stupid automobile.

Then it came to him, and he began to unwind the handkerchief from his thumb.

* * *

Silk hat in his left hand, John Milburn stepped up to the platform rail, gazed out over the crowd, and proclaimed, "Ladies and gentlemen—President McKinley!"

Having just retrieved his pince-nez from a waistcoat pocket, William McKinley placed them on the bridge of his nose, got to his feet, and moved to the center of the rail. Straightening the lapels of his black frock coat so that they hung unfurled on either side of his white waistcoat, he waited a moment for the applause to subside. Then, nodding twice to his left, twice to his right, and once over each shoulder to those gathered behind him, he began: "President Milburn, Director General Buchanan, Commissioners, Ladies and Gentlemen . . ."

Captain Driscoll felt his scalp tingling, as if he had drunk too much whiskey; he could see his still-sealed envelope at the bottom of the papers the President clutched in his left hand. He did not care that McKinley had not yet opened the letter. Once the Blackbird appeared over the Esplanade and circled back toward the estate—leaving fifty thousand awe-struck witnesses—all that would matter was his having the letter in his possession. Subsequent developments would be fueled by their own urgency.

* * *

". . . we give the hand of fellowship and felicitate with them upon the triumphs of art, science, education, and manufacture which the old has bequeathed to the new century."

From a distance Papa Joe kept an eye on Porter as he cranked his kinetograph. It pleased him to see the Edison man steal a glance at the sky every few seconds. He himself continued to look overhead. Any minute now he expected his grandsons to stake a claim on the new age. *The Twentieth Century*, he thought, hands stinging as he clapped at McKinley's words. *Our century*.

* * *

Seconds before the explosion that engulfed the carriage shed in flames, Buttonwood reached the side of the house opposite the carriage path. He had not known for sure that there would be an explosion when he tore a strip of lining from his coat, knotted it to his handkerchief, and stuffed an end into the automobile's fuel reservoir. Igniting his makeshift fuse, he had known only that there would be a fire, that the men from the barn would have to abandon the flight to fight the fire. He must return later to destroy the aerodrome and bring his own combustible fluid with him then. For now the shed fire would have to suffice.

As it happened, it was the explosion that saved his life.

Buttonwood had made it to the front corner of the house. He was about to tear through the brush and the maples to the road, but he came face to face with the bowlegged old timer. The man's face was weathered and full of white stubble, his smile revealing darkened stumps of teeth. He was smiling because he carried a shotgun, its barrel leveled at Buttonwood's chest.

"Cap'n Driscoll told me somebody might be lurkin' around," the old man said. "Told me to keep an eye out. So I do and I see you out the window. Now who are you and what—"

At that instant the shed went up with a *whoomph* that seemed to force the house and both men into an abrupt lean. The shotgun barrel swung away as the old man staggered sideways. Buttonwood snatched his revolver from his coat pocket in one fluid motion, grateful there was no hammer to catch the flap or to abrade his still tender thumb. He simply squeezed the trigger, and the man's head snapped back as if he had been smacked across the face with a plank.

* * *

"Modern inventions have brought into close relation widely separated peoples and made them better acquainted . . ."

Papa Joe no longer glanced over his shoulder. Now he was turned completely around, his back toward the President, his eyes searching the sky. Some of the men near him looked up from beneath their umbrellas and frowned at his rude disregard for McKinley. He did not care. His stomach had long since grown heavy with a more abiding concern: *What happened to*

Gus?

He struggled against the grisly answers served up by his imagination. But he was helpless to suppress visions of Gus lying broken amid the wreckage of the Blackbird. He tried to shake the vision and clenched his teeth so hard he nicked the side of his tongue.

*   *   *

"These buildings will disappear; this creation of art and beauty and industry will perish from sight, but their influence will remain. Our earnest prayer is that God will graciously vouchsafe prosperity, happiness and peace to all our neighbors, and like blessings to all the peoples and powers of earth."

Deafened by the applause and whistling, Captain Driscoll watched President McKinley return his papers, including the unopened letter, to the inside pocket of his frock coat. For some reason the Blackbird had failed to appear. The Captain was afraid to think what might have happened. *If Joseph loses Gus . . .* More than likely, there had been some mechanical failure. Gasoline engines were tricky that way. If the aeroplane had malfunctioned, at least tomorrow there would be another chance. Meanwhile, he could try to get the President's eye again and perhaps gain an audience to explain the aeroplane.

Standing his ground beside the cordon as the McKinleys' returned to the victoria, Captain Driscoll noticed the man loping toward the President and Milburn as they helped the First Lady inside. Both had their backs turned—as did the escorts congregating about them—and could not see the man drawing near. Gray suit, brown hat with a yellow band—Driscoll had the odd feeling he had seen this man before. Abruptly, he realized he had—last evening at the train station, the fellow collared by the policeman. With this realization came the certainty that the man he had suspected was up to no good then intended to harm the President now. He forgot his letter and the

Blackbird and cried, "Major, behind you!"

But his warning was swallowed by the commotion.

* * *

From the Chronicles of Augustus Lockhart:
Thursday September 5

This morning, as we gathered in the barn, we were startled by an explosion. Outside, we found the carriage shed in flames and thick black smoke curling into the sky. The Blackbird was atop the barn, but the demonstration was forgotten as we hastened to form a bucket brigade from the well in the yard. Our efforts proved useless, however. There were too few of us to save the shed. Nevertheless, we continued emptying our buckets on the dry grass around it for some time afterward to keep the house, barn, and Blackbird safe. The shed was reduced to a heap of timber, charred and flaking, through which we could see the blackened hulk of Captain Driscoll's Packard automobile. Somehow its fuel must have caused the explosion.

Soon Papa Joe and Captain Driscoll returned, my grandfather pushing Mac up the path at a dangerous speed because they had seen the smoke. Both men looked older than when they left this morning. Their imaginations must have prepared them for a scene much worse than the one they found. Papa Joe breathed with relief when he saw the Blackbird on the roof. Captain Driscoll shook his head sadly at the sight of his lost automobile.

Only after the Captain asked Danny where the sergeant was during all the excitement did we realize that Jonas Newcomb was missing. We spread out to search the property but could not locate him. Then, using long-handled rakes, Danny and Will sifted through the debris and poked around the Packard but found no sign of him. Either he has gone somewhere and not yet returned or he lies dead in the rubble, awaiting a more thorough search.

Reverend Banks wondered aloud if Jonas caused the fire—accidentally, he said when the Captain frowned at the suggestion. Captain Driscoll has known Jonas for many years and trusts him completely. "Why would he disappear?" Reverend Banks asked. Before the exchange could grow passionate, my grandfather prevailed upon us all, for the sake of the entire undertaking, to focus our efforts on tomorrow's demonstration. "Captain, the fire is out," he said. "These two hands, alone if necessary, will rebuild your carriage shed." Then he turned to Reverend Banks. "Do you have faith in Will, Portius? In his aeroplane and his ideas?"

Reverend Banks nodded.

"Is your faith based on knowing him?"

Again Reverend Banks nodded.

"Then accept Captain Driscoll's faith in Jonas as he accepts yours in Will. Tomorrow is what matters now. Everything we have worked for depends on the faith we have in each other."

Captain Driscoll's forehead creased in thought. "Joseph, last night when your horse made a racket we considered that somebody might've been skulking about."

"Probably spooked by a coon," said Papa Joe.

"Perhaps not." The Captain narrowed his eyes at my grandfather. "Suppose there was somebody. I told Jonas to keep a watchful eye. Maybe this stranger started the fire. Maybe he did something to the sergeant, took him away."

"Why would someone do that?" asked Danny.

"You may think your father addled, Daniel, but I have my share of enemies, business rivals and the like. Maybe they got wind of what we're doing here. Suppose someone saw the practice flights and wants to stop us."

Having been up in the Electric Tower, Papa Joe and I both said it was a possibility. We were silent for a time. The idea that we might have an enemy filled the air with new urgency.

"Then we must be on our guard tonight," said Papa Joe at last. "You and I, Portius, and Captain Driscoll. The others must sleep, but we three will take turns keeping watch. If somebody is trying to stop us, it's more important than ever that we succeed tomorrow."

"There is another matter," said Captain Driscoll. "In all this confusion I nearly forgot. I was trying to tell Joseph when we first saw the smoke." Then he described a young man he had seen trying twice to reach what he called striking distance of the President. "I feared he was up to some mischief. Today he came close enough to be of some danger with a knife or a pistol . . . but he just stopped and stood there, looking confused, more like a frightened boy than a madman."

"Do you think he wanted to attack President McKinley?" asked Reverend Banks.

"I don't know. Both the President and Milburn had their backs to him. Maybe he couldn't tell them apart. Maybe he was there to press his own petition into the President's hand. In any case, this man troubled me so much I shouted a warning, but I doubt anyone heard it. When he stopped short I felt foolish." Captain Driscoll shook his head. "Such an ordinary looking fellow, and for a minute there I had him dead to rights as the next Charles Guiteau."

Seventeen

Buttonwood was unable to sleep.

All night he lay in his narrow bed at the Clinton, staring into the darkness, waiting for the weight of his exhaustion to drag him backward into sleep. By rights he should have dropped off the instant his head hit the pillow. He'd had no real sleep for nearly two days. He had fled the sponsor's estate and walked off a week's shoe leather mingling with crowds at the fair. Later, with cabs impossible to come by, he'd been forced to stand on a streetcar, with people clustered about him like locusts. He should have been too tired to walk as far as he did after his evening meal—more than dozen blocks to the harbor and back. Sleep should have come to him easily.

But he had killed a man.

He had never killed before, had never thought of killing before buying the gun and sitting in the hotel barroom the other night. Then he had thought he might have to kill a dinge, but now, facing his second restless dawn, he saw only the old white man's face every time he shut his eyes, saw the dry, veined nose burst in a spray of blood. He tried to dislodge the image from his brain by reminding himself that his work was not yet done. He still must find a way to destroy the Lockhart aerodrome. (At least the President would be away most of today, his visit to Niagara Falls keeping him out of the range of surprise demonstrations.) The killing, he told himself again and again, had been a sad necessity.

By dawn, when sleep finally took him, he had begun to picture the old man's face as his head snapped back in a red mist. It was darker, more sinister, more like the faces of the men for whom he worked.

*   *   *

Today I am in the hands of God.

This is my first thought as I stir here in the barn. The hands of God are warm and gentle and comforting, even more so than my makeshift bed of straw and the blanket in which I am wrapped. In the hands of God I am safe from my enemies, from those who would keep me bound to the earth by chains and laws, from those who would crush me with their racialism or pluck me from the sky with their arrows of hatred. In the hands of God I cannot fall.

It is Friday. The light from the windows we cut high in the barn walls so many months ago finds me alone in the straw. My brother Will and the others are gone, but the Blackbird, disassembled, waits near the door. I have no idea what hour it is or how the others managed to rise and leave without waking me. It is not yet noon, or I would hear them on the roof, examining the rails and hauling up parts of the aeroplane with that squeaky pulley. But I hear only the music of birds and the occasional creak of these rough wooden walls in the breeze—and my heart, beating in my ears.

It is Friday, and as I shake the sleep from my body I am more alive than ever. My mind is churning, spinning, flying. My senses are alert and screaming. The morning air tastes unusually sweet. I can smell that the coolness will give way to a very hot day. Much will happen in the heat. Like Good Friday, this will be a day of transformation leading to the rebirth of a people. I am an agent of that transformation, that rebirth. I stand, the blanket draped over my shoulders, and walk to the wall that still holds the photographs of the Blackbird in flight. Today I am unafraid to see myself in them, to see my fragile body in a fragile craft, to imagine which thread in a grander fabric than any of us has ever dreamed bears my name.

It is Friday, and I am an instrument in the hands of God.

*   *   *

Surprised Pearl was absent from her scheduled Friday morning duties in the surgery, Lucas tried to sound casual as he asked where she was.

"I've given her the day off," his father said. "She stayed late last night and cleaned the operatory so she could go to the Exposition today with her father." In banded shirt sleeves, Dr. Westbeck stepped out of the consulting room and into the operatory. He opened the glass doors of a white cabinet and withdrew a covered instrument tray. "They plan to shake the President's hand, even if they have to wait in line all day." He set the tray on a table, then faced Lucas. "I don't have many patients today and you're not due at the hospital until later. Why don't you take the day off as well."

"Sir?"

"Take the day off." An uncharacteristic smile appeared amid the tangles of Dr. Westbeck's white beard. "Go to the Expo, why don't you? Maybe you can shake the President's hand too."

"I doubt I'll be lucky enough to see William McKinley," Lucas said, shrugging back into the tan suitcoat he had just begun to shed. "But I could do with a day at the fair."

*   *   *

Papa Joe felt an echo of his grandson's embrace all the way to the Exposition. The embrace had been a surprise, so unlike Gus, almost desperately firm, as if he feared he might never see his grandfather again. Drifting in for breakfast, Gus had been wrapped in his blanket as if it were a cocoon. He gazed at everyone with distant but vigilant eyes, his customary silence almost mystical. Sitting down to johnnycake and bacon, he had seemed detached from the talk at the table and continued to stare out the kitchen window, even as he sipped his third cup of coffee. After breakfast he had embraced Papa Joe suddenly and said, "A good day for it." Then he had pulled away and gone back to the barn to dress.

Now Papa Joe wondered if Gus had got it into his head that he was going to die today. When he was a slave, his granny had told him tales of people who dreamt their own deaths and sleepwalked through the next day until the moment they died. Some spoke freely of what they had seen in the night, resigned that this was their last day on earth. Others were tighter-lipped but couldn't escape wearing the otherworldly look that comes over your face when your name has been whispered in heaven. Papa Joe had been free too long, had read far too many books to put stock in slave superstitions. Still, Gus's demeanor had unsettled him.

On the way over he decided not to share his concerns with Captain Driscoll, who rode beside him in silence, adrift in his own worries. Jonas had not yet turned up, which made the possibility of an unseen adversary more likely. Had this affected Gus as well? Did he expect to be shot down in flight, like a game bird? Or was his dreaminess an effort to master simple fear? Papa Joe recalled an old Turkish proverb: No matter how far you've gone down the wrong road, turn back. The inverse, he knew, must also be true: No matter how far you've gone down the *right* road, *never* turn back. Enemy or fear, they had all come to far to turn back. Especially Gus.

* * *

Fully assembled, the Blackbird is now atop the barn, waiting for me. Will led us through a minute inspection of the engine components, the wing surfaces and buckling mechanisms, every nail, screw, hinge, coupling, and cable—until he was satisfied that every connection is secure and every part will perform as intended. Now that the aeroplane is locked in place, Will is in the barn, preparing me.

My brother's voice is level and comforting, gently urging me to recite the procedures yet again. Although I have flown dozens of times, this is a ritual we perform before each flight. Will believes that such recitations are necessary for my skills in the air to become second nature. He says when aeroplanes become practical, inspection of wings and engines will be commonplace to insure that the machines are safe. Examination of pilots will keep their flying skills keen.

"Once again," says Will, "to angle to the right for a change of direction of one hundred eighty degrees. . ."

I answer without pausing to think.

*　　*　　*

Papa Joe pulled off his hat and mopped his brow with his handkerchief. "Got to be eighty degrees," he said. Captain Driscoll was behind him, Ben Parker in front of him. Essie and Pearl stood in front of Ben, clad in pale summer dresses and sun hats, fanning themselves. In line for hours, the five of them had taken turns getting lemonade and using the comfort stations and passing around Essie's small parasol until everyone's arm had wearied of holding it.

"More like eighty-five," Captain Driscoll said.

His own face glistening with sweat and his slouch hat pushed back to reveal oiled hair plastered to his forehead, Ben Parker grinned. "Been awhile since you folks been south, huh?"

"A good while," Papa Joe said.

212 | Gary Earl Ross

"This is nothing next to a Georgia noon in July," Ben said.

"Or even North Carolina sun," Papa Joe said, "but it's still hot." He'd grown accustomed to Buffalo's changing seasons, to its long winters, indecisive springs, and kaleidoscopic autumns. With a third of the year cold and five months pleasantly cool or warm, late summer temperatures were sometimes unbearable.

"You from North Ca'lina?" Ben asked.

Papa Joe nodded, slowly.

"When'd you leave?"

"A couple hundred years ago."

Ben nodded, and Papa Joe sensed that he understood.

Ahead of Pearl more than two hundred people formed a line up to the east door of the Temple of Music, whose red and gold trim flickered flamelike in the sun. Behind Captain Driscoll the line stretching into the Esplanade seemed to number in the thousands. Papa Joe was relieved they had come early enough to get a good position. With only fifteen minutes reserved for the handshaking, there was no way this many people could file through to see the President.

Captain Driscoll fished out his watch, popped the lid. "Ought to get here any time now," he said. "Judging from all that cheering to the north, his train hit the station twenty minutes ago." He returned the watch to his waistcoat. "Think we'll make it inside before they shut the doors?"

"Hope so," Papa Joe said.

"He recognized me the other night, called me by name. Did I tell you that?"

Papa Joe smiled. "Yes, you did."

"Recognized me yesterday too," Captain Driscoll went on, as if he hadn't already recounted the moment. "Hadn't laid eyes on me since the war. But after all these years he still recognized me. That's what got my letter to him." He took off his own hat and pulled out a handkerchief to wipe his forehead and the back of his neck. "He's got to be here soon." He looked around, as if expecting the President to materialize beside him.

Papa Joe saw that Ben had bent down so Essie could whisper something into his ear. For a moment he looked confused, then concerned. He leaned past his sister to whisper something to his daughter, who shook her head, then nodded and took a step backward. Papa Joe tapped Ben on his shoulder when he straightened.

"I'm gonna trade places with Pearl," Ben said softly. "Looks like it's something to do with that fella in front of her."

Papa Joe narrowed his eyes at the back of the unassuming man with wheat-colored waves and slumped shoulders. He didn't look particularly offensive but Papa Joe frowned anyway. "Did he say something improper to her?" Anger tightened in his stomach. If Ben—or even he, a much older colored man—uttered an unseemly word to this man's wife or daughter, there was the very real possibility of a beating or worse. Lynchings, for the most part, remained the madness of the South but were common enough in the North. Still, Papa Joe was unafraid, too old to surrender to fear. "I'll have a word with him."

"No," Ben said. "Nothing like that. Must've looked odd to her is all." He shrugged. "Who knows?"

Just then a great cheer arose from the northeast corner of the grounds and rolled south like thunder to the Esplanade, then west toward where they stood.

"He's coming," Captain Driscoll said.

* * *

Papa Joe saw that far ahead of them the line was

beginning to move. Seconds earlier, Captain Driscoll had announced that it was two minutes past four and time the reception got underway, since the President had been inside for nearly five minutes. To those behind him he must have seemed unconscionably rude, but Papa Joe shared his worry—getting inside before those massive doors were shut. If the receiving line was stopped before Papa Joe and Captain Driscoll had an opportunity to speak with the President, it would be more difficult to arrange a demonstration later. They would have to transport the Blackbird and its trappings to Washington and secure a building large enough to house it and enough land to conduct flights. Then they would have to request an audience with the President and wait however many days or weeks it took, if they got in to see him at all. Captain Driscoll had already promised to undertake the expense of such an enterprise, if it became necessary. Papa Joe knew the Captain had entered into their arrangement in the hope that he would profit while upstaging the Exposition. Now it struck him as ironic that this white man had become a friend willing to gamble so much on the brainchild of an ex-slave's grandson.

From inside the Temple came organ music, and the line began to move.

"There will be no time to say hello," Captain Driscoll said. "He has a reputation for being astonishingly quick on these kinds of occasions. Before you know it, he's pulled you past, with the word hello still stuck to your lips, and he's doing the same to the next fellow. You've got to be quick yourself. We both do."

Papa Joe wiped his forehead and cheeks with his handkerchief and nodded.

Captain Driscoll continued, "Just ask him if he has read our letter about the aeroplane. I'll do likewise but will address him as Major McKinley. Our time soldiering together should buy us a few more seconds—and serious consideration. If Milburn is with him to introduce local leaders we may be able to linger a moment longer, perhaps long enough to tempt him out to the house for a personal demonstration."

Just then the line stopped short. After a few seconds it began to move again, then stopped once more, as if it were a creature of unwieldy size pausing to collect itself every few steps. So it moved for another minute or two, until it began to seem certain that they would reach the doors before the soldiers on either side pushed them shut. Not only would they meet the President, they would get a brief respite from the sun. Then the wait grew unexpectedly long, and Papa Joe heard Ben say, "If you can't go faster, at least let us by!"

Papa Joe glared at the man ahead of Ben, who had been gazing off in the distance when the line started to move again. Having noticed the emptiness in his eyes when he turned and looked up at Ben with an open but wordless mouth, Papa Joe pegged the man as dim-witted, someone who had trouble remembering his name or where he was. Wouldn't it be just their misfortune to be kept from the President by the inaction of a fool? But when he saw the man mop his own brow with a white kerchief wrapped around an injured hand, he admonished himself for his lack of charity. This poor fellow was suffering in the heat as much as anyone.

The closer they came to the doors, the more inviting and cool the interior looked. Then they were moving inside, into what Papa Joe thought must be a drop in temperature of ten or more degrees. Momentarily, as he took off his hat, he shivered, as if he were stepping into a tin-lined ice house and not an ornate concert hall. When his eyes adjusted to the change in brightness, he saw Essie, Pearl, and Ben ahead of him. Also he saw soldiers and policemen on either side of the aisle and above the organist's efforts heard somebody bark, "Get in line!" At first he thought the guard had snapped at Ben. Then he realized the order had been directed to someone who had stepped too far to one side as if trying to get an early view of the President.

Papa Joe was grateful that he did not need to get out of line to get a good look ahead. He was tall enough to see over the heads of just about anyone in front of him, except Ben. Papa Joe swallowed at the sight of William McKinley, in black frock coat and trousers and immaculate white waistcoat and collar, smiling and shaking hands. Another shiver rolled through him, and to his surprise his eyes moistened. To think, he had begun life as a slave, and now, after fifty years of stolen freedom, he was just footsteps away from clasping the hand of the President of the United States. Even if he had not been here for a higher purpose, the emotion of the moment would have overwhelmed him.

"Milburn is with him," Captain Driscoll said, caught up in his own emotions.

Papa Joe glanced back at the Captain, who must have seen the tears forming and placed a hand on his shoulder. "We are almost there, Joseph, so close to success that I can taste it. Can you taste it?"

Yes, he could taste it, like raw honey clinging to the tip of his tongue.

Just then there was some kind of disturbance ahead. One of the plainclothesmen, a large man with silvery hair, had crossed the aisle to intercept someone in line—a short heavy man in the coarse garb of an immigrant worker. The detective grasped him by his shoulders and seemed to peer into his face before inspecting his hands. Papa Joe believed the handling was rough enough to have resulted in a scuffle, if there had been the slightest resistance. But this luckless man looked appropriately terrified and raised his arms willingly to let the detective's hands slide inside his coat. Evidently satisfied that his prey was harmless, the detective retreated across the aisle and waved him forward. His trembling visible to those behind him, the worker reached for the President's outstretched hand.

Papa Joe noticed that to his left, near the plainclothesmen across from the President, stood Captain Louis Babcock, the young lawyer who was Exposition Grand Marshal and one of the blacksmith shop's best customers. In fact, it was Babcock's recommendation that landed Gus his job. Gus had long since sent a beautiful letter to express his gratitude, and Papa Joe had thanked Captain Babcock personally during a shoeing. Now he hoped to catch his eye and raise a hand in greeting—and as the idea arose, the opportunity presented itself. Nodding at another man beside the President, Babcock turned and started past the line—perhaps on his way to close the doors, Papa Joe thought, relieved they had made it inside. Beginning to smile, he was about to murmur hello to the passing Grand Marshal.

Then he heard the first shot.

Papa Joe flinched, something congealing in his throat. His eyes locked with Babcock's for the smallest fraction of a second, then snapped forward. Full comprehension of the horror taking shape before him took less than a heartbeat.

A second shot broke the ephemeral silence that followed the first, and a flaming kerchief fluttered to the floor. The man ahead of Ben was dropping into a shooter's crouch within a foot of the President, whose hands had flown to his chest as he rose on the balls of his feet. Ben's right arm was cocked, his fist above his shoulder. As he swung downward at the head of the assassin, one of the soldiers and one of the detectives dove toward them. All four men went down amid shouts and screams and the sudden cessation of organ music. The line, so orderly before the gunshots, instantly broke apart as people scrambled to get out of the way or see what was happening. Arms flailing, more soldiers piled onto Ben and the other three. Someone shouted, "Al, get his gun!" Meanwhile, President McKinley, a jagged rose taking shape in the center of his white waistcoat, slumped into the arms of the man behind him. Eased into a chair, he wheezed, "M-my wife . . . be careful, Cortelyou, how you tell her. Oh, be careful."

And Papa Joe thought, *My God!*

Eighteen

It is time.

Reverend Banks makes Will, Danny, and me join hands and kneel in prayer. A tremor is in his voice as he says that this is a crucial day for the American negro, a people strengthened by centuries of adversity. "The ships made us stronger, Father, as did the fields and shackles and whips. Out of that strength have grown patience, wisdom, and the will to endure. We seek now to rise, however heavy the boot in our back. What we accomplish today will bridge the start of this century to generations unborn who will inherit our success and build upon it. We ask that You look with favor upon our present enterprise and upon William and Augustus Lockhart. They chase the sky not as a challenge to You but as a celebration of the wondrous intellect You saw fit to bestow upon man. Theirs is the work of proud children who wish to show the Father they love the creation that love has inspired . . ."

Afterward I climb the ladder, with Will behind me. Atop the barn, I crawl into the hammock. Will helps me put my hands and feet into the control stirrups. Before he cranks the engine, he speaks to me. His words are muffled by the wadding in my helmet but I do not need to hear to know that he has told me he loves me. The howl of the engine overpowers my reply.

I am in position, goggles over my eyes. Will removes the wheel wedges as I note the start time in the Waterbury timepiece—quarter past four—and ease the lever forward. Then I am shooting down the track, teeth clenched against the vibrations that previously have caused me to bite my tongue. I have learned also not to glance to either side, for the sight of trees and fields racing past fills me with a confusion I dare not carry into the sky. Thus, my eyes are locked on the track. My ears surrender to the rattle and roar of my increasing speed. My brain leaps ahead to all that I must do to stay aloft. My heart stops as I near the upsweep at the end of the track . . .

And suddenly I am in the sky.

*   *   *

In the seconds that followed the shooting, there had been nothing but confusion—bodies colliding in the narrow aisle, shouting and weeping and curses hurled at the assassin, soldiers with bayonets and policemen with truncheons forcing everyone outside. Papa Joe had been struck hard on the elbow, whether by rifle butt or billy club he did not know. Now, right forearm and fingers tingling, he found himself outside, separated from the others and caught up in a mass of humanity that thickened steadily as word of the shooting spread.

In the minutes before a boxy black automobile marked AMBULANCE stopped outside the Temple, the crowd seemed to double in size. It surged toward the now locked doors with cries of "Kill the assassin!" and "Hang the bastard!" Soldiers blockaded the entrance. Not yet a mob, the crowd fell back before raised rifles, then parted to let the dark-uniformed ambulance men reach the building. People grew silent when the President was carried out on a stretcher and hefted into the back of the ambulance. Men snatched off their hats. Veterans saluted. Women wept into handkerchiefs. But as soon as the electric vehicle whined away, the gathering storm of mob anger returned. A man in a skimmer begin to remove rope from nearby stanchions. Another, in a faded cap and threadbare coat, shouted, "Lynch him!" Others echoed the cry, pushing toward the doors again. Soldiers worked their rifle bolts, and the crowd fell back once more, seething.

Fearing for their safety, Papa Joe looked about for his companions but could see none of them. Then he remembered Gus and lifted his gaze.

*   *   *

I am afraid I will feel dizzy from rising so rapidly and so high. I clench my teeth.

As I near the Electric Tower, I think of Icarus. I must keep my distance from the Goddess of Light so that her afternoon sunfire will not melt the wings in my soul. So much is at stake that I cannot let myself fail. I would find forgiveness in Will's eyes and Papa Joe's heart. I would find it in the words of Reverend Banks and even in the wallet of Captain Driscoll. What failure will deny me, however, is self-forgiveness for being the weakest link in the chain of this dream.

I must not fail.

Crossing over the Plaza and behind the Tower, I angle left. I imagine I am seen—a girl in the Tower cupola, tugging her mother's sleeve and pointing. An old man in the loggia below who removes his spectacles in utter amazement. A well-dressed couple who look up and gasp as they leave a Plaza restaurant. Perhaps spectators in the Mexican village are torn away from the four o'clock bullfight by this miracle in the cloudless sky.

Yes, the Blackbird is a miracle, steady and sturdy, four hundred feet above the ground.

This is my greatest height yet. It keeps me above minarets and flagpoles. I feared it would lessen control, but the winds are calmer than I dared to hope—as if the sun casting my liquid shadow upon the Goddess as I pass has stilled the currents. As I head south, then, I have only one concern, the minute hand on the Waterbury fixed near my eyes. I lost time in the climb, but I am confident I can reach the Temple of Music, then make a wide arc and pass over the Court of the Fountains on my return journey. Still, I am not Icarus, unmindful of warnings that would save my life. When I reach the midpoint of my time, I will turn back, wherever I am.

Below sprawls the Rainbow City, an artist's palette even more dazzling to the eye from above, its thoroughfares clogged with people, people who will stop and gaze up at—

Something feels wrong below. The people filling the streets are moving in one direction, as if drawn like rats by some unseen piper calling them to water. I do not understand. Ordinarily these streets are full of people who move in every direction, at random, their purposes known only to themselves. Now everyone appears to be heading south—toward a common destination. Ahead to my left lies the vast Esplanade, clogged with people heading west. Now I look down upon the blue panels in the dome of the Temple of Music and I understand. The President must be coming out and people are hurrying to catch a last glimpse of him before he leaves.

Hurrying in such a fever that someone could be injured...

I am almost over the Temple now. Somewhere down there Papa Joe and the Captain have accomplished their mission and await Mr. McKinley's departure. Pearl and her aunt and father have been looking skyward for me and by now see me and are proud. I cannot tell where the President is. With so many people packed together below, he must at least be in one of the doorways. I imagine him waving as he moves toward his carriage, smiling as he surveys the crowd, looking up because he has been told I am overhead . . .

Has he already seen me? Will he see me in his next breath?

But fate is the cruelest of engineers, for one glance at the Waterbury tells me that it is almost time to change course. Just seconds remain. If I delay too long . . .

Then that I notice the intensity of movement near the Temple, as if those massed outside are the waters of the Flood beating against the sides of the Ark. Again I do not understand. If President McKinley is coming out, why should anyone be trying so hard to get inside? If the Temple is surrounded and the doors are blocked, how can he get out?

It is time now. I begin my turn to the east.

People are streaming across the Triumphal Bridge, pouring into the Esplanade from all directions, surging toward the Temple of Music. I can only steal glances at the activity below if I am to keep control of the aeroplane. Yet there is anger beneath the energy of such movement. This is not a crowd but a mob, moving without thinking. Even at this height I sense the purity of their rage. In the absence of reason rage is often called blind. If they are blind they will not see me when I need most to be seen.

Despite the danger, I must circle back, fly over them again. I must be seen.

I turn left, sharply but careful not to tilt the wings to a degree at which I would lose control. The Blackbird shudders anyway. For one unholy moment, as I look below at those who would be at the end of my downward spiral, I am terrified. How many will die with me if I cannot right the aeroplane? The control cables tighten, sending vibrations through my arms and legs as I strain to level the wings. Then my right wing is dropping, my left rising, and once again I am nearing the Temple of Music.

The frenzy below still baffles me, though by now I must have been noticed. Here and there a few faces must have turned upward, but from so great a height I cannot tell. If the sound of the engine has not drawn more attention, the crowd must be exceptionally noisy. Why? Then comes the thought that something has happened to the President. I try to push it aside, to dismiss it as the outgrowth of the Captain's misgivings yesterday. Yet the notion persists. It seems the likeliest explanation for the imminent riot. Something has happened to McKinley . . .

But I have no more time to consider such things.

My next turn is wider than the last. Finally flying north, I will not look at the Waterbury. Whatever time I have lost in my curiosity and desire to be seen will not be restored with nervous glances. My sole consideration now is getting back in one piece. I ease the engine lever back a bit in the hope that I will not consume my remaining fuel before I reach the estate.

But I am not so fortunate. The engine sputters before the north rail station. By the time I pass through dying plumes of locomotive smoke, I know my fuel is spent.

* * *

Lucas had spent most of the afternoon on the Midway. At the Japanese village he sipped tea served by a geisha as he watched a trio of young male acrobats somersault, walk on their hands, and arrange themselves into an inverted pyramid. In the Beautiful Orient he sidestepped donkey boys hawking rides on cobblestone streets and watched fez-wearing men inside a chicken wire enclosure make the cigarettes he bought. He wandered about like a wide-eyed child, listening to the steam calliope and shoveling popcorn into his mouth. Later, at the gypsy camp, he felt decidedly more adult watching colorfully clad women roll and snap their hips in the scandalous couchee-couchee dance.

It was there that he heard of the attempted assassination.

As the dancers drifted back into their tents, Lucas went to the man who had halted the performance with the announcement. The spieler was not a gypsy himself but an old white man with leathery skin and bushy white hair. He frowned when Lucas asked directions to the hospital.

"I'm a doctor," Lucas said. "I may be able to help." It was shameful, he chided himself, that a member of the medical committee, even a nominal member, should need directions to the hospital. But he kept his embarrassment to himself.

"Not far at all," the spieler drawled, beginning to give directions that were a combination of words and gestures.

Having run the U-shaped path through the Midway, Lucas was winded when he reached the gray stucco building. Already a crowd had gathered, kept back by mounted police. Sweating, he had to push his way through, alternately apologizing and declaring his profession, first to the fairgoers, then the policemen, and finally the soldiers blocking the entrance. At the word doctor, two soldiers stepped aside to let him pass.

Just inside the archway was another cluster of men, in suits instead of uniforms, but somehow more menacing than the soldiers. Angrily chewing a cigar, a big man in a cocked derby held up a hand. Lucas saw in the lines of the palm a reddish tinge that looked like the residue of blood recently wiped away.

"Dr. Lucas Westbeck," he said. "I came as soon as I heard."

The big man looked over his shoulder at someone standing in the shadows of the main hall. "Dr. Westbeck," he said.

"Send him in, Foster, send him in."

Stepping into the cooler hall, Lucas was glad to see that the man who had called for his admittance was John Milburn. They shook hands. Milburn's eyes held tendrils of red and were ringed with worry. His shoulders sagged under the weight of the tragedy evolving at the fair he had labored so hard to bring to Buffalo. Lucas felt sorry for him.

"We've tried by telephone and sent messengers to reach your father and other medical men," Milburn said. "Some are already here." He indicated a gathering at the other end of the main hall. "We must assemble the best available surgical contingent as quickly as possible."

To Lucas the choice of a lead doctor was obvious. Roswell Park, Exposition medical director, was a world renowned surgeon. "Is Dr. Park here yet?"

Milburn shook his head. "He's in surgery in Niagara Falls. A special train is being readied for him. However, there is a question of whether we can delay until his arrival."

"What about the President's personal physician?"

"I don't know where Dr. Rixey is, but efforts are being made to find him."

Lucas nodded and moved past Milburn to his colleagues at the far end of the hall. There were eight or nine of them, but Lucas recognized only a few. There seemed to be a dispute in progress about the course of action to be taken. A dark-bearded stranger was wagging his finger in the face of a younger man. Lucas went to Herman Mynter, his former professor and his father's friend. Mynter was a rawboned man, with a long weathered face, ash-colored mustache, and soft blue eyes beneath eyebrows sun-bleached to near invisibility. Some years earlier he had been a surgeon for both the Royal Army and Navy in his native Denmark.

Mynter pulled Lucas aside. "Best not to get mixed up in

all that," he said with a faint accent. He inclined his head toward the disputants. "Out-of-towners on holiday and local rivalries, a volatile medical mix. That fellow Lee from St. Louis feels he ought to be in charge because he was medical director of the Omaha Exposition."

"How's the President?"

Mynter led him to the door of the operating room. Inside, pale and undressed, William McKinley lay atop a surgical table. His huge abdomen seemed to quiver beneath the sheet that covered it. Lucas noticed mounds under the sheet where wads of batting had been used to stanch the wounds. The room looked suitably equipped for emergency treatment, though the lighting left much to be desired. Here and there stood cabinets full of medicines, dressings, and supplies. Sinks were strategically located. Two nurses in starched white bib skirts hovered over one side of the table, preparing instrument trays. On the other side a bespectacled man with a dark mustache held the President's right hand in both of his and bent to listen. Between grimaces and sleepy pauses, McKinley was telling him something.

"He's been injected with morphine and strychnine to lessen the pain," Mynter said. "The man with him is his secretary, George Cortelyou." Mynter drew Lucas away from the door and explained what he had found during his examination. "The first bullet struck the sternum on the left but failed to penetrate, whether because of the sternum itself or a waistcoat button I cannot say for certain. I have not yet examined the bullet or the clothing. The second bullet entered the abdomen two and a half inches to the left of the midline, an inch and a half above the umbilicus, and five inches below the left nipple. Unless it's trapped in fatty tissue, it penetrated the stomach. Without prompt surgery, he will very likely die."

"Milburn said they were getting a special train for Park."

"It's nearly five now. Waiting until six-thirty or seven could be too late."

"I haven't much surgical experience," Lucas said, "but I'm willing to assist in any way . . ."

Mynter smiled. "Thank you, Lucas." He nodded toward the cluster of physicians, which had nearly tripled in size in the past few minutes and now had nervous Exposition officials pacing about the edges. "However, I see no shortage of capable hands. The question to be decided is who will lead the surgery if Park is not here."

Lucas did not understand. "Surely, you. Your experience as a military surgeon, your professorship in surgery at the medical college, your—"

Mynter cut him off with a sigh and an uplifted hand. "The choice is not mine to make. It's up to the President's physician or his wife or in their absence his secretary. Whoever chooses will do so based on what he is told about the men present." He shrugged. "If I am called upon to perform the operation, I should certainly consider having you participate." He smiled thinly. "I may yet make a surgeon of you, in spite of Mordecai's insistence on leaving you his practice."

Just then the secretary stepped out of the operating room and motioned Milburn away from the crowd. After an exchange of whispers, the secretary announced that Dr. Matthew Mann would lead the President's surgical contingent. A small man with tired eyes and a neat gray beard, Mann separated himself from the others and looked about the hall. "Dr. Wasdin," he said with quiet authority, "prepare to administer the ether." Then he named those who would assist him. Dr. Herman Mynter was among them; Dr. Lucas Westbeck was not.

As the medical team disappeared into the operating

room, Lucas was left to wonder why a gynecologist would be leading gunshot wound surgery on the President of the United States.

* * *

Nearly thirty minutes after the assassin was whisked away in a closed patrol wagon, with hundreds in angry pursuit, Papa Joe found Essie and Pearl near the Graphic Arts Building. Pearl had lost her hat and her aunt's parasol; the bottom of Essie's dress had been torn when someone stepped on the fringe. Arm in arm, they had made their way through the crush, managing to detach themselves only when the crowd heaved toward a wagon believed to be carrying the assassin away from the east door of the Temple. Thus, Essie and Pearl had been there when the actual gunman was bustled out the south door and shoved into the police wagon before most people knew what was happening. By the time the crowd shifted direction again, the driver was whipping his team across the Triumphal Bridge toward the Lincoln Parkway gate.

"What happened to Ben?" Papa Joe asked.

"He must still be inside," Pearl said, looking with concern at the Temple. Her hair was in disarray, her lower lip caught between her teeth. She would have looked like a frightened child if she had been shorter.

"They probably want to talk to him," Papa Joe said. "He was right behind the man. He'll have to testify." He took hold of Pearl's shoulders and stared into her moistening eyes. "No one's going to hurt him, Pearl. He's a hero, the man who saved the President."

Even as she nodded, the tears came, and Papa Joe drew her to his chest.

Essie began to pat her niece's back, then stiffened suddenly and looked up. "Papa Joe, I didn't think of it until just now," she said. "I'm sorry. Did Gus—"

"I think the Edison man missed him trying to get pictures of the crowd," he said. "But Gus was up there, all right, and I wasn't the only one who saw him." He closed his eyes and pressed Pearl closer to him. "I wasn't the only one."

*   *   *

They chanced upon Ben at the northern edge of the Court of the Fountains, surrounded by people who sounded excited. Papa Joe could feel Pearl tensing as they worked their way through to her father. When they reached the interior of the semicircle, they saw that four or five feet separated Ben from those closest to him. His crooked half smile when he saw them told them there was no danger, only that he was embarrassed at the attention.

"It's him, I tell you." A man in a dark jacket and coal shoveler's cap was pointing straight at Ben. "Ain't you the colored fella what jumped on the wretch what shot McKinley?"

"Well, I—"

"Sure you are," the man said. "I was there. I seen you." He pivoted to face the rest of the small assembly, his open hand thrust toward Ben. "This is the man. Pounced on the assassin like a lion, he did. Pounded him right into the floor. He saved the President."

Papa Joe looked at Pearl and raised his eyebrows as if to say, *I told you so.*

The people gathered around Ben applauded, and he shrugged self-consciously. The man who had proclaimed Ben's identity stepped toward him and seized his hand, pumping it hard. Others came forward to shake his hand, or touch his coat. One man asked for a button from his waistcoat. Another offered a quarter for it. "I'll give you a dollar!" a third said.

Ben surrendered the button, shaking his head in disbelief

at the unexpected price of safe passage. Then he yanked off another and another, handing them over for a dollar each, until his coat and waistcoat were both buttonless. Smiling awkwardly, he held out his hands, palms up, to show he had nothing more to give.

"What about that tie?" someone else shouted. "Two dollars!"

"Three!" A well-dressed woman came forth, coins in hand.

Ben's tie went, followed by his hat, lapel pin, admission ticket stub, Exposition program, matchbox, and souvenir pencil.

Calls rang out for other articles of clothing—waistcoat, jacket ("The sleeves look a little short anyway!"), and even his trousers. Someone suggested that he cut up his clothing and sell it off in small squares. "I'll give you five dollars apiece for your shoes!" someone else cried, only to be answered by a bid of twenty-five. Hands up, Ben took a step back and shook his head. "I need these shoes, and my shirt and trousers, and the buttons on my shirt and trousers. Please! Are you good people trying to leave me naked?" He laughed faintly, as though hoping that might appease them. "They'll sure enough take me to jail."

"Then you can get close to him and finish what you started." This came from a small man in a crisp checked suit. A cheer went up when he added, "I'd give you a thousand for your shoes if you had stomped the bastard to death when you had the chance."

When it was apparent that Ben would sell nothing more, the crowd began to disperse. There was talk of getting a rope and marching downtown to the jail. Several men, including the man in the checked suit, drifted off to find support for such an action. A few hung back to shake Ben's hand again before leaving. A tiny old woman walked straight up to him and tipped her head back to look him full in the face. "I wish I could have a lock of your hair," she said.

Ben smiled down at her. "Don't know if I got a lock, but I might be willing to spare a kink." He let out a deep laugh, and the old woman laughed with him before she toddled off.

Five men remained behind, pads open, pencils scratching, and hats pushed back.

"What's your name, fella?" one said, jaws pulverizing gum. He was a thickset man in a light suit, the handkerchief pocket of his jacket full of pencils. His face had reddened so in the heat that his forehead had begun to peel.

"You from the newspapers?" Ben asked.

They nodded, almost in unison, and rattled off their names and the names of their papers. Then one asked for Ben's name.

"James Benjamin Parker," he said, nervously. "My family and friends call me Ben." He grinned at Pearl, Essie, and Papa Joe.

"Damned if you ain't one of the biggest men I've ever seen, Ben Parker," a third man said, staring up at him. "Christ, look at those hands." In waistcoat and shirt sleeves, the man tapped his lower lip with the top of his pencil. "Hmm. Big Ben Parker. Kind of has a ring to it."

"Nah, Tommy," the gum-chewer scoffed. "Big Ben is a clock in England. Americans don't want to read that their President was saved by a British clock!"

Tommy frowned, then scratched his chin, squinting at Ben. "How about Big Jim then?"

"Big Jim sounds good," the first reporter said thoughtfully, his gum-chewing slowing to an occasional snap. "Big Jim Parker. Now that sounds American."

And then the questions came in a flurry:

"Where're you from, Big Jim? How old are you?"

"What brings Big Jim Parker to the Exposition?"

"Big Jim, when you took him down, what went through your mind?"

*   *   *

Linen suit coat ruined by the bloody nose he had got from a stray elbow, Captain Driscoll had been unable to locate Papa Joe and had gone to wait by his stanhope. Then he realized that Ben and the women had come by streetcar, that in all the madness of the afternoon Joseph would likely insist on giving the women a ride, especially if Ben was held over and questioned about his role in subduing the assassin. Since three would be enough of a squeeze in the two-seater and everyone was to come to his house anyway, Driscoll fished a pencil out of an inside pocket and wrote a note on the back of his program, which he left on the seat. Then he started back alone.

It had taken him a long time to extricate himself from the mob. Now, trudging across the tracks at the northern perimeter, he pulled out his watch and saw that it was just minutes before six. Nearly two hours had passed since the shooting, and in that time he had felt the most violent mix of emotions that he could recall since his war days.

His shock had been quickly replaced by rage so profound he would have hanged the assassin himself if he'd had rope and a tree. As his old comrade was carted, his anger gave way to worry that would gnaw at him until McKinley was out of danger. When the crowd became a mob, his rage came back, tempered only by concern that efforts to reach the assassin would result in injury, maybe even death, for citizens, soldiers, and policemen alike. Finally, there had been elation amid the fury, pure elation, for he had swung his eyes to the sky . . .

The Blackbird, looking like a free-floating box kite—

soaring, circling, circling again . . .

He had looked up and seen the future. A glance to either side told him that others had seen it too, and the realization left him breathless. As the Blackbird flew north out of sight, he was filled with an excitement that threatened to send his heart bursting out of his chest. They had done it. Joseph's amazing grandsons had done it.

Now, heading home, Captain Driscoll felt tired, emotionally and physically, and old. Despite his satisfaction at the flight, his back and bones ached, and his piles burned. He was wearily aware of his mortality. He had not imagined walking so near his own grave since before his involvement with the negroes and their flying machine, since Anna's death.

Death begets death, but with the negroes he'd found a way to embrace life, despite the cold curl of Death's beckoning finger.

He wondered if at this very instant McKinley lay dying. Or were the doctors who must surely be attending him by now saving his life? Then he remembered the man he had suspected of wanting to harm the President. In the confusion that followed the shots, he had been hustled outside too quickly to see the assassin's face. He was curious to know if this man and his were one and the same. Perhaps if he had shouted louder yesterday . . .

When he reached the path that wound through trees and brush to his house, he was grateful to be home, however bittersweet the homecoming. He would have the somber task of reporting what had befallen the President. On the other hand, he would be the first to congratulate Gus and Will. Whether McKinley lived or died, the flight of the Blackbird had been a success. However few had seen it, it had been noticed by more than enough people. Now Will could stage a public test reported in the newspapers. The government would have to pay attention.

Whatever happened with the Blackbird, Daniel would share in its ultimate prosperity—as he should, for having the foresight to support the idea. It would take many years for the aeroplane to go from this experimental stage to commercial use. Driscoll had no illusions about that. His one regret was the unlikelihood that he would live long enough to see Daniel swept into the pages of history alongside Will and Gus.

In shirt sleeves rolled up to the elbows, Daniel and Reverend Banks were waiting for him on the porch. Their faces were grave, and Daniel's eyes were red.

Captain Driscoll swallowed. "Is Gus all right?"

"His fuel burned up too quickly," Daniel said, slowly. "He had to glide in, right through the treetops, and he landed too hard. His arm's broken and the aeroplane's got a broken wing."

"It can be repaired," Captain Driscoll said, relieved. He mounted the stairs. "Thank God Gus is alive. You should have seen him up there, and you should have seen Ben. With all that happened—"

"Captain, that's not the worst," Reverend Banks said, softly. "There's something else."

Driscoll paused on the third step, mouth open in an unvoiced question.

Daniel moved toward him. "Father, we found Jonas . . . under the front porch. Somebody shot him . . ." His voice broke. "Somebody shot him in the face and dragged him underneath and left him there like a cat leaving a dead bird."

Not just someone, an enemy. Our enemy. Death begets death. Death inspires death. Sergeant, old friend. My God, not you . . .

Captain Driscoll felt a sudden dizziness wash over him and was vaguely aware of Daniel and Reverend Banks hastening down the steps to grasp his arms and help him sit. His single sad thought before the tears came was that he might never sleep well again. How could he when the sergeant was no longer in the world to watch over him?

*   *   *

Having slept the entire day, Eustace Buttonwood woke up hungry. He hurried into his clothes and went downstairs, intending to walk through the tavern and out the front door of the Clinton to a nearby eatery. But an oppressive sobriety hung in the air of the packed tavern and slowed his steps enough for him to catch snatches of conversation at tables he passed. There was talk of evil and the general state of misery in the world, talk of a good man who had never hurt anyone, talk of a lynching. Unable to find an empty seat, Buttonwood stood near the bar just as someone called for attention and raised a toast to William McKinley.

It was in this manner that he learned the President had been shot.

Nineteen

Saturday afternoon, in a ring of trees on the edge of the Driscoll estate, Papa Joe attended what would have been the second secret burial of his life, had he not been laid up with a gunshot wound on the first occasion, some fifty years earlier.

Reverend Banks conducted funeral services for Jonas Newcomb. The mourners gathered around a grave that looked too small for the irregular coffin waiting beside it. Captain Driscoll and Danny stood at the head of the grave. Will and Ben were on the right, and on the left, behind the coffin, were Papa Joe and Gus, his splinted right arm in a sling. At the foot of the grave were Essie and Pearl. Reverend Banks moved past Will and crouched to touch the coffin lid. After a moment of silence, he straightened and recounted the particulars of Jonas's life—orphaned early and never married, especially fond of rabbit stew and vinegar pie—all of which he had learned from the Captain the night before. Then he praised Jonas for his service—to the Grand Army of the Republic, to the cause of liberty, to the Driscolls. Finally, he opened his Bible to a page he had marked in the Book of Psalms.

"O God, to whom vengeance belongeth, shew thyself . . . Lord, how long shall the wicked triumph?. . . They break in pieces thy people, O Lord, and afflict thine heritage. They slay the widow and the stranger, and murder the fatherless . . . The Lord is my defence; and my God is the rock of my refuge . . . "

Friday night there had been much discussion of how Jonas had met his end. Everyone agreed that he must have confronted the man who destroyed the carriage shed and taken a bullet for his vigilance. That they had an enemy afoot was unsettling but not surprising. That he was willing to kill made him more than one of the Captain's business rivals. "Somebody," Papa Joe said, "does not want to see a colored man fly."

When Danny offered to summon the police, Captain Driscoll looked first at Papa Joe, who said nothing, and then at each of the others. Since Jonas had died defending the estate, he said after a few minutes, it was fitting that he be buried on it. "Sometimes the only way a body can rest is in a secret place," he said, and Papa Joe nodded. The few shopkeepers who'd known Jonas in passing would not question his absence. If anyone asked after him, they would say that he'd died while visiting a cousin out West. "And the sergeant wouldn't have wanted his death to harm our work, not when we're so close. No, he will rest here, in this ground, undisturbed." The Captain looked at Danny, as if waiting for an objection. When none came, he asked Papa Joe and Ben to piece together a coffin out of whatever planks they could find and Danny and Will to dig a grave. Driscoll promised to prepare the body himself.

Papa Joe was relieved. With an assassin in jail, police would have their hands full keeping lynch mobs at bay. How hard would they search for an anonymous murderer when they found five colored men right under their noses, even if one of them was the man who saved the President? And what would they make of the damaged flying machine in the barn? The Captain was right. Even a lone investigator could ruin their enterprise in some unforeseen way.

Captain Driscoll's grief was heavy, the kind that bent the

spine instead of wringing out tears. Papa Joe admired the way his friend bore it, the gentlemanly deference he showed Essie when he asked if she would select and brush a suit for Jonas. But he was most touched by the crack in Driscoll's voice when he said to Portius, "Reverend, I wonder if you would lead the service?" and to Pearl, "They tell me you have a lovely voice, child. Please sing for my friend."

And so Jonas Newcomb was laid to rest, in the faded blue G.A.R. uniform that Essie had found among his meager possessions, in a crude coffin and hastily dug grave, in the company of his only two friends, and in the presence of the colored men whose work he had died to protect. With Pearl's "Amazing Grace" still ringing in their ears, Captain Driscoll turned the first shovelful, then handed the shovel to Danny. As the shovel was passed from man to man, Papa Joe closed his eyes and prayed silently that Jesus would make room for Jonas in the Kingdom of His Father.

* * *

On Saturday evening Papa Joe took Gus back to the blacksmith shop. With a broken arm he would be of little use on the estate. Even if rebuilding the wing took just a few days, it would be weeks before Gus could fly again. That was fine with Papa Joe. Gus had done well, had earned a rest. Let him spend his days in a chair, with a book open in his lap. Evenings he could pass at the kitchen table, narrating details of his flight to Pearl, who had promised to record them in his chronicle. Papa Joe was just glad he had survived.

He waited until Gus had gone to bed before he scoured the newspapers he had purchased on the way home. The front page of each was crammed with accounts of the assassination attempt and the President's subsequent surgery. McKinley had been struck by two bullets. The first had been found in his clothing. The second had entered his stomach and remained lodged somewhere in his back. Despite failing to locate the bullet, surgeons were confident their efforts to repair the injury had been successful. A statement signed by all his doctors noted that McKinley was resting well and in no pain. Recovery seemed likely.

An early paper identified Ben as John Parker and the assassin as Fred Nieman. Later editions called Big Jim Parker a hero. The man he had wrestled to the floor turned out to be a Leon Czolgosz of Ohio, born in Detroit and lately a resident of John Nowak's saloon-hotel on Broadway. Apparently he was a disciple of anarchist Emma Goldman, called by several papers the most dangerous woman in America. Leon Czolgosz. Papa Joe tried to work his tongue around a pronunciation. Whoever this strange young man was and however his Polish surname hung in the air, he had shot the President. In all likelihood he faced a walk up the gallows steps or a sit-down in that new electrical chair. Fool or firebrand, he was now beyond the help of anyone but God.

Other articles reported that Mrs. McKinley was exhibiting commendable courage, the Vice President and the Cabinet were either in town or en route, and the Exposition would continue as scheduled. Here and there were accounts of the two previous presidential assassinations, Lincoln's by the actor John Wilkes Booth and Garfield's by the madman Charles Guiteau. The rest of each newspaper was occupied by local stories, regular features, and advertisements. But finally Papa Joe found the report he had been seeking, buried deep inside a late afternoon edition.

His chest tightened and hands trembled as he began to read.

CAPTIVE BALLOON? KITE?
FLYING MACHINE? OR LATE OMEN?

Fairgoers Report Peculiar Object in Sky Soon
After Tragedy Unfolds Inside Temple of Music

Having been thwarted in his murderous enterprise by soldiers and detectives, Leon Czolgosz, in police custody and bloodied from his struggle with guards, awaited justice in a small office near the Temple of Music stage. The recipient of his villainy, William McKinley, was on his way to surgery. Exposition thoroughfares were crammed with citizens eager for news of the President and clamoring for the assassin's neck. Then came a development completely unexpected. Dozens of witnesses reported an object high in the sky that appeared to be flying. According to those who claim to have seen it, it swooped and circled like a great bird, remaining in flight only a brief time. Then it headed north and disappeared.

It was described as having wings connected to a framework possibly capable of carrying of a man. Whether it carried a man is uncertain. While some claim to have heard a rumbling as it soared overhead, others insist that it was silent. One gentleman who refused to give his name suggested that the object was a flying machine intended to spirit away the assassin. Mr. Peter Wirth of the Exposition Company offered two possible explanations. "Quite likely the Captive Balloon ride," he said, "reflecting sunlight and manifesting itself as an illusion. Or perhaps a lost kite of unusual shape." He dismissed the notion that it was some type of flying machine. "Some of the finest minds in the country have been working for years to achieve heavier-than-air flight, but such an aerial conveyance has yet to be perfected. Whatever it was, this object was no aeroplane. As likely as not, it was a sad harbinger, minutes too late, of the attempt on the President's life."

Papa Joe felt the tightness slipping out of his chest, felt it replaced by a mixture of elation and relief. Not only had Gus and the Blackbird been seen, but the flight had made at least one newspaper. Papa Joe smiled as he creased and tore off the entire page, folding it and sliding it between the pages of his Bible. Enemy or no, there could be no denying what had happened over the Exposition. The Blackbird had not been a symbol of presidential destiny but a portent of the future of the negro race.

Whatever lay ahead for the President, the colored century had begun.

* * *

For the next several days Papa Joe went out twice daily to the kiosk on Broadway and Michigan to get newspapers fresh off the back of a horse-drawn wagon. The medical news was encouraging. At the Delaware Avenue home of John Milburn, the President was conscious and responding so well to treatment it would not be necessary to send for the Edison X-ray machine to locate the second bullet. By Tuesday, when the Vice President felt certain enough of recovery to announce his own departure, the President was able to turn himself in bed and asked to sit. His rapid gain indicated he would survive.

He will yet see Will's aeroplane, Papa Joe thought.

Meanwhile, from pulpits and newspapers alike came calls to stamp out anarchy once and for all. Avowed anarchists were being arrested all over the country. Emma Goldman herself was taken in Chicago, and one newspaper demanded that the Medusa of Anarchy be extradited to Buffalo. In one article Leon Czolgosz claimed that it was his duty to shoot McKinley. In another he declared jail food much to his liking and confessed to reporters that what he really wanted was to fire up a good cigar. *Careful boy*, Papa Joe thought. *You might get burnt.*

Papa Joe was pleased to see there was no shortage of articles about Ben. Business was increasing at Bailey's because fairgoers wanted to meet him and were prepared to wait to sit at a table he served. A *Courier* writer named Ben a "Don't Knock" for his courage, and negro groups around the nation were expressing their pride in "Big Jim Parker." Money and gifts addressed to Big Jim streamed into Exposition offices from as far away as Oregon and California.

By Wednesday the papers reported the President was out of danger. His stomach wounds had healed and he had begun to take liquid nourishment, beef broth he consumed eagerly. The doctors saw no alarming symptoms afterward. By Thursday he was having toast and coffee and asking for a cigar. His blood count showed no signs of poisoning. His sleep was natural and easy. Relieved, members of his Cabinet made their own plans to leave.

On Friday morning, however, Papa Joe was stunned to read that the President's condition had worsened after cathartic treatment for intestinal toxemia. Unable to digest solid food, he had been given calomel and castor oil as purgatives. Still, his heart showed signs of fatigue. The five p.m. *Enquirer* reported that Rooosevelt and the Cabinet, summoned in the night, were speeding back to Buffalo. Noting his repeated requests for cigars, one physician speculated that the relapse might be the result of tobacco heart, a weakening of the smoker's heart caused by deprivation of tobacco. Another named the elusive second bullet as the likely agent of an infection. Whatever the reason, the President was dying.

* * *

Late Saturday morning, several hours after the early papers announced the President had died at 2:15 a.m., the Westbeck home was in a state of agitation. With no patients scheduled in his surgery, Dr. Westbeck rattled about the house, proclaiming the flesh of anarchists unfit even for carrion-eaters. Mrs. Westbeck wrung her hands and said, "His poor, poor wife!" And in the parlor early that afternoon, with the air humid from the brief morning rain, both reproached their son as he readied himself for the tea to which he had been invited.

Pearl had been sent outside to stretch black mourning bunting between the front porch's columns and could not help overhearing the Westbecks through the open windows.

"Most inappropriate at a time like this," Dr. Westbeck said. "Here the President of the United States is not yet cold and you have to go lallygagging with some young lady!"

"Not some young lady," Lucas protested, "but the same Miss Wilcox whose cause Mother has championed these past six months."

"I said you should consider *marrying* her before some other suitor snatches her up," Mrs. Westbeck sniffed, "not sitting down to tea with her smack in the middle of a national crisis."

"Surely, this will be canceled," Dr. Westbeck said. "The Wilcoxes got back from their summer travels just a few days ago."

"They've already boarded their first houseguest of the season," Lucas said.

"Lucas," Dr. Westbeck said, "your impertinence is shameful! The Vice President is an old friend of Mr. Wilcox and was there because of what had happened to the President. Now that he is President, he will very likely be there again, which is all the more reason you mustn't go today."

"The newspaper says he's been summoned but I have no idea whether he has even reached the city." Then Lucas paused and took a deep breath. "Father, even if Mr. Roosevelt sits down to tea with us, which I doubt, given the needs of the nation, I will do nothing to embarrass the family name. The invitation was very gracious. Of course, it was posted before McKinley took a bad turn, but if she has not telephoned me to cancel, then I will not telephone her to withdraw. Look, this is not an affair of state, but it could become an affair of the heart. Miss Wilcox and I will have tea and talk and learn about each other and maybe learn to like each other. Mr. Roosevelt will probably be elsewhere. The wheels of history will turn without taking notice of either one of us."

The discussion ended, and Pearl knew what she must do. She prayed she had enough time.

* * *

Two hours later Lucas Westbeck stood in the library of the Wilcox home and waited for the wheel of history to turn, with him lashed to a spoke.

He had walked the several blocks in a daze, still amazed at the story Pearl had told him so hastily in the front hall. He readily agreed to convey her sealed note to the President, should an opportunity present itself, but once he knew the essence of the message, uneasiness rose in his chest. There was little hope the President would have any use for Pearl's claim. He might even have Lucas locked away. Maybe he could leave the envelope somewhere in the house, thereby detaching himself from its bizarre contents.

A negro flying machine. The idea was fantastic, too wild

to be true. He'd dismissed it immediately. But she asked him to recall the marks on the arms of Andrew Ridgewater, fatally injured in a fall. He remembered having accepted Gus's explanation of the rope burns. A block and tackle as they worked on a roof. That was certainly more credible than an aeroplane accident. But Pearl persisted, handing him a newspaper article she had torn from a page in the pile by the hearth. Clearly *something* had been in the sky the day McKinley was shot, though Lucas remained unconvinced it was a negro flying machine, especially with that stripling Gus at the controls. But then he recalled something else from the day the Ridgewater boy died.

He had arrived at the hospital after the Dedication Day festivities and learned of Andrew's death. Finding the mother with the giant blacksmith, he'd drawn near and overheard something he did not understand. He had considered it a figure of speech and forgotten it, until now.

God didn't intend anybody to fly, Mrs. Ridgewater had said. *Especially colored folks.*

Now, waiting in the library for Cornelia Wilcox, Lucas paced. It was a comfortable room the size of two parlors, but still it felt too small to contain his agitation. He looked about for a place to leave Pearl's note. Most of the wall space was occupied by books and some by paintings. Here and there were stuffed chairs in dusty slipcovers, a stuffed footstool, a rocker, and a small desk already covered with papers. To the left of the fireplace loomed a three-paned bay window with a cushioned seat and to the right two tall front windows. All the windows were open, the afternoon breeze cutting through the rank heaviness of books that had been closed too long in the summer heat. A wing chair sat before each front window, on either side of a small table that held a silver tea service.

Perhaps the mantel. He crossed the room to the fireplace, fingers sliding inside his jacket toward the letter Pearl had given him. Then, lower lip caught between his teeth, he hesitated and withdrew his hand.

A very old book with a torn binding lay on the narrow mantel. *St. Martin's Summer* by Anne H.M. Brewster. He picked it up, opened it, and saw an inscription on the flyleaf:

> *To Cornelia,*
> *On her Fourteenth Birthday*
> *April 18, 1866,*
> *From her Father*

"Lest you think me remarkably preserved for a woman born in 1852, I must tell you that book belonged to my late mother."

Lucas turned to face Cornelia Wilcox and immediately felt his tension shift from Pearl's letter to the most intense blue eyes he had ever seen. She was a small woman of about twenty, with a softly rounded chin and high cheekbones. Her shimmering dark hair was pulled back in a bun. She wore a simple white lawn dress with a high collar and black crepe on one sleeve. She came forward and offered her hand, which Lucas took, unable to tear his gaze from her eyes.

"I'm so glad you accepted my invitation, Dr. Westbeck—especially in the face of tragedy. I've always felt the best way to approach death is to live as normally as possible." She gestured toward the chairs beside the tea service. "Please sit, and call me Nina."

"After you," Lucas said. "I agree. It's a terrible thing, but life, and the country, must go on. And please call me Lucas." When he had taken the chair nearer the fireplace, he held up the book. "You say this belonged to your *late* mother?"

"Yes," Nina said.

"Then the Mrs. Wilcox who is a friend to my mother is not your real mother?"

"Gracie—Mary Grace—is the only mother I've ever known," she said. "She is both my stepmother, and my aunt. You see, my real mother died when I was just a few weeks old, and her sister cared for me. Eventually, Father married her."

"Ah." Lucas nodded.

She reached over and took the Brewster book from his hand. "I've read this many times, whenever I wonder about her, who she was, what she liked. It helps me feel closer to her." She laid the book aside and lifted the cosy from the silver teapot. "Now, you must be wondering why I asked you here today." She set gilt-edged cups on saucers and began to pour.

"I won't tell you what my mother hopes," Lucas said.

"I can imagine." Nina smiled. "I'm not interviewing you to become my husband." She handed him his tea. "Someone else has pledged himself to that role. Being a lawyer's daughter, however, I have a mind for particulars." She smiled again.

"I don't understand," Lucas said. He stirred in sugar.

She cast him a sly sidelong glance. "I asked him to furnish me with character references."

Lucas's arm froze before the teacup could reach his lips. "You're joking, of course." He studied her for a moment and saw that she wasn't. He felt the beginnings of a smile tugging at the corners of his mouth. He sipped his tea.

"You were high on his list of hoped-for endorsements."

He smiled broadly then. She was quite beautiful, he decided, in a devilish sort of way. Too bad she was unavailable. Of course, a bad reference could reverse that. "Who is this . . . applicant?"

"Henry," she said. "Henry Bull."

"Henry? Good old Henry? Why, I—"

Just then there was the tramp of boots on the verandah, and the front doors banged open. The vestibule filled with voices and heavy footsteps. A balding man with a neatly waxed mustache stepped into the library. Lucas recognized Mr. Wilcox and was about to offer a greeting, but the harried-looking lawyer cut him off with the urgency of his words to his daughter.

"Nina, fetch your mother, and have the servants make room in here. Milburn's house is all wrong, with the body in one room and the widow in the next. He'll have to be sworn in here."

Lucas felt himself drawn to his feet by the unexpected force of history, for there behind Mr. Wilcox stood Theodore Roosevelt.

The next half hour was consumed by preparations for the President's taking the oath of office. Someone was dispatched to secure appropriate clothing for the travel-weary Roosevelt, while others mounted a search for a Bible. Slowly, the library filled with Cabinet members and city politicians, Exposition officials, and finally, on condition there be no photography, newspaper reporters. Standing silent in a rear corner, Lucas was surprised that he knew so many of those present—Milburn and his wife, Dr. and Mrs. Mann, Dr. Park. He recognized a couple of the judges, Secretary of War Elihu Root, and from the hospital McKinley's secretary. Lucas was overwhelmed and must have looked it, for Nina, beside him, squeezed his hand.

At last all was in readiness. In borrowed frock coat and striped trousers, Theodore Roosevelt stood before the bay window, right hand clutching his lapel and right heel nervously tapping the hardwood floor. His gold-rimmed glasses glinted as he turned to face the more than forty witnesses. Someone called for the Bible and someone else answered that none could be found. "You must swear him with uplifted hand then," came an authoritative voice.

Secretary of War Root stepped forward and exchanged a few private words with Roosevelt. Then they stood facing each other in the light of the open bay window. A stray blue jay fluttered to the sill outside the window, its chirping clearly audible in the expectant silence. Roosevelt turned to look at the bird, which lingered briefly, then flitted away. In the momentary rustle of witnesses shifting weight from one foot to the other and pressing forward, Nina stood on tiptoe to whisper into Lucas's ear: "'Hope is the thing with feathers that perches in the soul.'"

He looked at her, confused.

"Miss Emily Dickinson," she said, squeezing his hand again.

Secretary Root spoke. "Mr. Vice President, I—I. . ." His voice wavered, then cracked. He began to weep, as did many others. Tears were visible on Roosevelt's cheeks as well, but he stood unflinching as he waited for the Secretary to collect himself. Finally, after trying twice more, Root was able to continue.

"I have been requested on behalf of the Cabinet of the late President, at least those who are present in Buffalo, all except two, to request that for reasons of weight affecting the affairs of government you should proceed to take the Constitutional oath of President of the United States."

When one of the judges came forward and asked Roosevelt to raise his right hand, Lucas thought about the line of poetry Nina had recited. It struck him that the hope of a nation now rested on this one man. Shouldering such a burden was a responsibility unlike any other. It was hope that made people go on when the gods seemed lined up against them, when the fury of nature or the madness of men took all that they had and left them for dead. To carry the hope of a people meant being the last man to surrender it, to die while holding it aloft. Then he remembered Pearl's letter in his breast pocket and knew that what he had seen in her eyes was hope, a hope that reached beyond her and perched in the souls of a people, her people.

He carried their hope in his pocket. He swallowed at the weight of it, a burden he could not bear to keep. He would share it, he decided, forthrightly and openly, when the new President came around to shake his hand.

Top: Exposition Emergency Hospital After the Shooting
Bottom: McKinley's Casket Arrives at City & County Hall
Courtesy of University at Buffalo Libraries

Twenty

It had poured through the night.

In the morning, when Papa Joe urged Mac onto the Driscoll estate, the turf was sodden and the wheel ruts narrow channels of mud. The underbrush was laden with water, and the sky was dark with the threat of more rain. The air held the promise of a seasonal change. Papa Joe felt Gus shiver beside him on the seat, felt the ache of the dampness in his own joints.

It was a miserable day for a funeral.

Sunday morning. At this hour people all over town would be on their way to church or already seated. The ride through the city, however, had been unusually quiet, even for the Sabbath. Papa Joe had no idea how many congregations were in the area, but he was certain that today prayers and sermons in every one would exalt the fallen President. After services, many of the worshipers would forego the ease of their day of rest to head downtown and join an already long line of mourners waiting to view the remains of William McKinley.

After a private ceremony in the Milburn house, the funeral cortege would proceed along Delaware to the City and County Hall, where the body would lie in state in the rotunda. Wheeling the stanhope across Delaware at Summer to reach Elmwood, Papa Joe and Gus had seen the lines forming along both sides of the route two hours before the processional was to begin

"How long will he lie in state?" Gus asked as they drove north.

"Paper says from noon to five," Papa Joe said. "That

won't be enough time for all the folk who want to pay their respects." He knew that Captain Driscoll would be determined to try, and he snapped the reins to speed Mac along. He owed it to the Captain to give him his chance to bid McKinley farewell.

Now he climbed down and gazed for a moment at the barn and the blackened remains of the carriage shed. Then he reached for the reins to tie Mac to the post, but Gus had taken hold of them with his left hand, looping them around the boards of his splint. Papa Joe regarded him with obvious doubt. "You sure you can hold him with your arm like that?"

Gus smiled, almost indulgently. "No trouble, Papa."

"I'm sure Captain Driscoll would be willing to drive. He knows how to handle a horse."

Mac snorted, almost as if dismissing the idea.

Gus laughed. "I think Mac wants me."

Shaking his head in self- reproach, Papa Joe mounted the back steps. He had to keep reminding himself that Gus was no longer the sickly child who had consumed so much of his waking worry. He was now a man, restless to get back to work after a week of sitting and reading. When the aeroplane was made public, history would record him as the first man to fly. He could handle an old horse he'd known and fed and brushed since his childhood, even with his arm in a sling. Gus deserved not to be fretted over like a foundling with the grippe. It was going to be difficult not to fear for him, but Papa Joe told himself he would have to try.

Captain Driscoll unbolted the door. He was in a mackintosh, an umbrella hooked over his forearm and black crepe high on his sleeve. "Good morning, Joseph," he said, as Papa Joe stepped into the kitchen. "I'm glad you're here. The streetcar line is a close enough walk that I've been lax about getting a new carriage. But today the public cars will be filled, and every hack I tried to reserve yesterday was already booked. I'm indebted to you for coming out on such a bleak day."

"There are no debts between friends," Papa Joe said. "Gus is in the rig, waiting for you."

Captain Driscoll furrowed his brow. "Daniel wanted to come," he said, "if there's room."

"I plan to stay here," Papa Joe said. "Daniel should be able to squeeze in. If there's time, I'll pay my respects later. Meanwhile, I thought I'd see how the repairs are coming. I haven't seen Will since. . ." He hesitated, recalling Jonas's funeral and the Captain's palpable grief.

"I'm glad you're staying," Captain Driscoll said. "I had misgivings about leaving Will here alone. He's out in the barn. He was standing watch when I went out to wake Daniel." He sighed. "We have been keeping sorely disparate hours, but someone is always awake."

"You should have sent for us sooner," Papa Joe said. "Gus is eager to get back to work."

Captain Driscoll shrugged. "Oh, we've managed well enough. Not a night has gone by that we haven't had someone out here—Reverend Banks or Ben. Mrs. Banks has kept us all well fed. These days my businesses practically run themselves, so I've kept my share of the vigils too."

Papa Joe saw the truth of that in the Captain's tired eyes.

"Gus needed you, so we decided not to disturb you for at least a week," Captain Driscoll said. "I wouldn't have sent the message last night, except you have no telephone and Reverend Banks has a worship service to lead and—"

"Captain, the lines get longer as we speak," Papa Joe said.

Driscoll reddened and grinned. "Of course." He called over his shoulder for Daniel to come downstairs, then said,

"Listen to me, prattling on like an old fool."

*　　*　　*

Shotgun cradled in the crook of his arm, Papa Joe walked up to the barn as the stanhope disappeared down the path. The air inside was cool, the light tinged with gray. The Blackbird sat in the middle of the floor, wingless but fitted with cables and wheels that looked new. The engine had been scoured and polished and now gleamed. The aeronautical hammock had been replaced with fresh canvas. Four wing sections lay on their sides along the north wall. The wooden struts and cotton sateen on all four looked new, as did the hinges and pulley assemblies. Nearby lay the propellers, burnished to a shine. Tools and small parts were scattered elsewhere across the floor.

His back against another wall, lips slightly parted, Will was seated on a pile of hay, asleep. Papa Joe stared at him, finding consolation in his breathing but in nothing else about his unkempt appearance. He looked exhausted, pouches beneath his eyes even in sleep, cheeks peppered with stubble. He seemed to have lost weight, and one of his braces had fallen from his shoulder. Papa Joe wanted to wake him and drag him into the house and shovel food into him. Instead, he set down the shotgun and quietly moved to one of the makeshift beds. He picked up a blanket, shook it free of straw, and covered Will from his chest to his ankles. Then he got a chair from a corner and sat facing the barn door, the shotgun across his knees. Occasionally, he gazed at his grandson and wondered, *My God, what have we done to you?*

An hour later Will woke with a start and lurched forward as if throwing himself out of a bad dream. After a moment he sank back and wiped his eyes with the heels of his hands. Inhaling deeply, he noticed the blanket now rumpled in his lap and Papa Joe seated nearby.

"Must have fallen asleep."

"Go on back to sleep," Papa Joe said. "You need it. Sleep for a week, I'll be right here."

Will remained motionless a moment, as if considering Papa Joe's advice. Then he took another deep breath and got to his feet, brushing straw off his trousers, pulling up his errant brace. "Can't. Too much to do." His first step looked unsteady. He hesitated before trying a second.

"Will—"

"What time is it?"

Papa Joe pulled a watch from his coat pocket. "Quarter to noon." He closed his watch, slid it away. "You know, I worked hard all my life so my family wouldn't have to shake hands with the missed-meal cramps. I bet you can't remember the last time you ate."

Will managed a shamefaced grin. "Yesterday noon."

"No wonder you look so hungry." Papa Joe rose and took hold of Will's arm. "Let's go see what the Captain's got put by." Then he led his grandson out into a light rain.

Bread, bacon, eggs. Will washed down the last of it with coffee, and Papa Joe thought he saw something ignite in his grandson's eyes. The past few months had changed Will. The whole endeavor had taken a grievous toll on him. He looked older as well as tired, an appearance surely aggravated by his guilt over Andrew and his concern for his brother. All the talk about what his invention would mean for the race or Captain Driscoll's business couldn't have helped. After he finished his breakfast, however, the old Will was back, the excitement in his eyes undeniable.

"Have you looked at it?" he asked.

Papa Joe did not know quite how to answer. "There are some new parts," he began.

Will shook his head. "Not just new cables and stirrups and fabric," he said. "I've made a few design changes, to lengthen the glide after fuel is spent, to improve front cable control. What happened to Gus—and Andrew—"

"Will," Papa Joe said, gently. He placed his hand on Will's forearm. "Don't blame yourself for Gus or Andrew. Everybody who climbed aboard knew he could get hurt."

"I've made it safer and stronger," he said. "I'll explain how when we go back to the barn."

Papa Joe withdrew his hand. "How soon before it can fly?"

Will smiled. "A week. Ten days at most."

Papa Joe frowned as he picked up his own coffee. "But your brother won't be ready, not with his arm in a splint."

"There's no need to worry about Gus," Will said. "I'm going to fly it myself this time."

Papa Joe swallowed, and his coffee bubbled back up on him, souring his mouth. "You?"

"Yes."

"But . . . but I thought . . ."

"Thought what? If something happens to me, you can't build another aeroplane?"

Papa Joe felt ice crystallize in his bloodstream. That was exactly what he thought, what everyone thought, had always thought. He said nothing.

Will leveled his eyes at him. "This has been on my mind for a long time. My notes, my calculations, my drawings— they're all here. This work can survive me. It should survive me. Nothing should depend on one man."

Papa Joe set down his coffee cup and folded his hands.

"Besides, I've seen the look in Gus's eyes," Will continued. "Even when we pulled him out with a broken arm, he had that same look in his eyes. Joy. Total joy. I can imagine what it's like up there—the wind and the speed and looking down on the trees. I imagine it exhilarates the soul like nothing else, but I want to know what it feels like, even if I have to die to do it."

Papa Joe was silent, eyes focused on his hands. *Another time, another skin*, he thought, *and the company of men who look at the world through the same lens*. Then he nodded slowly and murmured, "I understand." He unfolded his hands and held Will's face in them, felt his own eyes moisten. "I've never discouraged you in anything, and I won't start now."

"Thank you," Will said. "Now, let me show you what we've done this week."

Drawn by Will's enthusiasm, Papa Joe was halfway to the barn when he realized that he had left the shotgun leaning against the sideboard in the kitchen. "Will, go ahead," he said. "I'll be along directly." He turned and started back, quickening his pace as the rain increased. Before he reached the steps he saw a man with an umbrella walking up the path alongside the house.

Papa Joe took the steps two at a time and was back on the porch with the shotgun by the time the man reached the rear of the house. He held the gun casually but was ready to swing up the barrel and shoot if it became necessary. He remained on the porch, out of the rain.

The stranger was a small man with a neatly trimmed mustache and striped gray suit. A pipe was in his mouth. The bottoms of his trousers were soaked, as if he had been walking through wet underbrush. His hat was tilted back in a manner that suggested confusion. For a moment, eyes fixed on the shotgun, he said nothing. Then he spoke, his voice uneasy. "Excuse me, I'm looking for . . ." He consulted a paper from his inside pocket. "For a Mr. Driscoll."

Papa Joe tightened his grip on the shotgun. "He's not

here right now."

"I see." The man hesitated, chewing his pipe stem, and said, "Then perhaps I could speak to—" He glanced down at the paper again. "William Lockhart?" He raised his eyes to meet Papa Joe's. "Are you William Lockhart?"

Something about those eyes, Papa Joe thought. They were oddly familiar, though he was sure he had never seen this man before. "What do you want with William Lockhart?"

The man took out his pipe and made an audible effort to steady his voice. "I was sent here from Washington," he said. He knocked his pipe bowl out on the handle of his umbrella, then slid the pipe into his left coat pocket. "I wish you'd put that gun away. It makes me nervous. I mean you no harm. I've come to see about the flying machine."

Papa Joe neither raised nor lowered the shotgun. With right forefinger inside the trigger guard and left hand on the barrel, he continued to hold it across his midsection. "Flying machine?"

"Yes, the flying machine. I was sent here to inspect it."

Papa Joe swallowed and felt a lump in his chest where relief and doubt began to wrestle. Had the letter to McKinley brought this man to them? It was possible. He'd had the letter a whole day before his assassination. Surely he could have read it and set in motion a review of its claims. Still, Papa Joe was wary. "Does Washington do business on Sundays now? Especially during the President's funeral?"

The man clicked his tongue. "My good fellow, Washington conducts business *all* day, *every* day." He took a deep breath, then let it out as if it would carry his exasperation with it. "President McKinley was a great man. He'll be remembered with the likes of Washington and Lincoln. But we have a new President now, and the business of government must go forward."

"What part of the government do you represent?"

The response was immediate and suffused with importance. "The War Department, of course. I came here with the Secretary of War. Obviously, he is otherwise engaged today. We all leave tomorrow to escort the President's body back to Washington. I was asked to come here today on behalf of the Secretary—and the new President—to see this flying machine."

"How did you get here?"

"I already told you, I came with the Secretary—"

"No," Papa Joe said. "How did you get *here*, today?"

"I took a cab. It let me off out front." The man stuffed the paper back into his pocket and withdrew a watch from his waistcoat. "It'll be back for me in an hour. Less, now that you've wasted so much time jabbering at me. I knocked at the front door but got no answer so I came around back. Now, I'm about one minute away from walking out of here and never coming back. I will tell Mr. Root it was all a mistake."

"Mr. Root's name I know," Papa Joe said. "Yours I don't."

The man glared at him, an impertinent negro with a shotgun. "Briggs," he said finally. "Samuel Briggs."

Papa Joe chewed his own lip and studied Briggs for nearly half a minute before deciding he posed no danger. "Mr. Briggs, I'm Joe Lockhart, William's grandfather." He lowered the shotgun and came off the porch to shake Briggs's hand. "I'm sorry about all the questions."

"I understand," Briggs said, sounding relieved. He raised his umbrella as high as he could to permit Papa Joe beneath it. "With an invention like this you can't be too careful. Let me assure you, though, that Washington is interested. If it works."

"It works," Papa Joe said. He shifted the shotgun to his

left hand and held it beside his leg, the barrel pointing at the ground. "It flew over the Exposition the same day the President was shot and got written up in a newspaper, but nobody knew what it was."

"Really?" Briggs licked his lips and smiled. "Then I must see this machine."

"Let's go on up to the barn. I'll let Will show it to you. He can tell you how it works and how he came to invent it."

"William invented it?"

Papa Joe smiled at the amazement in Briggs's voice. "Yes."

The rain grew even heavier as they climbed the grassy rise to the barn. Inside, Briggs half closed his umbrella as if about to shake off the water, but the sight of the Blackbird arrested his movements. At first he was speechless, eyes blinking rapidly and lower lip quivering. Then he dropped his umbrella and pushed his homburg so far back on his head that it threatened to fall off. "This is really it?"

"Yes," Papa Joe said. He waved Will over from the workbench and introduced him to Briggs. "He's here from Washington . . . about the aeroplane. From the War Department."

Will stepped back, his mouth open. Presently, his disbelief was replaced by a smile, and he wiped his hands on a rag from his pocket. "Honored to meet you, sir." He shook Briggs's hand.

"The honor is mine, son," Briggs said. He gazed past Will toward the components leaning against the wall. "Those are the wings, I take it?"

"Yes, sir," Will said.

"And when they are attached to this machine, will it fly?"

"Yes, though there's more to it . . ."

"We have pictures," Papa Joe added, indicating the far wall.

Briggs moved across the barn, stepping over the items that littered the floor. "So you have," he said. He scrutinized the photographs mounted on the wall. His Adam's apple rose and fell with swallows of excitement. He turned back to Will and Papa Joe. Fighting breathlessness, he said. "I must see your designs, your equations. You must tell me how it works!"

"The engine turns those blades, which forces air beneath the wings," Will said. "The air gathers and lifts the wings. In the simplest sense, that's what makes it fly. But it's a much more complex process that keeps it in the air." He led Briggs to the workbench and flipped open one of his leather-covered notebooks. "Here, take a look at these diagrams."

Pleased, Papa Joe spent the next several minutes watching his grandson walk the War Department man through the genesis of his aeroplane. Will was patient and careful, moving from diagrams to calculations to photographs to indicate one aspect or another of the mechanics of flying. Always he came back to the Blackbird itself, to this connection or that cable, to the curve of the wings or the tooling of the propellers. He explained how the blades must spin in opposite directions and demonstrated with cupped hands, palms down, how the wings would lift the aeroplane. He described the damage sustained at the end of its last flight and the repairs and modifications he had made. Finally, Will said, "There's very little fuel in it right now, just enough for a half minute or so." He cranked the engine and pointed to the now chainless gear wheels that would drive the propellers.

Through it all Briggs had been quiet and reflective, nodding attentively, but wide-eyed like a schoolboy discovering his own sense of wonder when he least expected to do so. Papa Joe's one regret was that Captain Driscoll and Gus and everyone else who had worked so hard to bring the Blackbird into existence were not here to share this moment. He felt obligated to watch intently, to commit the nuances of Will's exchange with the government man to memory so he could describe them to the others later.

Now the engine coughed and sputtered as its fuel reservoir went dry. No one spoke as the high-pitched whine of the gear wheels diminished, then ceased. Papa Joe looked from Briggs to Will and back. Briggs appeared thoughtful, hands deep in his coat pockets. Will leaned slightly forward, as if waiting for questions.

"Remarkable," Briggs said at last. "Utterly remarkable."

"Now what?" Papa Joe said. "A demonstration?"

"Of course," Briggs said. "However, timing is critical."

"It will be ready to fly again in seven to ten days." Will looked at Papa Joe. "Maybe sooner if we find more help."

"It is unlikely that War Department officials will gather here for a demonstration in seven to ten days." Briggs shook his head. "With all due respect to Buffalo, the President was just killed here. I doubt the government desires to remain any longer than it must or to return any sooner than necessary." He looked almost apologetic. "Besides, affairs of state are complex. Attention will be elsewhere." He began to pace.

"There must be something," Papa Joe said. "You said Washington is interested. That's why they sent you."

Briggs stopped a few feet away and faced them. "Washington is interested. In fact, it's already spent a considerable sum on flying machine development. Yours is far from the only proposal under review. Our nation's leaders can't just drop everything and come here for an exhibit. Other inventors have brought their machines to Washington." His face began to soften. "Perhaps I can arrange to have you demonstrate yours there as well."

"You can do that?" Papa Joe asked.

"I can try," Briggs said. "I have some discretion in the discharge of my duties."

Will wrinkled his brow. "That would involve great expense. Transportation of machinery and men, lodgings, a test site . . ."

Briggs smiled. "The government will pay for it, all of it."

"For a machine you haven't yet seen fly?" Papa Joe felt the stirrings of a new uneasiness. "You have that much discretion?"

"Actually, no," Briggs said. "But I may have a way." He took a deep breath and tried to fix them both with his eyes. "I will need to take your notebooks with me."

"What?" Will stiffened, as if he had been slapped.

Perhaps it was Briggs's eyes or the tone of his voice when he repeated his request, but something went cold in Papa Joe, even as Will shook his head and began to explain the role his notebooks played in reassembly. The coldness sat in the middle of Papa Joe's belly, a living thing with tendrils of ice that curled around his innards and slithered up his spine, that froze his heart in fearful certainty. The man's eyes held his half a clockstroke longer than they should have, and he knew he had seen them before. Where or when he could not say, but that he had done so meant Briggs had not come to town with Elihu Root. He was not the man he claimed to be.

Briggs was the enemy—and knew he'd been recognized as such.

Papa Joe tried to swing the shotgun up as Briggs

snatched a hand from a side pocket. Fumbling to get his finger inside the trigger guard, he saw the pistol in the man's right hand, saw Briggs crouching, saw the halo of fire envelop the cylinder. The first bullet smacked into his left shoulder, his mind embracing the memory of his previously having been shot there before it registered the sound and the pain; the second cracked his left collarbone. He heard Will scream, "Papa!" in a voice too distant to belong to someone nearby. Twitching on his back, he listened to the third and fourth shots but did not feel them.

Until he heard Will fall beside him.

His upper chest and shoulder on fire, Papa Joe tried to work his lips, to call Will, but did not know whether he could make a sound. His eyes, blinking and wet, looked straight up, at the rafters and the windows. He was keenly aware of the rain on the roof, the stubbornness of his own heart, his grandson's stillness. Footsteps drew near, and he felt a wave of molten lead roll through his arm as the shotgun was torn from his left hand. He heard it clatter to the packed earth floor. Then a shadow loomed over him, and through his tears Briggs came into view, smoking pistol still in hand.

"I have to take the notebooks," he said. "And the pictures. That's the only way I'll get my job back. When I show these to the Old Man, whoever sent that wire discharging me is going to be very sorry. We'll see who's useless then."

Papa Joe did not understand, could not understand.

Briggs returned the gun to his side pocket and produced a thin metal flask from an inside breast pocket. He held it so Papa Joe could see it. "This time the fire will be complete."

This time Papa Joe understood and felt the fingers of his right hand close into a fist so tight he thought his bones would crack. But he could move nothing else, not yet. He heard Briggs moving about, gathering papers. He listened to the sound of a single shoe sweeping straw into piles. He heard the snaps of blankets unfurled and in his mind's eye saw them draped over the piles of straw. Next came the belch of the flask vomiting up whatever it contained.

The searing on his left side had begun to follow the rhythm of his heart. He started to feel again. His legs, he knew, were at odd angles, his knees aware of their arthritis. He realized also that he was lying atop something which pressed hard into his backbone. It took him a moment to understand what it was, a moment he spent straining to hear Will, praying for the sound of pained movement or labored breathing. But he heard nothing. A rancid bubble of hatred formed in his throat. He struggled to keep himself still, to harness the howl gathering in his soul. Tears trickled down into his ears. The fingers of his right hand uncoiled.

Then he heard the scrape of a lone match, followed by the sudden inhalation of a small fire determined to feed quickly, and he was afraid.

Briggs appeared over him again, Will's notebooks in his arms. He looked down at him once, then stepped over him on his way to the door.

No, Papa Joe thought. *No!* Then he heard Briggs stop and pivot and mutter a curse. Shoes scraped this way and that and came near him at last.

"You landed on my umbrella," Briggs said. "How in the hell I am supposed to keep these papers dry in all this rain?"

Still, Papa Joe thought. *Don't bat an eye.* He remembered another stillness, another time of blood, a night fifty years earlier. *Don't bat an eye.* He had believed then that he would die, that he would stand before God with warm blood on his hands and impenitence in his heart. Now the thought of doing so kept him motionless and tensed, ready for what must come next.

Briggs kicked him.

He groaned but lay still. *Still, however much pain . . .*

Kicked him again.

As if satisfied Papa Joe was near enough dead, Briggs knelt beside him and set down the bundle of notebooks. He worked his hands under Papa Joe's burning shoulder, tried to roll him just enough to his right to free the umbrella.

Still. Don't breathe.

"My God, you're a big buck," Briggs said, teeth squeaking as he heaved.

Then Papa Joe's shoulder was high enough for the umbrella to be pulled free. Briggs snatched it up with one hand and let him fall backward.

Rolling back into place, Papa Joe twisted just enough to shoot his right arm out toward the smaller man's throat. Agony screamed through his left shoulder, his left side, as he rocked onto them. But he clenched his teeth against it in the hope that relief would come the instant he closed his hand around something vital. He missed the neck, clamping instead onto the lower jaw and squeezing the cheeks so hard he could feel Briggs's teeth cutting into them.

Surprised, Briggs dropped the umbrella and tried to speak as he clawed at the tightening hand, but his tongue, trapped between cheeks and teeth, felt to Papa Joe like a desperate snake caught in a vise. Briggs swatted and scratched but failed to dislodge his grip as Papa Joe leaned into him even more. Papa Joe worked his last two fingers down far enough to curl into Briggs's Adam's apple. Next he slid his thumb down and continued to press. Then his entire hand, his massive hand, sculpted by years of plantation labor and half a century of blacksmithing and strengthened by the memory of having once before crushed a gullet, was around his enemy's throat.

He tightened his grasp, tried to make a fist with Briggs's skinny neck in it, felt resistant muscle giving way, cartilage beginning to crack.

Papa Joe's pain sharpened as the man's hands scrabbled for something to hold on to, perhaps for the gun in his pocket. He did not know whether Briggs could reach the gun and did not care. Samuel Briggs, or whatever his name was, would die today, as Cobb Sparks and the original Joseph Lockhart had died fifty years before, at the hands of an adversary made stronger by the theft of his humanhood. Even if he managed to shoot Papa Joe again, he would die kicking and gurgling and shedding bloody tears. He would die at the hands of a black man who would never die quietly himself.

Papa Joe hissed and gave a final squeeze, and it was over.

He released the limp Briggs, and suddenly shivering, slumped onto his back. His brain began to reel. The space behind his eyes throbbed. His breathing grew shallow. He heard the fire crackling louder, saw it licking its way toward the top of one wall. He knew he must move, must pitch onto his good side and somehow get hold of Will and crawl toward the door. And soon, for the fire would burn fast and clean. But he needed a moment to catch his breath, to collect his strength, to feel warm again. *Just a moment, Lord.*

Just a moment, Will. Just a moment. Then I will come to you, son, and help you out of this place. I promise. We will lie for a time in the cleansing wash of the rain and begin our healing beneath God's open sky. Then, with whatever life I have left, I will come back inside and gather your papers. You will build another Blackbird, and all who love you will help. You and Gus will take turns flying it. You will pluck God's diamonds out of the sky and the world will know that when the Lockharts walked through it they were as worthy as any men alive.

But first, son, I need a moment . . . just . . . one . . . mo—

Twenty-One

Like everyone else in the packed courtroom, Captain Driscoll wanted justice, and blood.

He had been there the morning of Monday September 23 for the reading of the charge and jury selection. He had been seated in the same corner the next afternoon, when the jury foreman raised a slip of paper and read, "Guilty of murder in the first degree." Today, Thursday, he was back again for the afternoon sentencing, only this time he had been unable to reach a seat, despite his early arrival. He stood in the crush of spectators on one side, beneath a tall arched window that admitted gray autumn light. He stood between two men in dark clothing—one beardless, the other with whiskers down to his waistcoat—and behind a fat man in a tweed suit. And he waited.

Like the crowd, Captain Driscoll was restless as District Attorney Penney questioned Leon Czolgosz about his background, education, and religious upbringing. No one gave a damn whether his parents were living or dead, whether he drank too much or had a criminal history. No one cared about his statement to the court. He had said what anyone would have predicted, that he acted alone, that neither his family nor anyone else had a part in his crime.

None of that mattered to Driscoll, for the first time he saw Czolgosz in court he knew with a certainty newspaper photographs could not give that this was the man he had twice seen trying to get close to the President. That he had managed eventually to do so filled Driscoll with a mixture of anger and shame, the latter because he had failed to intervene. If he had, McKinley would still be alive, as would Joseph and Will, and the Blackbird would be the future of the nation instead of a pile of incinerated wood and metal where his barn had stood. Whoever he had been, the man whose charred remains had been found in the rubble along with Joseph and Will would have had no chance to destroy the aeroplane once the President had seen it.

But the bitterest irony had come in the early evening hours, after the rain had stopped and the fire had burned itself out. Police had removed the bodies. Daniel had taken a badly shaken Gus to Reverend Banks. More than a week would pass before anyone officially tried to piece together what had happened, but Driscoll *knew*. Their enemy had found them. Jonas's killer had come back to finish his destruction. Seated on his front porch and starting his third glass of whiskey, he found himself wondering who the man had been and how he had convinced Joseph to let him get so close. Presently, he heard hoofbeats and the creaking of chassis springs and was surprised to see an open carriage, side lights flickering, coming up his path. His surprise tripled when the smartly dressed passenger proved to be William Loeb, personal secretary to President Roosevelt.

He had come, he said, about the flying machine.

Driscoll envisioned the unrecognizable mass peeking through the fallen timber out back and shook his head without speaking. Then he buried his face in his hands and wept. He wept for the dead, all of them, and for those who must move through their vacated spaces. He wept for a woman whose absence still chilled his bed, for a friend who would never fish beside him again and a friend who would never join him with a pole the first time, for a boy who died believing in his friend and an imagination stolen from a world in desperate need of it. He wept for a gentle leader whose celebration of prosperity would ever be clouded by his martyrdom. Most of all he wept for himself, for he had tried to shape the future and failed, had stood on the threshold of this new century with men bold enough to infect others with a glimpse of tomorrow. But all their visions had succumbed to bullets and fire.

Czolgosz, then, would always be more than the man who shot McKinley. For the rest of his life Driscoll would remember him as he did the nameless assassin in his barn, as a wanton killer of dreams. Such men belonged in hell and now he waited to see this one consigned to its flames.

Finally, the assassin's identity and fitness for sentencing established to the satisfaction of the court, Justice White took less than a minute and spent no emotion in passing sentence:

"Czolgosz, in taking the life of our beloved President, you committed a crime which shocked and outraged the moral sense of the civilized world. You have confessed your guilt, and, after learning all that can at this time be learned of the facts and circumstances of the case, twelve good men have pronounced your confession true and have found you guilty of murder in the first degree. You declare, according to the testimony of credible witnesses, that no other person aided or abetted you in the commission of this terrible act. God grant it may be so. The penalty of the crime of which you stand convicted is fixed by statute, and it now becomes my duty to pronounce its judgment against you. The sentence of the court is that in the week beginning on October 28, 1901, at the place, in the manner, and by the means prescribed by law you suffer the punishment of death."

Were it not blasphemous, Captain Driscoll would have

prayed that God have no mercy on his soul.

*　　*　　*

In a narrow corner room off the Ascension sanctuary, Pearl watched her father's face for any indication that he might change his mind about leaving. But he wouldn't look at her. Instead he gazed out the half-open door at her Uncle Portius, in gray street clothes instead of cassock and collar, as he stood in his pulpit to address the unusual Friday night gathering.

Pearl moved to the door and looked out upon a sea of colored faces. There was barely standing room left.

"The man is a hero, a true-to-life hero." Reverend Banks paused to let his words sink in. "He was next in line behind the assassin and threw himself upon Czolgosz before that reprobate could fire a third shot, which may have struck and killed someone in addition to the President." He patted his brow and nose with a white handkerchief. "Ben Parker is a hero who risked his life to bring down a criminal, yet the only colored man called to testify at the trial was the janitor who was on the other side of the room. Now the newspapers are saying Ben lied, that he wasn't there at all. One of the soldiers says there were *no* negroes in the Temple of Music when President McKinley was shot, apparently not even the janitor called to the witness stand . . ."

Bitter laughter rippled through the assembly.

"My wife, Mother Essie, was there with her brother Ben, and my niece was there with her father, and poor Brother Lockhart—" His voice broke, and he paused a few seconds. "Brother Lockhart was there, may the Lord keep him safe and warm in his final rest. At least three other negroes and this soldier saw none. Are we wisps of air, lost to the eye? Does light stream through us as it does through glass? Are we invisible except when we bend our backs in labor? No, no, and no. We must stand and be seen, as Ben stood and was seen. Have they forgotten, all who watched his struggle with the assassin? Who took mementoes from his person? Ben is a true American, a first among equals. We must tell the world the truth, scream it if necessary . . ."

Pearl's father looked crestfallen when he turned to her. "I can't stay," he said softly, "not when they're calling me a liar, when they want me to be in one of their freak shows." He pulled away from the door and sagged against a wall. "Probably want me to share the stage with Esau, to prove he's *our* missing link and not theirs." His eyes glistened.

"Give Uncle Portius a chance," Pearl said. She pushed the door nearly closed and put a hand on her father's arm. "That's why he's having this meeting, why the other ministers and their congregations have come out for it. Everybody is here because of you, to stand behind you because of what you did. You *are* a hero and nobody will let history forget it. A hundred years from now, when they tell the story of the assassination, Big Jim Parker will be a part of it."

"Big Jim." He grinned and shook his head. "A hundred years is a long time to carry a name my mama didn't give me."

"Papa—"

"It's all right, child." He stood up straight, wiped his eyes, and ran a hand over his hair. "I'll go out there and take a bow when Portius calls me, but I still have to go. Mr. Ross, who puts out the colored magazines—he wants me to be a traveling agent selling his new gazetteer. Don't mean I won't be back, it just means I got to go for now. Do you understand?"

"Yes," she said, in a small voice. What she understood was that her father was going out of her world again, seeking solace once more in another place, another life. Her insides twisted.

"Portius knows I have to go," her father said. "Essie too. They already promised to look after the money I'm leaving you."

Pearl swallowed and said nothing. She didn't want his money. She wanted him.

"It's almost three thousand, from donations," he said. "I figure you and Gus will need it when you get married."

Pearl felt her cheeks grow warm. "What makes you think I'm going to marry Gus?"

Her father smiled. "He wants you. He may be a little fella but he's got the heart of a lion, and when a lion wants something bad enough, he usually gets it." Her father's face grew serious, his eyes holding hers. "And right now he needs you, Pearl. His whole family's gone. He needs to belong to somebody. He needs to belong to somebody before he gets too scared to try." He drew her to him and held her for nearly a minute. "You'll marry him," he whispered. "I know you will. Tall as you are and short as he is, your children'll be somewhere in between." He chuckled. "At least nobody's gonna call my grandson Big Jim."

Pearl smiled, even as tears filled her eyes.

*   *   *

From the Chronicles of Augustus Lockhart:
Sunday November 10

Mac is mine now. Every day I feed him, brush him, and muck out his stall. Several times a week I hitch him to the stanhope and take him out for a stretch. Sometimes I simply slip on his bridle and take hold of the reins and walk beside him for a block or so down Broadway. However soothing I try to make my voice, however gently I pat the powerful cords in his thick neck, he seems unconvinced of my ownership. In those moments when I am caught in the glare of one of his great eyes, I cannot shake the belief that I am being tolerated in my grandfather's absence, as if Mac is waiting patiently for his return. The more time that passes without Papa Joe saying familiar things or stroking him with familiar rhythms, the more wistfulness I sense in that old horse. Maybe all that is my imagination. Perhaps his eye is just a black mirror in which I see my own sadness, my own loneliness.

To the world Papa Joe and Will were working on the Driscoll estate when they were surprised and shot by a thief that Papa Joe managed to kill before he died. Neither the police nor newspaper men questioned the mangled remains of the flying machine, accepting the Captain's statement that the whole mess was farm machinery. The Blackbird, then, remains a secret—for all the good secrecy has done anyone.

I must not be bitter. Bitterness makes me feel ungrateful for the kindness of my friends . . .

A few weeks after my grandfather and my brother were laid to rest in the churchyard, visits from my friends began to lessen. Danny has gone to work for his father's company, and Captain Driscoll has promised me a job—as a chronicler of his business affairs and a recorder of documents. I am to report as soon as I have settled matters pertaining to the blacksmith shop, which I must sell. Reverend and Mrs. Banks still stop over one evening a week and Sunday afternoon to bring me food and church news. I look forward to Sundays especially, because Pearl comes with them.

Before my splint and wrappings were removed, she offered to continue transcribing my chronicle but I could see no point then. Later, with my arm healed, I could not bring myself to open this notebook. Sleep eluded me most nights—until the small hours before dawn, when sheer exhaustion overwhelmed the memory of finding Papa Joe and Will in the smoldering ruins of the barn. For a long time I could barely bring myself to rise from my bed, let alone put words to paper in some attempt to make sense out of all that happened.

Lately, however, the house and shop have seemed cavernous, full of unsettling sounds and uncertain motions. Some nights it feels as though someone is rambling about out front, and I picture my grandfather at his anvil or working his bellows, exercising the freedom that he cherished so deeply. Sometimes I see Will, peering into the wind shaft in which he tested his miniatures or hunched over his drawing table to refine his designs. I know it is the wind that tricks me, that stirs loose boards or rattles chains and ironwork suspended from pegs, that fills my head with longed for images of those I mourn. Or are better memories trying to push aside the blackened flesh that awaits me each night on the inside of my eyelids? Whatever the reason, it sometimes seems my dead family will not permit me to withdraw from the labors of the past year. Thus, it is with a sense of duty that I now take up the pen, lest all of Will's work be lost and the passion for freedom that inspired it crumble into dust along with him and Papa Joe.

I know what I must do.

Earlier today, after church, I asked Reverend Banks if Pearl might accompany me for a ride. Because I had not been to Ascension since the funeral, I half-expected him to deny my request and to chide me for my lapse of faith, as he sometimes does on his Sunday visits. But the sight of me seemed to bring a heaviness into his eyes, and he embraced me as a father would a prodigal son. For a time neither of us spoke. Then he said, "I'm so happy to see you getting out, Gus."

Pearl and I were both silent for much of the long ride, sharing a lap blanket against the November chill. Mac's hooves clattered along on asphalt and cobblestones, his shoes clanging every now and then on a section of trolley track. Only when we neared the grounds of the now closed Exposition did Pearl ask our destination. I could not answer at once. I steered Mac over to the curb. When we reached the fence near the West Amherst gate I reined him to a stop so we could gaze past the fence at the quiet Rainbow City.

The flagpoles were bare. The buildings had long since begun to fade, the pastel walls to chip and crack. Some of the windows were broken. Many fixtures and decorations were missing, the result of a scramble for souvenirs in the closing days of the fair a week or so ago. Large work wagons were scattered here and there. Come Monday work crews will continue the dismantling they began three or four days ago. The buildings will be emptied, their contents and adornments sold off to defray the cost of the Exposition, already greater than expected. By spring the halls and pavilions will be gone, the canals filled, the gardens plowed under, and the walkways and fountains torn up. Eventually the land will be sold and put to other uses.

Since Leon Czolgosz's electrocution at Auburn Prison nearly two weeks ago, there has been talk of keeping the Temple of Music as a monument to President McKinley. I doubt that will come to pass. It was made with temporary materials. Its first winter would likely be its last. Silent witness to history, the Rainbow City—all of it—will come down within seven or eight months, and the city that surrounds it will advance through this new century to its intended purpose.

As will we to ours.

Pearl and I stared at the Exposition for a long while before I found the words. I began by telling her that for a time it had been our century—the colored century, as Papa Joe put it. For a time it seemed we might change the lot of our race by giving the world its most desired ancient dream. Together we were a bold blackbird soaring over a resplendent rainbow, the first men to inherit the sky from the balloonists and gliderists.

Regardless of whether history noticed, together we had tried and succeeded. Together we could succeed once more, at anything.

Pearl studied me for a long moment, a look I could not read passing over her face. "You want to build another Blackbird," she said finally. Her words lacked the hesitancy of a question. "You want to fly again."

"Yes," I answered. I could not explain it to her then, but flying has made of me something new, something different. It has filled me with a confidence I previously lacked, a sense of purpose it would have taken me a lifetime to find elsewhere. I watched my brother closely and listened carefully. I even have a few of his drawings and some of his notes. With time and patience I believe I can build another Blackbird. With so many others at work on aeroplanes, this new one will likely not be the first in the air. Nevertheless, it will still be a fine achievement, a symbol of negro diligence and a tribute to Will and Papa Joe and Andrew. "I want to make a new Blackbird," I said. "But there's something I must do first, even if I never fly again."

Then I told her that I want to write a book about my brother and his aeroplane. If the Blackbird cannot fly, at least its story can be told. Who better to tell it than the one who was there to chronicle it? Who better to explain it than the first man to fly, although he will never be first in the eyes of the world? The book might have to remain hidden, passed down from parent to child for a hundred years before it sees the light of day. Even then it might never come out or will likely never be believed. But the book will be known to a family, a strong American family, who will read it again and again, who will believe in it and use its principles of industry and imagination as the guiding forces in their lives. Our descendants will be Lockharts and will face obstacles with what Papa Joe liked to call the Lockhart will to overcome.

"There is no better legacy we can give our children and grandchildren," I said. Holding Pearl's eyes with my own, I waited for her to question my inclusion of her as the matriarch of unborn Lockharts. She said nothing. She simply smiled, and deep in my heart I knew that one day, together, we would find our way back to the sky.

Inherit the Sky—An Epilogue

When once you have tasted flight, you will forever walk the earth with your eyes turned skyward—for there you have been, and there you will always long to return.

–Leonardo da Vinci

May, Present Day

Half seated on the front bumper of her mother's old silver Saturn, Denise Lockhart gazed across the water at the neon pulse of Fort Erie, Ontario.

It was a warm night. The river made a soft sucking sound as it lapped against steel pilings beneath the concrete riverwalk. Less than a mile to the left, arching over the river, the bridge to Canada was illuminated by moving headlights and blossoms of mercury vapor atop steel stems. A hundred yards to the right two men stood at the walkway railing, holding fishing poles out over the swift black water. Seven or eight other cars were scattered throughout the gravel parking lot, their windows steamed. Overhead, in the absence of clouds, there were stars.

Forearms resting on her knees, Denise looked up at the stars and tried to remember how old she had been when she first noticed that their positions changed over time. Seven, maybe eight, even before the Christmas her parents gave her the first of several telescopes. She remembered how her father would drive her away from the glare of the city two or three nights a month, often down here to the foot of West Ferry Street, sometimes south of Buffalo into the country, so she could open her tripod to gaze up at God's diamonds, which had been the family name for stars as far back as she could recall. There had been fewer lights in the Canadian village across the river then, and more stars had been visible. She remembered studying their names in her first field guide to the night sky.

She had been drawn to the daytime sky as well. When she was ten, her parents took her older brothers and her to California to visit their Uncle Carl. Somehow, her father had arranged for all three children to visit the cockpit of the jet that carried them. She was careful to touch nothing but was not shy about pointing and asking questions of the pilot and co-pilot. They indulged her and smiled as they directed their answers to her brothers. Clearly, they considered her curiosity a waste of time. What good would it do a little black girl to ponder such things as altimeter, airspeed indicator, VOR receiver, and engine pressure ratio? She smiled back at them, and committed everything they said to memory.

A science teacher at her inner city high school had asked why she was determined to take advanced placement physics in her junior year. "Aeronautical engineering is highly competitive," he said. "With your height and your looks and that honey-brown skin you stand a better chance of becoming a model." She said, without hesitation, "The sky's in my blood." But she couldn't tell Mr. Gill about the Book, her great-grandfather's handwritten account of the first airplane to make sustained flights. She had learned that lesson years before in Sunday school, when Mrs. Bowden took her to Reverend

Davis for lying after she told Ricky Moses her great-grandpa Gus was the first man to fly. Afterward, her father explained that the Book was a family secret. There were only six copies—the handwritten original and first typed copy, both sealed in plastic and kept in her family's fireproof safe, and four photocopies of the typescript, each bound and in the possession her grandfather's four children. The story was not meant to be shared with anyone outside, except by action. "Gus gave us the Book so we would know all things were possible," her father said, pulling her onto his lap before bed that night. "He didn't want us to spend all our time convincing other people he flew. He wanted to show us that we could fly ourselves."

And fly the Lockharts did.

Both her brothers were fliers, Junior for the Air Force and Linc for the Navy. Her father James had flown F-111 missions in Vietnam, and his brother Carl had served on a helicopter gunship. Uncle Carl's son Thaddeus was a surgeon with the Air Force School of Aerospace Medicine, his daughter Carla the proprietor of her own flying school in Texas. Denise's cousin Parker Flint, a year her senior and the oldest of Aunt Essie's six children, worked as an aerial firefighter somewhere out west. Denise herself held a doctorate in astrophysics, though she had got her private pilot's license while still an undergraduate.

Neither of her aunts nor any of her remaining seven cousins was in any way attached to the aerospace industry. Four cousins were in graduate school, one in English literature, one in biochemistry, and two in elementary education. Jay was an arts administrator, Pearl Ann a fledgling lawyer. Marisa would finish high school with honors next month. Grandpa Willy Joe, himself a Tuskegee Airman, and Great-grandpa Gus, the only African-American in the Lafayette Escadrille killed in action in

World War I, would have been proud of them all.

And so would Papa Joe. According to Gus's Book, he had been a runaway slave and had stood somewhere near this very place . . .

A car crunched gravel and stopped in the space to the right of hers—a Ford Escape hybrid, she knew without looking. The ignition died and the door opened.

"Thought I'd find you here, Baby Girl."

Denise smiled at the sound of her father's deep voice and his pet name for her. To her brothers and friends she had always been Nisey, lanky girl jock and wide-eyed honor student. Most of her professors had insisted on Ms. before her surname. Now her colleagues called her Dr. Lockhart. But to James Lockhart, Sr., she would always be Baby Girl, the stick-thin infant whose rare viral pneumonia had moved him to tears and prayers. She looked over her shoulder and saw his dark face and salty beard awash in the glow of the dome light. He grinned at her and climbed out of his Escape. He sat beside her on the front bumper of the Saturn. Earlier this evening, watching him, she had wondered whether he was putting on weight. Now she was unsure. Her father was a big man who carried himself well; the car barely moved.

"You cut out on your own party," he said. "Your aunts and uncles and cousins came from all over the country for this, and Junie and Linc got special leave."

"I know," she said. "But it was getting kind of crowded in there. I started feeling kind of overwhelmed and needed some air." She shoved her hands into the pockets of her black nylon jacket. "Guess I never expected a surprise party—or a family reunion in May."

"Well, it is a special occasion . . ." Then he fell silent, as if feeling her embarrassment at all the attention, and patted the knee of her jeans. "All the airport hopscotching you had to do today to get home, I'd have figured you were too tired to come such a long way for air."

"You know why I'm here," she said and felt him nod beside her.

"Yeah, I know. I used to bring you down here, remember." He inhaled deeply. "All three of you. Now you're here for the same reason I started coming as a boy. Your brothers never much cared for this part of our family history. Junie was knee-high to a duck when he started asking me about the cars with their windows all fogged up." Chuckling, he turned to her. "But this place always meant something to you. You were always as haunted by it as I was."

"I'm drawn to this spot whenever I come back to town," she said. "It's not the best place to see Canada or study the stars or even to fish—and I never came here to make out because I just knew you'd catch me."

Her father chuckled. "Caught Junie here once, trying to make me a grandpa, but that's between you and me. I never told your mother."

"Junie told me about it years ago. He said you were really pissed."

"Oh yeah, but not because of the sex . . ."

"Because of the sacrilege," Denise said. "This ground feels sacred. It's important to the Lockharts. It's almost a point of convergence for the ancient elements—where earth, air, fire, and water meet. It's like these stars influenced our destiny."

Her father let out a whistle. "All the time and money it took to make her an astrophysicist and she really believes in alchemy and astrology."

"No, silly." She nudged him with an elbow and began to point. "There's Cygnus and Draco and that W is Cassiopeia, and there, Lacerta the Lizard. They're stars, some of them already dead and their light just reaching us. They don't influence our lives and loves and real estate ventures, at least not the way the astrology books say. But they might have an effect on an individual, and his choice might influence so many other lives."

"Papa Joe," her father said.

"Yes, Papa Joe. According to Gus, he got to this spot and was ready to cross into Canada but didn't go. Why not? I mean, there had to be a bounty on him. They could send him back from any place in the union, right? Those folks were serious about slavery and racial supremacy. They said the Bible wanted slaves to be submissive so it must be mental illness that made them run away—and the bastards even came up with a name for it, *drapetomania*."

Her father threw back his head and laughed. "Damned if you do, damned if you don't. What was that other disease, the one that afflicted free blacks?"

"*Dysaethesia aethiopica*—shiftlessness from mental lethargy," Denise said. "One craziness after another. So why would Papa Joe take a chance with somebody else's birth papers? Why not just cross the river and make a life for yourself away from all these made-up insanities, where slave hunters couldn't lay a hand on you? I've always wondered about that."

"Gus says he stayed for love."

She shook her head, shook out the residues of her own failed relationships—the men who'd felt threatened by her education and her dreams. Long before her thirtieth-seventh birthday, last August, she had decided that being alone with a dream was far better than being with a dreamless man.

"We've both read Gus and we both know he was a romantic," Denise said finally. "There had to be something else, something Gus didn't know and Papa Joe wouldn't tell. Who was the real Joseph Lockhart and how did Papa Joe get his identity? I mean, those yellow papers Gus kept in the Bible, they had to be important with bounty hunters looking for runaways. I can't imagine this man just gave them up and rode off into the sunset. And why all the talk about the stars being God's diamonds? Papa Joe probably followed Polaris like a lot of runaways, but I've never understood the diamond thing. I imagine he must have stood here looking at the water and the fires in the village on the other side, then maybe looking up at the stars and seeing something that made him stay. His choice made the rest of us possible."

"Choice is the point of freedom," her father said. "We don't know what his name was before he got here because he decided not to be that man anymore. He *chose* to be Joseph, somebody else. He was the first link in the Lockhart chain. We begin right here."

"Will and the Blackbird," Denise said. "Gus and the Book. As for *le Petit Lion*, if Gus hadn't crashed his Spad during a recon flight, would your father have gone down to Tuskegee when he got the chance? If he had never learned of his great-grandfather's decision not to go to Canada, would he have come back here? What about you and Uncle Carl? Who and what we are, or ever will be, may pivot on what one runaway slave saw in the night sky. Can you imagine? The whole idea is just so . . ." She sucked her teeth, unable to find the right word to complete her thought.

"It bothers you," her father said. "Not knowing. Even with all we do know—and we know a lot more than most black folks—it still bugs me that so much about us is lost."

"Always knew I came by this curiosity honestly," she said, squeezing his hand. "You know, I've calculated what stars and planets were where around the time he was supposed to cross. There were no phenomena then, no comets or meteor showers—just stars, a night like this."

"Sometimes a night like this is all you need to make you think about your place in the universe."

Denise smiled. "I wonder what would have become of us if he had gone to Canada."

For a time neither of them said anything.

Then her father slid an arm around her shoulders. "Whatever happened to make him stay, I know one thing for sure."

"What's that?"

"Canada doesn't have a NASA branch office, and tonight we would not be celebrating somebody's acceptance into the astronaut training program."

Denise felt herself flush.

He pulled her to him and kissed her forehead. "Proud of you, sugar. Proud as I can be."

Her eyes filled. "Thanks, Daddy."

"Now, why don't you leave all this philosophical speculation for another night?" He drew a finger along her right temple and pushed one of her short curls back into place. "The river and the village and all those stars will be here tomorrow and every night for a long time." He sighed. "And so will Papa Joe. This is his spot." He stood and stretched. "So come on back to the house before the cake and ice cream are all gone and everybody starts heading back to their motels." He hovered over her a moment, then tapped her shoulder. "Real ice cream, too, not that freeze-dried crap they force-feed mission specialists. What's it called, Heavenly Hubble Hash?"

She laughed, wiping her eyes. "All right," she said. After a moment she got to her feet.

Her father moved to his car and opened the door. "God's

diamonds." He took a final look skyward. "They must have been beautiful hanging there in the heavens like that, without all the ambient light we have today. Maybe Papa Joe was just too breathless to move." He got behind the wheel.

Denise opened the door of the Saturn as the Escape hybrid purred to life. With one foot inside and listening to her father back away through the gravel, she paused to take her own last look at the stars and the lights and the water. Presently, she pictured the river as it must have looked a century and a half before—no riverwalk, just a sloping muddy bank, rushing water beneath the moon and stars. *This is his spot.* She imagined a man there at the edge, a young man—still a boy, really—who had braved a fearful journey alone and perhaps now waited for signal fires to tell him it was safe to cross. By all accounts he was a giant of a man, dark and powerful. She imagined him at the river's edge, staring northwest at freedom as water soaked into his boots and the sharp breeze cut through the rough shirt taut against the muscles of his shoulders and back. God, Papa Joe must have been beautiful! She imagined him turning for a farewell look at the country of his birth and his bondage, turning to see what he was leaving behind.

They were the deepest, wisest eyes I have ever seen, and they glittered like diamonds in the night sky, Gus had written. *My grandfather was a dreamer, you see, a man who gazed into the future as easily as most men look back at the past.*

Then, in her mind, his gaze found hers and they were looking at each other across nearly sixteen decades. There were no photographs of Papa Joe, but the face in her vision was his. She was sure of it, as if genetic memory were giving her this privileged glimpse into the past. It was a broad and determined face, eyes alight with intelligence and the fever of hope. Perhaps in her eyes he saw the future he could not abandon, unformed dreams that would come to pass only if he stood his ground as a man.

And he was in the perfect place to dream—America, where some dream of riches, others dream of freedom, and a select few dream of doing wondrous things.

Denise shook her head but the image persisted. Blinking, she saw him nod at her and smile. The smile widened, imprinting itself on her memory before he turned away. Smiling back, she slid into the Saturn and cranked it. She left him there at the water, gazing up at the diamonds she longed to explore, earthbound in body and eye, yet drawn to the celestial ballet by something greater than himself. Silently, she thanked God for Papa Joe and prayed that in this next phase of her life she would honor his spirit by doing wondrous things. Then she started for home, hoping there was still cake left—and real ice cream.

Historical Notes:

Although some of the people and events portrayed are historical, this is a novel. I have taken storyteller's license with some details of the Pan-American Exposition and turn of the century Buffalo: The city had two black churches, not three, and the meeting in support of James Benjamin Parker took place on September 27, 1901 at the Vine Street A.M.E. There was no Buckett's Brigade or Pan-American Doll Works. The pickaninny float came earlier in the parade than depicted here. The undeveloped land north of the Exposition is larger and hillier in the novel than it was in reality. While the Ellicott Square was indeed the world's largest office building, and the Vitascope Hall in its basement the world's first dedicated cinema, the meeting Captain Driscoll describes as having been held there is entirely fictitious.

Some of the African-Americans who tried to bring an exhibit to the Exposition—like Mary Talbert and Reverend J. Edward Nash—were later part of the 1905 Niagara Movement that led to the founding of the NAACP. Despite an Internet rumor to the contrary, Mason, publisher, and tobacconist James Ross was not my ancestor. Apart from a mother in Georgia, according to *Leslie's Illustrated Weekly*, James Parker had no relatives. *Aeroplane* and *negro* (lowercase N) were spellings in use at the time. Eugene Jacques Bullard of France's Lafayette Escadrille was the only black pilot of WWI.

The Edison Exposition films attribute camera work to Edwin S. Porter (who directed the 1903 action hit *The Great Train Robbery*) and James H. White. The species of the bird that landed on the window sill during Theodore Roosevelt's inauguration was not reported.

I trust that liberties taken will be viewed as narrative conveniences and not an attempt to rewrite history, for which I have a deep fondness and the greatest respect.

Gary Earl Ross

Suggested Reading:

Ault, Phillip H. *By the Seat of Their Pants: The Story of Early
    Aviation.* New York : Dodd, Mead, 1978.

Balibar, Francoise, and Jean-Pierre Maury. *How Things Fly.*
    New York: Barron, 1987.

Belfer, Lauren. *City of Light.* New York: Dial Press/Random
    House, 1999.

Bilstein, Roger E. *Flight in America 1900-1983: From the
    Wrights to the Astronauts.* Baltimore: Johns Hopkins
    University Press, 1984.

Brooks-Bertram, Peggy, Barbara Seals Nevergold, and Lisa C.
    Francescone. *Uncrowned Queens, Volume 1: African
    American Women Community Builders in Western New
    York.* Buffalo: Uncrowned Queens, 2002.

Dale, Henry. *Early Flying Machines.* New York: Oxford
    University Press, 1994.

Dwiggins, Don. *Famous flyers and the Ships They Flew.* New
    York: Grosset & Dunlap 1969.

Fox, Austin M. *Symbol and Show: The Pan-American Exposition
    of 1901.* Buffalo: Western New York Wares, 1987.

Freedman, Russell. *The Wright Brothers: How They Invented the
    Airplane.* New York: Holiday House, 1994.

Grant, Kerry S. *The Rainbow City: Celebrating Light, Color,
    and Architecture at the Pan-American Exposition,
    Buffalo, 1901.* Buffalo: Canisius College Press, 2001.

Halpern, John. *Early Birds: An Informal Account of the Beginnings of Aviation*. New York: Dutton, 1981.

Hart, Philip S. *Flying Free: America's First Black Aviators*. Minneapolis: Lerner, 1992.

Johns, A. Wesley. *The Man Who Shot McKinley*. South Brunswick, NY: A.S. Barnes, 1970.

Lewis, David Levering, and Deborah Willis. *A Small Nation of People: W.E.B. Du Bois and African American Portraits of Progress*. New York: Amistad, 2003.

Loos, William H., Ami Savigny, and Robert M. Gurn. *The Forgotten "Negro Exhibit": African-American Involvement in Buffalo's Pan-American Exposition, 1901*. Buffalo and Erie County Public Library and The Library Foundation of Buffalo and Erie County, 2001.

Soper, Barabara. *Carnival of Rainbows: A Novel of the Pan-American Exposition*. Philadelphia. Xlibris, 2001.

Web Sites:

Doing the Pan
   http://panam1901.bfn.org/

Illuminations: Revisiting the Buffalo Pan-American Exposition
   http://library.buffalo.edu/libraries/exhibits/panam/index.html

Uncrowned Queens
   http://wings.buffalo.edu/uncrownedqueens/C/index.html

Discussion Questions:

1. Historical novels shed light on past times. By seeing through the eyes of characters, listening to their voices, walking in their shoes, history comes alive. Most of *Blackbird Rising* takes place in 1901 in Buffalo, New York. The book showcases the Pan-American Exposition and a bygone era where a modern city begins to flourish. What aspects of life at the turn of the twentieth century surprised you? What aspects are similar to today?

2. Central to *Blackbird Rising* is the plight of African Americans. In the arc of over one hundred and fifty years, from pre-Civil War America to the present day, the reader learns how the road to freedom was elusive and circuitous. Slavery, prejudice, segregation, and even the rule of law, weighed heavily and proved constant impediments for African Americans who sought to live equal and free. Still, through hope and perseverance, the African American community grew and became a support to its members. In reading this novel, discuss how African Americans helped each other to advance in this society.

3. Papa Joe Lockhart was a runaway slave who survived many trials. Still, he managed to carve out a life for himself, his family. What were Papa Joe's strengths that made him succeed in personal and professional matters? What beliefs did he have that are admirable? What outside forces helped him become such a strong, loving man?

4. In *Blackbird Rising* we learn the invention of the airplane came about by the repeated concerted study and experimentation of industrious inventors from many places and times. While flying is commonplace today, history will remember flight as a challenge that inspired many. With the skies now conquered, what inventions can be imagined for the future? What problems do we wish to solve to make the world a better place?

5. The Chronicles of Augustus Lockhart include many poetic phrasings and insightful sayings. To name one: "…you can judge a man by how easily laughter comes to him. A man who cannot laugh at the surprises that add texture to his day, the peculiarities of his fellow men, and particularly his own failings is a man who suffers from an impoverishment of character." What other excerpts are memorable and why?

6. The subtitle for *Blackbird Rising* is: *A Novel of the American Spirit*. References throughout this book echo such sentiment: *And he was in the perfect place to dream—America, where some dream of riches, others dream of freedom, and a select few dream of doing wondrous things.* The United States of America is often cited as being a beacon to the rest of the world for its ingenuity. In what way is the American Spirit expressed in *Blackbird Rising?* In what ways does this spirit manifest in our country today?

About the Author:

Gary Earl Ross is a language arts professor at the University at Buffalo Educational Opportunity Center and playwright-in-residence for the Ujima Company. His honors for writing include a LIFT Fiction Fellowship for his short stories, first place commentary awards from the New York Associated Press and the New York Broadcasters' Association for his public radio essays, a Saltonstall Foundation grant for play writing, and an Edgar Allan Poe Award from Mystery Writers of America. His books and staged plays include *The Wheel of Desire and Other Intimate Hauntings*, *Shimmerville: Tales Macabre and Curious*, *Sleepwalker: The Cabinet of Dr. Caligari*, the children's tale *Dots*, *Picture Perfect*, *The Best Woman*, and *Matter of Intent* (winner of the Emanuel Fried Outstanding New Play Award and the Edgar from MWA). Ross also edited *Nickel City Nights*, *Erotic Writing in Western New York*. *Blackbird Rising* is his first novel.

Praise for the work of **Gary Earl Ross**:

The Wheel of Desire and Other Intimate Hauntings (Short Stories)

"[S]potlights human connections as its common thread, skillfully drawing readers into the inner folds of its own seductive resonance . . . universal themes of joy, pain, sex and wonder, with peeks into . . . obsession and solitude."

—*The Boox Review*

Shimmerville: Tales Macabre and Curious (Short Stories)

"[A] George Orwell meets Ralph Ellison narrative premise. . . Readers impressed by *The Wheel of Desire* will find even more to like in the allegorical and interconnected tapestry of narratives in *Shimmerville*."

—*Buffalo News*

Matter of Intent (Winner of the Edgar Award for Drama, Mystery Writers of America)

"[T]ouches upon a variety of tough issues that include incest, rape and racism. It is a play that will make you think not only about the 1960's, but also about the present. This is a real mystery with a surprise ending."

—*Buffalo Criterion*

The Best Woman (Drama)

"[A] Clinton-esque senator running for president against an Condoleeza-esque conservative Republican, African-American woman. The play derives a great deal of its fun from thinly disguised references to current events. [I]nspire[s] delighted audience reaction . . . Ross's writing is witty and provides a rapid pace for [the] actors who play the central combatants."

—*Artvoice*

CPSIA information can be obtained at www.ICGtesting.com
Printed in the USA
266837BV00004B/2/P

9 780981 707044